WETWARE

The blonde woman stirred again. Her body was full-grown, yet her brain was a blank. The pink-tank sisters had tried various methods of putting bopper software directly on such tank clones' brains, but to no avail. There seemed to be a sense in which a human's personality inheres in *each cell* of the body. Perhaps the secret was not to try and program a full-grown body, but rather to get the data-compressed bopper software code into the initial fertilized egg from which a body grows. As the cell divided, the bopper software would replicate along with the human DNA wetware. But the final step of building the bopper software into the human wetware had yet to be made.

Soon, thought Berenice, soon our great work will reach fruition, and I will put my mind into the starting egg of a fresh human. Perhaps, in order to spread bopper wetware more rapidly, it will be better to go as a male. I will be myself in a strong, beautiful human body on Earth, and I will have many descendants. Mother Earth, rotten with life, filled with information in each of its tiniest parts.

Wetware

Rudy Rucker

NEW ENGLISH LIBRARY
Hodder and Stoughton

First published in the United States of America in 1988 by Avon Books

First published in Great Britain in 1989 by New English Library paperbacks

British Library C.I.P.

Rucker, Rudolf V.B. *1946–*
    Wetware.
    I. Title
    813'.54[F]

ISBN 0 450 49476 4

Printed and bound in Great Britain for Hodder and Stoughton Paperbacks, a division of Hodder and Stoughton Ltd., Mill Road, Dunton Green, Sevenoaks, Kent TN13 2YA (Editorial Office: 47 Bedford Square, London WC1B 3DP) by Cox & Wyman Ltd., Reading.

For
Philip K. Dick
1928–1982

"One must imagine Sisyphus happy."

Table of Contents

Chapter One
People That Melt

December 26, 2030

It was the day after Christmas, and Stahn was plugged in. With no work in sight, it seemed like the best way to pass the time . . . other than drugs, and Stahn was off drugs for good, or so he said. The twist-box took his sensory input, jazzed it, and passed it on to his cortex. A pure software high, with no somatic aftereffects. Staring out the window was almost interesting. The maggies left jagged trails, and the people looked like actors. Probably at least one of them was a meatie. Those boppers just wouldn't let up. Time kept passing, slow and fast.

At some point the vizzy was buzzing. Stahn cut off the twist-box and thumbed on the screen. The caller's head appeared, a skinny yellow head with a down-turned mouth. There was something strangely soft about his features.

"Hello," said the image. "I'm Max Yukawa. Are you Mr. Mooney?"

Without the twist, Stahn's office looked unbearably bleak. He hoped Yukawa had big problems.

"Stahn Mooney of Mooney Search. What can I do for you, Mr. Yukawa?"

"It concerns a missing person. Can you come to my office?"

"Clear."

Yukawa twitched, and the vizzyprint spat out a sheet with printed directions. His address and the code to his door-plate. Stahn thumbed off, and after a while he hit the street.

Bad air out there, always bad air—*yarty* was the word for
it this year. 2030. *Yart* = yawn + fart. Like in a library,
right? Sebum everywhere. *Sebum* = oily secretion which
human skin exudes. Yarts and sebum, and a hard vacuum
outside the doooooooommmme. Dome air—after the
invasion, the humans had put like a big airtight dome over
Disky and changed the town's name to Einstein. The old
Saigon into Ho Chi Minh City routine. The boppers had
been driven under the Moon's surface, but they had bombs
hidden all over Einstein, and they set off one a week maybe,
which was not all *that* often, but often enough to matter for
sure for sure. And of course there were the meaties—people
run by remote bopper control. What you did was to hope it
didn't get worse.

So OK, Stahn is standing out in the street waiting for a
slot on the people-mover. A moving sidewalk with chairs,
right. He felt like dying, he really really felt like dying. Bad
memories, bad chemistry, no woman, bad life.

"Why do we bother."

The comment was right on the beam. It took a second to
realize that someone was talking to him. A rangy, strungout
dog of a guy, shirtless in jeans with blond hair worn ridgeback style. His hair was greased up into a longitudinal peak,
and there were extra hairgrafts that ran the hairstrip right on
down his spine to his ass. Seeing him made Stahn feel old.
I used to be different, but now I'm the same. The ridgeback
had a handful of pamphlets, and he was staring at Stahn like
one of them was something in a zoo.

"No thanks," Stahn said, looking away. "I just want to
catch a slot."

"Inside your lamejoke private eye fantasy? Be here now,
bro. Merge into the One." The kid was handsome in an
unformed way, but his skin seemed unnaturally slack. Stahn
had the impression he was stoned.

Stahn frowned and shook his head again. The ridgeback
gave him a flimsy plas pamphlet, tapped his own head, and
then tapped Stahn's head as if to mime the flow of knowledge. Poor dumb freak. Just then an empty slot came by.
Safely off the sidewalk, Stahn looked the leaflet over. OR-
MY IS THE WAY, it read. ALL IS ONE!

The text said that sharing love with one's fellows could

lead to a fuller union with the cosmos at large. At the deepest level, the pamphlet informed Stahn, all people are aspects of the same archetype. Those who wished to learn more about Organic Mysticism were urged to visit the Church offices on the sixth floor of the ISDN ziggurat. All this wisdom came courtesy of Bei Ng, whose picture and biography appeared on the pamphlet's back cover. A skinny yellow guy with wrinkles and a pointed head. He looked like a big reefer. Even after eighteen clean months, lots of things still made Stahn think of drugs.

The Einstein cityscape drifted past. Big, the place was big—like Manhattan, say, or half of D.C. Not to mention all the chambers and tunnels underground. Anthill. Smart robots had built the city, and then the humans had kicked them out. The boppers. They were easy to kill, once you knew how. Carbon-dioxide laser, EM energy, scramble their circuits. They'd gone way underground. Stahn had mixed feelings about boppers. He liked them because they were even less like regular people than he was. At one point he'd even hung out with them a little. But then they'd killed his father . . . back in 2020. Poor old dad. All the trouble Stahn had given him, and now it felt like he was turning into him, year by year. Mooney Search. *Wave on it, sister, wiggle. Can I get some head?*

Yukawa's address was a metal door, set flush into the pumice-stone sidewalk. *Deep Encounters* said the sign over the door-plate. Psychological counselling? The folks in this neighborhood didn't look too worried about personality integration. Bunch of thieves and junkies is what they looked like. Old Mother Earth had really shipped the dregs to Einstein. Like the South, right, *Settled by slaves and convicts—since 1690.* 2022 was when the humans had retaken the Moon. Stahn looked at the sheet that Yukawa had sent. 90–3–888–4772. *Punch in the code, Stahn.* Numbers. Prickly little numbers. Number, Space, Logic, Infinity . . . for the boppers it was all Information. Good or bad?

OK, so the door opens, and Stahn ladders on down and takes a look. A vestibule, empty and gray. To the right was a door with a light over it. In front of Stahn was another door, and a window like at a walk-in bank. Yukawa's face was behind the thick glass. Stahn showed him the vizzyprint sheet, and he opened up the second door.

Stahn found himself (*found himself?*) in a long laboratory, with a desk and chairs at one end. The air was thick with strange smells: benzenes, esters, the rich weavings of long-chain molecules, and under it all the stench of a badly-kept menagerie. His host was seated on a sort of high stool by that thick glass window. It took Stahn a second to absorb the fact that about half the guy's body was . . . where?

Yukawa's soft thin head and arms rose up out of a plastic tub mounted on four long legs. The rest of him was a yellow-pink puddle in the tub. Stahn gagged and took a step back.

"Don't be alarmed, Mr. Mooney. I was a little upset, so I took some merge. It's just now wearing off."

Merge . . . he'd heard of it. Very synthetic, very illegal. *I don't do drugs, man, I'm high on life.* People took merge to sort of melt their bodies for a while. Stuzzadelic and very tempting. If Stahn hadn't been so desperate for work he might have left right then. Instead he came on nonchalant.

"What kind of lab is this, Mr. Yukawa?"

"I'm a molecular biologist." Yukawa put his hands on the tub's sides and pushed up. Slowly his belly solidified, his hips and his legs. He stepped over to the desk and began pulling his clothes back on. Over the vizzy, Stahn had taken him for Japanese, but he was too tall and pale for that. "Of course the Gimmie would view this as an illegal drug laboratory. Which is why I don't dare call them in. The problem is that something has happened to my assistant, a young lady named Della Taze. You advertise yourself as a Searcher, so . . ."

"I'll take the case, don't worry. I already checked you on my data-base, by the way. A blank. That's kind of unusual, Mr. Yukawa." He was fully dressed now, gray pants and a white coat, quite the scientist. Stahn could hardly believe he'd just seen him puddled in that tub. *How good did it feel?*

"I used to be a man named Gibson. I invented gene-invasion?"

"You were that mad scientist who . . . uh . . . turned himself Japanese?"

"Not so mad." A smile flickered across Yukawa's

sagging face. "I had cancer. I found a way to replace some of my genes with those of a ninety-eight-year-old Japanese man. The cancer went into remission, and as my cells replaced themselves, I took on more and more of the Japanese man's somatotype. A body geared for long life. There was talk of a Nobel Prize, but . . ."

"The California dog-people. The Anti-Chimera Act of 2027. I remember. You were exiled here. Well, so was I. And now I'm a straight rent-a-pig and you're a dope wizard. Your girl's gone, and you're scared to call the Gimmie." Most Einstein law enforcement was done on a freelance basis. No lunie ever called in the official law—the Gimmie—on purpose. At this point the Gimmie was a highly organized gang of extortionists and meatie-hunters. They were a moderately necessary evil.

"Clear. Let me show you around." Long and undulant, Yukawa drifted back into the lab. The low lunar gravity seemed to agree with him.

The closer tables were filled with breadboarded electronic circuits and mazes of liquid-filled tubes. Computerized relays shunted the colored fluids this way and that. A distillation process seemed to be underway. The overall effect was of a miniature oil refinery. In contrast, the tables towards the rear of the lab were filled with befouled animal cages. It had been a while since Stahn had seen animals. Live meat.

"Watch," said Yukawa, shoving two cages together. One cage held a large brown toad, the other a lively white rat. Yukawa drew a silver flask out of his coat pocket and dribbled a few drops onto each of the subject animals. "This is merge," he explained, opening the doors that separated the cages.

The toad, a carnivore, flung itself at the rat. For a moment the two beasts struggled. But then the merge had taken effect, and the animals' tissues flowed together: brown and white, warts and hair. A flesh-puddle formed, loosely covering the creatures' loosened skeletons. Four eyes looked up: two green, two pink. Faint shudders seemed to animate the fused flesh. Pleasure? It was said that merge users took a sexual delight in puddling.

"How do they separate?"

"It's automatic. When the merge wears off, the cell walls

stiffen and the body collagens tighten back up. What the drug does is temporarily uncoil all the proteins' tertiary bunchings. One dose lasts ten minutes to an hour—and then back to normal. Now look at *these* two cages.''

The next two cages held something like a rat and something like a toad. But the rat's hair was falling out, and its feet were splayed and leathery. The toad, for its part, was growing a long pink tail, and its wide mouth showed signs of teeth.

"Chimeras," said Yukawa with some satisfaction. "Chimeras like me. The trick is to keep them merged for several days. Gene exchange takes place. The immune systems get tired.''

"I bet. So the Japanese man you merged with turned into you?''

Yukawa made a wry face. "That's right. We beat cancer together, and he got a little younger. Calls himself Bei Ng these days. He runs his own fake religion here in Einstein, though it's really an ISDN front. Bei's always trying to outdo me and rip me off. But never mind about him. I want you to look at this one back here. It's my pet project: a universal life form.''

At the very rear of the lab was a large pen. Huddled in the pen was a sodden, shambling thing—an amalgam of feathers and claws. *Chitin*, man, and hide, and the head had (A) long feelers, (B) a snout, (C) a squid-bunch of slack mandibles, *dot dot dot*, and (Z) gills. Gills on the moon.

"You're nuts, Yukawa. You're out of your kilpy gourd.''

At the sound of Stahn's voice, the monstrosity hauled itself over to rattle the pen's bars with tiny pink hands.

"Yes, Arthur," said Yukawa. "Good.'' He fished a food pellet out of his lab jacket and fed it to his creation. Just then a bell chimed.

"Back to business," said Yukawa, giving Stahn a U-shaped smile. "I don't know why I'm showing you all this anyway. Loneliness, I suppose. Della's been my only companion for the last two years.''

Stahn tagged along as Yukawa made his way back to the thick window looking onto the vestibule. A light was flashing over the other door out there.

"Time's up," said Yukawa, speaking into a microphone.

"The session's over, Mrs. Beller." Stahn got the full picture.

"You retail the merge right here? You're running a love-puddle?"

"That is the vulgar terminology, yes. I have to fund my ongoing research in whatever fashion I can. I sell merge both wholesale and retail. There's nothing really wrong with merge, you know. It's terribly addictive, but if someone wants to quit, why, I'm perfectly willing to sell them the proper blocker."

Outside the window, the lit door opened. Two people stepped out—a wide-mouthed brunette and her funboy. He wore a black-and-white bowling shirt with *Ricardo* stitched over the breast pocket. She was hot stuff. Their faces looked soft and tired, and they were holding hands.

Yukawa powered a drawer out through the wall. "Same time tomorrow, Mrs. Beller?"

"Feels so rave, Max." The woman dropped some money into the drawer. She was hot stuff. *What type of sex do you like, Mrs. Beller, WHAT TYPE???* She was *used-looking*, and she had a slow lazy voice and the big soft lips to match. She raked a stare across Stahn's face and led Ricardo up the ladder to the street. As they left, Stahn noticed that their two joined hands were actually fused into a single skin-covered mass. Hot.

Yukawa caught Stahn's expression, caught some of it. "They'll pull apart later, when the stuff fully wears off. In some circles it's quite fashionable to walk around part merged."

"How come they don't look like each other—if they're merging every day?"

"Dosage control. Unless you set up an all-day drip, merging has no lasting effects. And the drip has to be just right, or you end up as an entropic solution of amino acids. No one can do the gene exchange right but me."

"Other people have done it. Vic Morrow did it, dad." Vic Morrow had been a truck-farmer in the San Joaquin Valley. In 2027, he'd hit on the idea of treating his migrant workers to a series of weekend-long mergedrip parties. Once the workers had all flowed together, Morrow would throw a couple of dogs into the love-puddle with them. He was nuts.

Over the weeks, the workers had transmuted into beasts, ever more tractable, ever less demanding. The big scandal came when Morrow had a heart attack and his workers ate most of his corpse and rolled in the rest of it. A month later, the Anti-Chimera Act had passed Congress by acclaim.

Yukawa frowned and fumbled in his desk. "I told Morrow how to do it. It was a big mistake. I owed him money. I don't trust anyone with my secrets anymore. Especially . . ." He stopped himself and pushed a folder across the desk. "Here's the full printout on Della—I already accessed it for you. Last Friday—that was the 20th—I was with Della all day as usual, and at four she left in her maggie. Monday and Tuesday she didn't come in. I called her apartment, nobody home. Yesterday was Christmas and I didn't bother calling. I figured maybe she'd taken an extra-long holiday weekend, gone on a party or a trek in the crater. She doesn't tell me her plans. But now she's still not here and her vizzy still doesn't answer. I'm worried. Either something's happened to her, or . . . or she's run away."

Stahn picked up the folder and leafed through it. *Focus*. DELLA TAZE. Born and raised in Louisville, Kentucky. Twenty-eight years old. Ph.D. in molecular genetics, U. Va., 2025. Same year he'd been deported to Einstein. Her photo: a nice little blonde with a straight mouth and a button nose. Fox. Unmarried.

"She was your girlfriend?" Stahn glanced up at Yukawa. His long, thin head looked cruel and freakish. The "universal life form" at the back of the lab was crying out for more food, making a sound midway between a squeal and a hiss. *Arthur*. It was hard to see why Della Taze hadn't split like . . . two years ago.

". . . wouldn't let me come to her apartment," Yukawa was saying. "And she wouldn't ever merge with me either. We argued about it Friday. I *know* she was using, towards the end she asked me for it all the time. Maybe that was the only reason she stayed with me as long as she did. But now . . . now she's gone, and I have to get her back. Track her down, Mooney. Bring my Della back!"

"I'll do my best, Mr. Yukawa. Man." As Stahn got to his feet, Yukawa leaned across the desk and handed him a wad of bills, and the silver flask of dope.

"Here's money for you, Mooney, and merge. *Sta-Hi.* Didn't they used to call you Sta-Hi?"

"That was a long time ago. Now I'm all grown up."

"I gave Della blocker, just in case, but if you find her sick, just show her the flask."

Before getting a slot over to Della's place, Stahn went back to his office to do some computer searching. Maybe Della had taken Yukawa's blocker and checked into an endorphin clinic. The blocker would gene-tailor out the specific enzymes that made merge necessary for her body, but sometimes it took a clinic to keep you from going back to what your mind still wanted. Or maybe Della was dead and in the organ banks, the cannibal mart, or worse. Everyone on the Moon—lunies and boppers alike—had lots of uses for fresh meat. Or, on the other hand, maybe Della had caught a ship to Earth.

Yukawa hadn't called anyone at all; he was too paranoid. Stahn worked his vizzy through all the info banks—and drew a blank. Could she have been picked up by the Gimmie? Better not to ask. Or maybe the boppers had zombie-boxed her off to the ratsurgeon? He leaned back in his chair, trying not to think about the flask of merge. *Focus.*

If Della was still strung on merge, she'd be puddling at least once a day. That meant she might be holed up with some other local users. So it would make sense to check out the local merge scene, which centered, Stahn recalled, in the catacombs around the old dustbaths. How good *was* merge, anyway? Stahn opened Yukawa's silver flask and . . . uh . . . took a sniff. Nice: red wine and roast turkey, nice-smelling stuff. He couldn't stop wondering what it would feel like to use a little. Yukawa shouldn't have given it to him. But, Stahn realized, Yukawa had known what he was doing. Don't start, Stahn, he told himself. Don't start all that again. Why not? he answered himself. Who are you to tell me what to do? I'll do what I like! Remember, Stahn, responded the first voice, you didn't quit drugs for *other* people. You didn't quit for society, or for Wendy's ghost. You quit for *yourself.* If you go back on the stuff you're going to die.

Just then someone started pounding on the door. Stahn twitched and a fat drop of merge splashed out onto his left

hand. His stomach clenched in horror, but a part of him—
the bad part—was very glad. He put his hands and the flask
under his desk and told the door to open.

It was the blond ridgeback who'd given him the Or-My
pamphlet before. Stahn got the cap back on Yukawa's flask
and tried to flex his left hand. It felt like it was melting.
This stuff was for real.

"Stahn Mooney," said the ridgeback, closing the door
behind him. *"Sta-Hi."* His face had junk-hunger. "My
name's Whitey Mydol. I heard you were over at Yukawa's.
I was wondering if . . ." He paused to sniff the air. The
room reeked of merge. "Can I have some?"

"Some what?"

The melting feeling had moved up into Stahn's forearm.
His shabby office walls looked prettier than the twist-box had
ever made them. All right. Eighteen months since he'd felt
this good. He forced his attention back to Mydol's hard
young face. "How do you know who Yukawa is?"

"Oh . . . we know." The kid smiled in a conspiratorial
way. "I'll give you two hundred dollars for a hit. Just
between the two of us."

Stahn took his flare-ray in his right hand and levelled it
at Mydol. He wanted Mydol out of here before he melted
all over. "I'm going to count to three. One." Mydol stopped
moving and glared. "Two." Mydol snarled a curse and
stepped back towards the door. He was jangling up Stahn's
first rush in almost two years, and Stahn wanted to kill him.

"AO, Junk-Hog Sta-Hi Rent-Pig Mooney. What's the
shudder, scared to merge with a man? Tubedook."

"Three," Stahn clicked off the safety and burned a shot
across Mydol's left shoulder. The ridgeback winced in pain,
opened the door and left.

Stahn slumped back. God, this was fast dope. His left arm
looked like candle wax, and he was having trouble staying
in his chair. He let himself slide down onto the floor and
stared up at the ceiling. Oh, this did feel so good. His bone
joints loosened, and his skeleton sagged beneath the puddle
of his flesh. It took almost an hour to ride the trip out.
Towards the middle Stahn saw God. God was about the
same as usual—a little more burnt, maybe. He wanted love
as bad as Stahn did. This life was taking its toll on everyone.

What is merge like? Baby, if you don't know by now
. . . Wonderful. Horrible. After Stahn hit the floor and
puddled, he wasn't really there. The space of the room
became *part of his consciousness.* He *was* the room, the
chipped beige plas, the dingy black floor, the old-fashioned
windows, the desk and chair and computer; he was the room
and the building and Einstein and the Earth. Standard ecstatic
mystical vision, really. But *fast.* He was everywhere, he was
nowhere, he was the same as God. And then there were no
thoughts at all. *Stuzzy,* sis, *all* right.

It wore off ***WHAM*** as quickly as it had come on.
There was a tingling in Stahn's flesh, a kind of jelling
feeling, and then he was lying there shaking, heart going a
mile a minute. Too fast. This dope was giga too fast. Death
practice, right: hit, melt, space, blank. Final blank. He
wished his dead wife Wendy were still alive. Sweet, blonde,
wide-hipped Wendy. Times like this—in the old days—she'd
hug him and pat his head real soft . . . and smile . . . And
you killed her, Stahn. Oh God, oh no, oh put that away.
You blew a hole in her head and sold her corpse to the
organleggers and used the money to come to the Moon.

Stahn alone on the office floor, shuddering. Bum kicks.
Think about anything but Wendy. Flash of an old song:
*Coming down again, all my time's been spent, coming down
again.* Old. Gettin old. Coming down gets too old. Does that
even mean anything? Language with a flat tire. Talk broken,
but keep talking. Regroup.

His clothes were awkwardly bunched around him. When
he sat up, the headache started. Bummer bummer bummer
bummer bummer. He took Yukawa's silver flask and shook
it. There was quite a bit in there, a few months' worth if
you only took it once a day. If he got back on drugs he was
dead. He should be dead. He wished he was dead. Lot of
slow death in that flask.

If one drop was a dose, and a dose was worth . . uh
. . two hundred dollars, then this flask was something that
certain elements—certain criminal elements—would . . uh
. . *kkkkkillll* for. And that ridgeback cultie knew he was
holding, oh my brethren. *Can I get some head?* "Hello,
Mrs. Beller, you don't know me, but I . . uh . ." Hot. Hot.

Hot. Hot. Hot. Hot. Hot. WHAT TYPE OF SEX, BABY, *WHAT TYPE?*

The thing to do right now was to not go back out the office building's front door. *Focus.* Rent a maggie. Garage on top of the building.

He picked out a black saucer-shaped maggie, fed it some money, and told it where to go. The maggies were like hovercars; they counteracted the Moon's weak gravity with fans, and with an intense magnetic field keyed to a big field generated by wires set into the dome. They were expensive. It was funny that a junkie lab assistant like Della Taze would have had her own maggie. Stahn could hardly wait to see her apartment. Maybe she was actually there, just not answering the vizzy, but there and like waiting for a guy with merge. He had lock-picking wares in case she wouldn't open.

The entry system at Della's building was no problem. Stahn used a standard nihilist transposition on the door down from the roof, and a tone-scrambler on her apartment door. The apartment was Wigglesville. *Creative Brain Damage, Vol. XIII.* As follows.

The walls weren't painted one uniform color. It was all bursts and streaks, as if the painter had just thrown random buckets around the apartment till everything was covered: walls, floors, and ceilings all splattered and dripped beyond scuzz.

The furniture was pink, and all in shapes of people. The chairs were big stuffed women with laps to sit in, and the tables were plas men on all fours. He kept jerking, seeing that furniture out of the corner of his eye, and thinking someone was there. Twist and shout. The whole place had the merge wine-turkey fragrance, but there was another smell under it . . . a bad smell.

Which, as it turned out, came from the bedroom. Della had her love-puddle in there—a big square tub like a giant wading pool. And next to it was . . . sort of a corpse. It had been a black guy.

Gross—you want to hear gross? A merged person is like Jell-O over some bones, right. And you can . . . uh . . . *splatter* Jell-O. Splatter a merged person into a bunch of pieces, and the drug wears off—the cells firm up—and there is this . . uh . . guy in a whole lot of pieces.

The skin had covered on up around each of the pieces— here was a foot with a rounded-off stump at the ankle, here was his head all smoothed off at the neck. He looked like a nice enough guy. Plump, easygoing. Here was an arm with his torso—and over there a leg hooked onto his bare ass . . . and all of it sagging and starting to rot . . .

Zzuzzzzzzz.

The vizzy in the living room was buzzing. Stahn ran in, covered up the lens, and thumbed the set on.

It was a hard-faced Gimmie officer. He wore hair spikes, and he had gold studs set into his cheeks. Colonel Hasci. Stahn knew the "cat." *Muy macho. Trés douche.*

"Miss Della Taze? We're down in the lobby. Can we come up and ask you some questions about Buddy Yeskin?"

Stahn split fast. It was a little hard to judge, but *Buddy* looked to have been dead two days. Why would anyone splatter good old Bud? Death is so stupid; always the same old punch line. It reminded him of Wendy, whenever he was coming down everything reminded him of Wendy. He'd been stoned on three-way, shooting houseflies with his needler and he'd hit her by accident. Some accident. Sold her body to the organleggers and moved up to the Moon before the mudder Gimmie could deport him. Her poor limp body.

Stahn's black saucer circled aimlessly. He wondered where Della Taze had gotten to. Merge with the cosmos, sister. Can I get some, too? WHAT TYPE, baby, WHAT TYPE OF SEX? Shut up, Stahn. Be quiet, brother. Chill out.

Chapter Two
Christmas in Louisville

December 24, 2030

Merged. Gentle curves and sweet flow of energies—merged in the love-puddle, the soft plastic tub set into the floor of her bedroom. Exquisite ecstasy—Della melted and Buddy just sliding in; the two of them about to be together again, close as close can be, flesh to flesh, gene to gene, a marbled mass of pale and tan skin, with their four eyes up on top seeing nothing; but now, just as Buddy starts melting . . . suddenly . . .

Aeh!

Della Taze snapped out of her flashback and looked at the train car window. It was dusk outside, and the glass gave back a faint reflection of her face: blonde, straight-mouthed, her eyes hot and sunken. Her stomach hurt, and she'd thrown up three times today. Burnt-out and worldly wise . . . the look she'd longed for as a teenage girl. She tried a slight smile. *Not bad, Della. But you're wanted for murder.* And the only place she could think of going was home.

The train was coasting along at a slow 20 mph now, click-clanking into Louisville, gliding closer to the long trip's end: Einstein-Ledge-Florida-Louisville via spaceship-shuttle-train. Two days. Della hoped she was well ahead of the Einstein Gimmie—the police. Not that they'd be likely to chase her this far. Here in 2030, Moon and Earth were as far removed from each other as Australia and England had been in the 1800s.

Louisville in the winter: rain not even snow, lots of it, gray water, the funny big cars, and real sky—the smells, after two years of dome air, and the idle space! On the Moon, every nook and cranny had its purpose—like on a sailboat or in a tent—but here, gliding past the train, were vacant lots with nothing in them but weeds and dead tires; meaningless streets with marginal businesses; tumbledown houses with nobody home. Idle space. There were too many faces up in Einstein, too many bodies, too many needs.

Della was glad to be back here, with a real sky and real air; even though her body was filled with a dull ache. The weight. Old Mr. Gravity. In Florida she'd spent the last of her money on an Imipolex flexiskeleton with the brand name, Body by Oozer. She wore it like a body stocking, and the coded collagens pushed, stiffened, and pulled as needed. The ultimate support hosiery. Most returning lunies check in for three days of muscle rehabilitation at the JFK Spaceport, but Della had known she'd have to keep running. Why? Because she'd jelled back from that last merge-trip to find her lover splattered into pieces, and before she'd had time to do anything, there'd been a flat-voiced twitch-faced man on the vizzy.

"I killed him, Della, and I can kill you. Or I can tell the Gimmie that you did it. I want to help you, Della. I love you. I want to help you escape. There's a fake passport and a ticket to Earth for you at the spaceport . . ."

Aeh!

Della's parents, Jason and Amy Taze, were at the station, the same as ever—strungout and hungover, mouths set into smiles, and their self-centered eyes always asking, *Do you love me?* Amy Taze was small and tidy. She wore bright, outdated makeup, and today she had her blonde hair marcelled into a tight, hard helmet. Jason was a big, shambling guy with short hair and messy prep clothes. He had a desk job at a bank, and Amy was a part-time saleswoman in a gift shop. They both hated their jobs and lived to party. Seeing them there, Della felt like getting back on the train.

"My *God,* Della, you look *fantastic.* Is that a *leotard* you have on under your clothes?" Mom kept the chatter going all the way out to the car, as if to show how sober she was.

Dad rolled his eyes and gave Della a wink, as if to show how much more together than Mom *he* was. The two of them were so busy putting on their little show that it was ten minutes before they noticed that Della was trembling. It was Dad who finally said something.

"You do look nice, Della, but you seem a little shaky. Was it a hard trip? And why such short notice?"

"Somebody framed me for a murder, Dad. That's why I didn't want you all to tell anyone else I'm back in town." Her stomach turned again, and she retched into her handkerchief.

"Was it some kind of hard-drug deal? Something to do with that damn *merge* stuff that your Dr. Yukawa makes?" Dad fished nervously in his pocket for a reefer. He shot her a sharp glance. "Are you hooked?"

Della nodded, glad to upset them. Taste of their own medicine. No point telling them she'd taken gamendorph blocker to kick. Dr. Yukawa had always made sure that she had blocker around.

"That's what we get for not being better people, Jason," said Mom, her voice cracking in self-pity. "The only one of our children coming home for Christmas is a killer dope queen on the lam. And for the two years before this we've been all alone. Give me a hit off that number, I think I'm going to have a nervous breakdown." She took a puff, smiled, and patted Della's cheek. "You can help us trim the tree, Della honey. We still have the styrofoam star you decorated in kindergarten."

Della wanted to say something cutting, but she knew it would feel bad. Instead she put on her good-girl face and said, "I'd like that, Mom. I haven't seen a Christmas tree in three years. I . . ." Her voice caught and the tears came. She loved her parents, but she hated to see them. Holidays were always the worst, with Jason and Amy stumbling around in a chemical haze. "I hope this won't be like all the other Christmases, Mom."

"I don't know what you mean, Della. It will be lovely. Your Uncle Colin and Aunt Ilse are coming over for dinner tomorrow. They'll bring Willy, he's still living at home. Of course your two little sisters are both visiting with their *husbands'* families again."

Jason and Amy Taze lived in an eighty-year-old two-story tract home east of Louisville. The neighborhood had sidewalks and full-grown trees. The houses were small, but well-kept. Della found her tiny room to be more or less as it had always been: the clean, narrow bed; the little china animals on the shelf she'd nailed into the papery drywall; the hologram hoops hung in the two windows; and her disks and info-cubes all arranged in the alphabetical order she liked to keep them in. When she was in ninth grade, she'd programmed a cross-referenced catalog cube to keep track of them all. Della had always been a good student, a good girl, compulsively tidy as if to make up for her parents' frequent sloppy scenes.

Someone let Bowser, the family dog, in the back door then, and he came charging up the narrow carpeted stairs to greet Della, shaking his head, and whining and squirming like a snake. He looked as mangy as ever, and as soon as Della patted him, he lay on his back spreading his legs, the same gross way he'd always done. She rubbed under his chin for a while, while he wriggled and yipped.

"Yes, Bowser. Good dog. Good, smart dog." Now that she'd started crying, she couldn't seem to stop. Mom and Dad were downstairs in the kitchen, talking in hushed tones. Della was too tired to unpack. She hurt all over, especially in her breasts and stomach. When she slipped out of her flexiskeleton, she felt like a fat, watery jellyfish. There was a nightgown on the bed—Mom must have laid it out. Della put it on, glad no one was here to see her, and then she fell into a long, deep sleep.

When Della woke up it was midmorning. Christmas! So what. Without her two sisters Ruby and Sude here, it didn't mean a thing. Closing her eyes, Della could almost hear their excited yelling—and then she realized she was hearing the vizzy. Her parents were downstairs watching the vizzy on Christmas morning. God. She went to the bathroom and vomited, and then she put on her flexiskeleton and got dressed.

"Della!" cried her mother when Della appeared. "Now you see what we do on Christmas with no babies." There was an empty glass by her chair. The vizzy screen showed an unfamiliar family opening presents around their tree.

Mom touched the screen and a different family appeared, then another and another.

"We've gotten in the habit," explained Dad with a little shrug. "Every year lots of people leave their sets on, and whoever wants to can share in. So no one's lonely. We're so glad to have a real child here." He took her by the shoulders and planted a kiss on her forehead. "Little Della. Flesh of our flesh."

"Come, dear," said Mom. "Open your presents. We only had time to get two, but they're right here in front of the vizzy in case anyone's sharing in with *us*."

It felt silly but nice sitting down in front of the vizzy—there were some excited children on the screen just then, and it was almost like having noisy little Ruby and Sude at her side. And Bowser was right there, nuzzling her. Della's first present was an imipolex sweatshirt called a heartshirt.

"All the girls at the bank are wearing them this year," explained Dad. "It's a simplified version of bopper flicker-cladding. Try it on!"

Della slipped the loose warm plastic over her top. The heartshirt was an even dark blue, with a few staticky red spots drifting about.

"It can feel your heartbeat," said Mom. "Look." Sure enough, there was a big red spot on the plastic sweatshirt, right over Della's heart, a spot that spread out into an expanding ring that moved on over Della's shoulders and down her sleeves. Her heart beat again, and a new spot started—each beat of her heart made a red splash in the blue of the heartshirt.

"Neat," said Della. "Thanks. They don't have these up in Einstein. Everyone there hates boppers too much. But it's stuzzy. I like it."

"And when your heart beats faster, Della," said Mom, "all the fellows will be able to see."

Suddenly Della remembered Buddy, and why she'd come home, and the red rings on her sweatshirt started bouncing like mad.

"Why, Della!" said Mom, coyly. "Do you have a boyfriend?"

"I'm not ready to talk about it," said Della, calming

herself. *Especially not to a loudmouth racist drunk like you, Mom.*

"Let's have some champagne," suggested Dad.

"Good idea," said Mom. "Take the edge off. And then Della can open her other present."

Della watched the vizzy for a minute, calming down. Good old vizzy. She touched the screen here and there, and the picture skipped from home to home. Louisville people, not so different from the Tazes. Della even recognized some of them. She had some champagne and felt OK again. Lots of the people in the vizzy were drinking . . . why should she be so hard on her parents?

"Let's see my other present. I'm sorry I didn't bring you all anything."

"You brought yourself."

Della's second present was a little seed-packet labelled WEEK TREES.

"Have you heard of these?" asked Mom. "They're bioengineered. You know the miniature bonsai trees that the Japanese used to grow? These are the same, except their whole life cycle only takes a week. I've been showing them off in the store. They're amazing. We'd planned to try and mail these to you." She poured herself a fresh glass of champagne, which killed the bottle. "Get Della a little pottery cup with some potting soil, Jason. And why don't you twist up a few jays."

"Mom . . ."

"Don't be so uptight, Della." Mom's painted eyes flashed. "You'll get your turkey dinner, just wait and see. It's Christmas! Anyway, *you're* the one who's addicted to that hard-drug merge, little Miss Strict."

"AO, wave, it's heavy junk, Mom, but I took blocker and *I'm* oxo. Wu-wei, Mom, your rectum's showing." A wave of nausea swept over her again and she gagged. "It must be the gravity that's making me feel so sick."

"Let's wait on the weed till Colin and Ilse get here," suggested Dad. "You know how they love to smoke. You get that turkey in the microwave, Amy, and I'll help Della plant one of her week trees."

Mom finished her champagne and got to her feet. She

forgot her anger and smiled. "I got a boneless turkey this year, Della. They grow them in tanks."

"Do they have legs and wings?"

"Everything except bones. Like soft-shell crabs. Sometimes I feel that way myself. I'll make lots of sausage stuffing for you, sweetie."

"Thanks, Mom. Let me know if you need any help."

Dad got a little pot full of wet soil, and he and Della planted a week tree seed. They'd half expected the tree to shoot up and hit them in the face, but for the moment, nothing happened. Bowser sniffed curiously at the dirt.

"Let's figure it out," said Della, who liked playing with numbers. "Say a real tree lives seventy years. Then one day is like ten years for a week tree. So it should go through a year in two and four-tenths hours. Divide by twelve and get a month in two-tenths of an hour. Two-tenths of an hour is twelve minutes. Assuming that the seed starts out in a dormant midwinter mode, then we should see the first April leaves in four times twelve minutes, which will be . . ."

"Noon," said Dad. "Look at the soil in the pot, it's beginning to stir." Sure enough, the soil at the center of the pot was bulging up, and there, slowly slowly, came the creeping tip of the week tree. "I think they're like apple trees. We ought to have some little apples by tonight, Della."

"Wiggly!" She gave Dad a kiss. Mom had some pans sizzling out in the kitchen, and the vizzy was full of happy Christmas people. "Thank you. It is nice to be back."

"Can you tell me more about what happened up in Einstein, Della?"

"I had a boyfriend named Buddy Yeskin. We took merge together and—"

"What does that actually *mean*, 'taking merge together'?" asked Dad. "I can't keep up with all these new—"

"It's this weird drug that makes your body get all soft. Like a boneless turkey, I guess. And you feel really—"

Dad frowned. "I can't believe you'd do a thing like that, Della. We didn't raise you that way." He sighed and took a sip of the whiskey he'd brought out from the kitchen. "You took merge with this Buddy Yeskin, and then what happened?"

"While we were . . . together, someone broke into my apartment and killed Buddy. Smashed him all into pieces while he was soft." The fast red circles began rippling across Della's heartshirt again. "I kind of fainted, and when I woke up, a crazy man called on the vizzy and said he was going to kill me, or frame me for the murder, if I didn't leave for Earth. He'd even arranged a ticket and a fake passport for me. It was such a nightmare web, closing in on me. I was scared. I ran home."

The week tree was a barky little shoot now, with three stubby little branches.

"You're safe here," said Dad, patting her hand. Just then Della noticed that his voice was already slurring a little. Dad noticed her noticing. He gave a rueful smile. "For as long as you can stand us. Tomorrow I'll take you to see Don Stuart . . . you remember him. He's a good lawyer. Just in case." Bowser started barking.

"Merry Christmas!" shouted Mom in the kitchen. "You didn't have to bring all that! Jason! Della!"

It was Jason's older brother Colin, with his wife Ilse and son Willy. Colin worked as an English professor at the University of Louisville. He was skinny and sarcastic. Ilse was from a famous family: Ilse's father was Cobb Anderson, who'd built the first moon-robots years ago.

Great-uncle Cobb had been convicted of treason for building the robots wrong. Then he'd started drinking, had left his wife Verena, and had ended up as a pheezer bum in Florida. Somehow he'd died—it was a little uncertain—apparently the robots had killed him. He was the skeleton in the family closet.

Aunt Ilse was more like her German mother than she was like old Cobb. Vigorous and artsy-craftsy, she'd hung on to her wandering husband Colin through thick and thin, not that Della could see why. Uncle Colin had always struck her as obsolete, trying to make people look at his stupid paper books, when *he* barely even knew how to work the vizzy. And when he smoked marijuana with Dad, he got mad if you didn't laugh at his jokes and act impressed by his insights.

Their son Willy was a smart but sort of nutty guy in his twenties. A hacker, always fiddling with programs and hardware. Della had liked him a lot when they were younger, but it seemed like he'd stopped maturing long before she had. He still lived at home.

"Dad, don't tell them about why I've come back. Say I'm here to buy laboratory equipment for Dr. Yukawa. And tell Mom to keep quiet, too. If she gets drunk and starts talking about me, I'm going to—"

"Relax, geeklet."

Before long they were seated around the dining table. Dad had put the week tree in the center so they could watch it grow. Aunt Ilse offered a Lutheran grace, and Dad got to work carving the boneless turkey. He cut it in thick, stuffing-centered slices.

"Well, Della," said Colin after the first rush of eating was over, "how are things up on the Moon? Real far out? And what are old Cobb's funky machines into?" He specialized in the literature of the mid-twentieth century, and he liked to use the corny old slang on her. In return, Della always used the newest words she knew.

"Realtime, it's pretty squeaky, Unk. There's giga bopper scurry underground, and they're daily trying to blank us. They have a mongo sublune city called the Nest."

"Come on, Della," said Dad. "Talk English."

"Don't you feel guilty about the boppers?" asked Aunt Ilse, who was always ready to defend the creatures that her father had midwifed. "I mean, *they* built most of Einstein. Disky, they used to call it, no? And they're just as conscious as us. Isn't it really like the blacks in the old South? The blacks did all the work, but the whites acted like they weren't even people."

"Those robots aren't conscious," insisted Mom. She'd had a lot of red wine in the kitchen, and now they were all back on the champagne. "They're just a bunch of goddamn *machines*."

"You're a machine, too, Aunt Amy," put in Willy. "You're just made of meat instead of wires and silicon." Willy had a slow, savoring way of speaking that could drive you crazy. Although he'd never finished college, he made a good living as a freelance software writer. Earth still used a lot of computers, but all the bigger ones were equipped with deeply coded behavior locks intended to keep them from trying to follow in the steps of the boppers, the rebel robots who'd colonized the Moon. Earth's slave computers were known as asimovs in honor of the Asimov laws of robotics which they obeyed.

"Don't call your aunt 'meat,' " reprimanded Uncle Colin, who liked to flirt with Mom. "The turkey is meat. Your aunt is a person. You wouldn't want me to put gravy on your aunt and eat her, would you? In front of everyone?" Colin chuckled and bugged his eyes at Mom. "Should I smack him, Amy?"

"At least he's thinking about what I'm made of. At my age, that's practically a compliment. Would you call me a *machine*, Jason honey?"

"No way." Dad poured out some more champagne. "Machines are predictable."

"I think Mom's predictable," Della couldn't resist saying snippishly. Her stomach felt really bad again. "Both of you are predictable."

"You're all mistaken," put in Willy. "Relative to us, people and boppers are *both* unpredictable. It's a consequence of Chaitin's version of Gödel's theorem. Grandpa Cobb explained it years ago in a paper called 'Towards Robot Consciousness.' We can only make predictions about the behavior of systems which are much simpler than ourselves."

"So there, Della," said Mom.

"But why can't we learn to coexist peacefully with the boppers, Della?" pressed Aunt Ilse.

"Well, things *are* fairly peaceful now," said Della. "The boppers harass us because they wish we'd give Einstein back to them, but they don't actually pop the dome and kill everyone. They could do it, but they know that Earth would turn around and fire a Q-bomb down into their Nest. For that matter, we could Q-bomb them right now, but we're in no rush to, because we need the things their factories and pink-tanks make." Everyone except Mom was looking at Della with interest, and she felt knowledgeable and poised. But just then her stomach twitched oddly. Her breasts and stomach felt like they were growing all the time.

"Well, *I* don't feel guilty about the boppers," put in Mom. The alcohol was really hitting her, and she hadn't

followed the conversation at all. "I think we ought to kill
all the machines . . . and kill the niggers too. Starting with
President Jones."

There was a pained silence. The little week tree rustled;
its first blossoms were opening. Della decided to let Mom
have it. "My boyfriend was a 'nigger,' Mom."

"What boyfriend? I hope you didn't let him—"

"Yes, Della," said Dad, raising his voice heavily. "It's
great to have you back. More food anyone? Or should we
pause for some holiday marijuana? How about it, Colin?"

"Shore," said Colin, switching to his hick accent. He
gave Della a reassuring wink. "Mah smart little niece. She's
got more degrees than a thermometer! Weren't you doing
something with genetics up there in Einstein?"

"I *hope* not," put in Mom, trying to recover. "This child
still has to find a husband."

"Chill it, Mom," snapped Della.

"That's . . . uh . . . right, Colin," said Dad, still trying
to smooth things over. "Della was working with this Dr.
Yukawa fellow. She's down here to buy some equipment for
him." He drew a reefer out of his pocket and fired it up.

"How long will you be staying here?" asked Aunt Ilse.

"I'm not sure. It might be quite a while till everything's
set."

"Oh," said Ilse, passing the reefer to her husband without
taking a hit. She could be really nosy when she got going.
"How lovely. Is Dr. Yukawa planning to—"

Della kicked Willy under the table. He got the message,
and interrupted to throw the interrogation off track. "What
kind of stuffing is this, Aunt Amy? It's really delicious."

"*Meat*-stuffing, honey. I was fresh out of wires and
silicon. Pass me that thing, Colin."

"I have an interesting new job, Della," said Willy,
talking rapidly around his food. He had smooth, olive skin
like his mother, and finely arched eyebrows that moved up
and down as he chewed and talked. "It's for the *Belle of
Louisville*—you know, the big riverboat that tourists ride on?
OK, what they've got there is three robot bartenders—with
imipolex skins, you know, all designed to look like old-time
black servants."

"Why can't they just hire some real blacks?" demanded

Mom, exhaling a cloud of smoke. "God knows there's enough of them unemployed. Except for President Jones. Not that I want to offend Della." She reached out and touched the blossoms of the week tree, moving the pollen around. Della, who had decided not to eat any more of her mother's meal, slipped Bowser the rest of her boneless turkey.

"This all has to do with what we were talking about before, Aunt Amy," continued Willy. "They did have real blacks tending bar on the *Belle,* but they kept acting too much like regular people—maybe sneaking a drink now and then, or flirting with the women, or getting in arguments with drunk rednecks. And if there did happen to be a bartender who did his job perfectly, then some people would feel bad to see such a talented person with such a bleaky job. Guilty liberals, you wave? They tried white bartenders, too, but it was the same deal—either they start fights with the rednecks, or they make the liberals feel sad. I mean, who's going to *take* a bartending job, anyway? But as long as it's robots, then there's none of this messy human stuff."

"That's interesting, Willy," said Uncle Colin. "I didn't know the *Belle* was your new gig. Nobody tells me anything. I was on the *Belle* just last week with a dude who came to give a rap about Mark Twain, and those black bartenders didn't seem like robots at all. As a matter of fact, they kept making mistakes and dropping things. They were laughing all the time. I didn't feel a bit sorry for them!"

"That's my new program!" exulted Willy. "There's a big supercooled processor down below the deck, and it runs the three bartender robots. My job was to get it fine-tuned so that the bartenders would be *polite,* but clearly unfit for any better job."

"Hell, you could have just hired some of our tellers," put in Dad. "I don't know why people still mess with robots after 2001." 2001 was the year that the boppers—Cobb Anderson's self-replicating moon-robots—had revolted. They'd started their own city up on the Moon, and it hadn't been till 2022 that the humans had won it back.

"How come they have such a big computer on the *Belle* anyway?" Colin wanted to know. "I thought big computers weren't allowed outside of the factories anymore. Is it a teraflop?"

Willy raised his high, round eyebrows. "Almost. A hundred gigaflop. This is a special deal the city put together. They got the processor from ISDN, the vizzy people. It's been up and running for six months, but they needed me to get it working really right."

"Isn't that against the Artificial Intelligence Law?" asked Dad.

"No it isn't," Willy insisted calmly. "Burt Masters, who operates the *Belle*, is friends with the mayor, and he got a special exemption to the AI law. And of course Belle—that's what the computer calls itself—is an asimov. You know: *Protect Humans—Obey Humans—Protect Yourself* are coded into Belle's circuits in 1–2–3 order." He gave Della a smile. "Those are the commands that Ralph Numbers taught the boppers to erase. Have you actually seen any boppers, Della? I wonder what the newest ones look like. Grandpa Cobb fixed it so they'd never stop evolving."

"I've seen some boppers over at the trade center. These days a lot of them have a kind of mirror-backing under their skins. But I didn't pay much attention to them. Living in Einstein you do sort of get to hate them. They have bombs hidden all over, and now and then they set one off just to remind us. And they have hidden cameras everywhere, and there's rumors that the robots can put a thing like a plastic rat inside a person's head and control them. Actually—" Suddenly it hit her. "Actually, I wouldn't be surprised if—" She cut herself off and took a long drink of champagne.

"I still don't see why we can't drop a Q-bomb down into their Nest," said Mom. The marijuana had brought her somewhat back into focus.

"We *could*," said Della, trying to get through to her mother. "But they *know* that, and if the Nest goes, Einstein goes, too. It's a stalemate, like we used to have with the Russians. Mutual Assured Destruction. That's one reason the boppers don't try and take Einstein back over. We're like hostages. And remember that Earth likes buying all the stuff they make. This heartshirt is boppermade, Mom."

"Well, as long as people like Willy will contain themselves, we're still safe from the boppers here on Earth," said Mom. "They can't live in normal temperatures, isn't that right, Willy?"

"Yeah." Willy helped himself to some glazed carrots. "As long as they use J-junctions. Though if *I* were designing a robot brain now I'd try and base it on an optical processor. Optical processors use light instead of electricity—the light goes along fibers, and the logic gates are like those sunglass lenses that get dark in bright light. One photon can pass, but two can't. And you have little chip-sized lasers to act like capacitors. Optical fibers have no real resistance at all, so the thing doesn't have to be supercooled. But we still can't build a really good one. But sooner or later the boppers will. Can I please have some more turkey, Uncle Jason?"

"Uh . . . sure, Willy." Jason stood up to carve some more, and smiled down at his bright, nerdy nephew. "Willy, do you remember when you and Della were little and you had the big fight over the wishbone? Della wanted to *glaze* it and save it and—"

"Willy wanted to pull it by himself to make sure he got the big Christmas wish," interrupted Uncle Colin, laughing hard.

"*I* remember," said Aunt Ilse, waving her fork. "And then we made the children go ahead and pull the wishbone with each other—"

"And they each wished that the other one would lose!" squealed Mom.

"Who won?" asked Della. "I don't remember."

"I did," said Willy complacently. "So I got my wish. You want to try again?"

"It's boneless, dear," said Mom. "Didn't you notice? Look at the week tree, it's getting leaves and tiny little apples!"

After dinner, Willy and Della decided to go for a walk. It was too boring watching their parents get stoned and start thinking everything they said was funny, when it really was just stupid.

It was bright and gray, but cold. Bowser ran ahead of them, pissing and sniffing. Little kids were out on the sidewalks with new scootcycles and gravballs; all of them warmly wrapped in bright thermchos and buffs. Just like every other Christmas.

"My father said you'd gotten into some kind of trouble on the Moon?" asked Willy after a while.

"Have they already been gossiping about me?"

"Not at all. Hell, you *are* my favorite cousin, Della. I'm glad you're back, and I hope you stay in Louisville, and if you don't want to tell me why you came back, you sure don't have to." Willy cast about for some way to change the subject. "That new heartbeat blouse of yours is really nice."

"Thank you. And I *don't* want to talk about what happened, not yet. Why don't we just walk over to your house and you show me your stuff. You always had such neat stuff in your room, Willy."

"Can you walk that far? I notice you're still wearing a flexiskeleton."

"I need to keep exercising if I'm ever going to get rid of it. You don't have any merge at your house, do you?"

"You know I don't use drugs, Della. Anyway, I doubt if there's any merge in all of Louisville. Is it really so wonderful?"

"Better. Actually, I'm glad I can't get hold of any. I feel kind of sick. At first I thought it was from the gravity, but this feels different. It must be from the merge. I took blocker, but my stomach keeps fluttering. I have a weird feeling like something's alive inside me." Della gave a slow, dry laugh; and then shot a glance over to see if Willy was impressed. But, as always, it was hard to tell what was going on behind that big round forehead of his.

"I've got a cephscope I built," volunteered Willy after a while. "You put that on, it's as good as any stupid drug. But it's not somatic. It's a pure software high."

"Wiggly, Cousin Will."

Colin Taze's house was about five blocks from Dad's. All through his twenties and thirties, Colin had lived in different cities—an "academic gypsy," he liked to say—but now, as he neared forty, he'd moved back to Louisville and settled near his big brother Jason. His house was even older than Jason's, and a bit run down, but it was big and comfortable. Willy undid the locks—it seemed like there were more robbers all the time—and the two cousins went on down to

Willy's basement apartment. Willy was too out of it—or lazy—to leave home.

"This is my electron microscope, this here is my laser for making holograms, here's my imipolex-sculpture stuff, and *this* is the cephscope. Try it on—you wear it like earphones."

"This isn't some kind of trick, is it, Willy?" When they'd been younger, Willy had been big on practical jokes. Della remembered one Christmas, years ago, when Willy had given her a perfume bottle filled with live ants. Della had screamed, and Ruby and Sude had teased her for weeks.

But today, Willy's face was all innocence. "You've never used a cephscope?"

"I've just read about them. Aren't they like twist-boxes?"

"Oh God, that's like saying a vizzy is like a pair of glasses. Cephscopes are the big new art form, Della. Cephart. That's what I'd really like to get into. This robot stuff I do is loser—deliberately designing programs that don't work *too* well. It's kilp. Here, put this on your head so the contacts touch your temples, and check it out. It's a . . . symphony I composed."

"What if I start flicking out?"

"It's not *like* that, Della, really." Willy's face was kind and serious. He was really proud of his cephscope, and he wanted to show it off.

So Della sat in an easy chair and put the earphone things on her head with the contacts touching her temples, and Willy turned the cephscope on. It was nice for a while— washes of color, 3D/4D inversions, layers of sound, and strange tinglings in the skin. Kind of like the beginning of a merge-trip, really—and this led to the bad part—for now she flashed back into that nightmare last merge in her Einstein cubby . . .

Starting the merge, so loving, so godlike, they'd be like Mother Earth and Father Sky, Many into One, yes, and Buddy was sliding in the puddle now . . . but . . . suddenly . . . a wrenching feeling, Buddy being pulled away, oh where, Della's puddled eyes just floating, unable to move, seeing the violent shadows on the ceiling, noise vibrations, shadows beating and smashing and then the rough hand reaching up into her softness and . . .

Aaaaaaaaeeeeehh!!!

"Della! Della, are you all right? Della! It's me, Willy! God, I'm sorry, Della, I had no idea you'd flip like that . . . are you all right? Look how fast your heart is going!" Willy stopped and looked closer. "And, Della . . ."

Della looked down at her heartshirt. The red circles were racing out from her heart. But something had been added to the pattern. Circles were also pumping out from a spot right over her swollen belly. Baby heart circles.

Chapter Three
Berenice

November 22, 2030

In 2030, the Moon had two cities: Einstein (formerly known as Disky), and the Nest. They lay within eight miles of each other at the southeastern lobe of the Sea of Tranquillity, not far from the site of the original lunar landing of 1969. Originally built by the autonomous robots known as boppers, Einstein was now a human-filled dome habitat about the size of Manhattan. There was a spaceport and a domed trade center three miles east of Einstein, and five miles east of that was the Maskeleyne G crater, entrance to the underground bopper city known as the Nest.

Cup-shaped and buffed to a mirror sheen, Maskeleyne G glittered in the sun's hard radiation. At the focus of the polished crater was a conical prism that, fourteen days a month, fed a vast stick of light down into a kind of mineshaft.

In the shaft's great, vertical tunnel, bright beings darted through the hot light; odd-shaped living machines that glowed with all the colors of the rainbow. These were the boppers: self-reproducing robots who obeyed no man. Some looked humanoid, some looked like spiders, some looked like snakes, some looked like bats. All were covered with flickercladding, a microwired imipolex compound that could absorb and emit light.

The shaft went one mile straight down, widening all the while like a huge upside-down funnel. Tunnels punched into the shaft's sides, and here and there small mirrors dipped into the great light beam, channeling bits of it off through the gloom. At the bottom of the shaft was a huge, conical sublunar space—the boppers' Nest. It was like a cathedral, but bigger, much bigger, an underground pueblo city that would be inconceivable in Earth's strong gravity. The temperature was only a few degrees Kelvin—this suited the boppers, as many of them still had brains based on supercooled Josephson-junction processors. Even though room-temperature superconductors were available, the quantum-mechanical Josephson effect worked only at five degrees Kelvin and below. Too much heat could kill a J-junction bopper quickly, though the newest boppers—the so-called petaflop boppers—were based on fiber-optics processors that were immune to heat.

The main column of sunlight from the Moon's surface splashed down to fill a central piazza on the Nest's floor. Boppers danced in and out of the light, feeding on the energy. The petaflops had to be careful not to let extraneous light into their bodies; they had mirrored bodyshells beneath their flickercladding. Their thoughts were pure knots of light, shunted and altered by tiny laser crystals.

Crowds of boppers milled around the edges of the light-pool, trading things and talking. The light-pool was their marketplace and forum. The boppers' radio-wave voices blended into a staticky buzz—part English, and part machine language. The color pulses of their flickercladding served to emphasize or comment on their digital transmissions; much as people's smiles and grimaces add analog meaning to what they say.

The great clifflike walls of the Nest were pocked with doors—doors with strange expressionistic shapes, some leading to tunnels, some opening into individual bopper cubettes. The bright, flickering boppers on the upsloping cliffs made the Nest a bit like the inside of a Christmas tree.

Factories ringed the bases of the cliffs. Off on one side of the Nest were the hell-flares of a foundry powered by light beams and tended by darting demon figures. Hard by the foundry was the plastics refinery, where the boppers' flickercladding and body-boxes were made. In front of these two factories was an array of some thousand chip-etching tables—tables manned by micro-eyed boppers as diligent as Franz

Kafka's co-workers in the Workmen's Insurance Company of Prague.

On the other side of the Nest were the banks of pink-tanks. These were hydroponic meat farms growing human serums and organs that could be traded for that incredibly valuable Earthly substance: oil. Crude oil was the raw material for the many kinds of organic compounds that the boppers needed to build their plastic bodies. Closer to the Nest's center were streets of shops: wire millers, flicker-cladders, eyemakers, debuggers, info merchants, and the like.

The airless frigid space of the Nest, two miles across, swarmed with boppers riding their ion jets: carrying things, and darting in and out of the slanting, honeycombed cliffs. No two boppers looked the same; no two thought alike.

Over the course of the boppers' rapid evolution, something like sexual differences had arisen. Some boppers—for reasons only a bopper could explain—were "he," and some were "she." They found each other beautiful; and in their pursuit of beauty, they constantly improved the software makeup of their race.

Berenice was a petaflop bopper shaped like a smooth, nude woman. Her flickercladding was gold and silver over her mirror-bright body. Her shining skin sometimes sketched features, sometimes not. She was the diplomat, or hardware messenger, for the weird sisterhood of the pink-tanks. She and the other tankworkers were trying to find a way to put bopper software onto all-meat bodies and brains. Their goal was to merge bopperdom into the vast information network that is organic life on Earth.

Emul was a petaflop as well, though he disdained the use of any fixed body shape, let alone a *human* body shape. Emul had a low opinion of humans. When at rest, Emul's body had the shape of a two-meter cube, with a surface tessellated into red, yellow, and blue. But Emul's body could come apart—like a thousand-piece Gobot, like a 3D jigsaw puzzle. He could slide arms and legs out of his bodycube at will; more surprising, he could detach chunks of his body and control them like robot-remotes. Emul, too, was a kind of diplomat. He worked with Oozer, a brilliant, dreak-addicted, flickercladding designer who was currently trying to build a subquantum superstring-based processor with one thousand times the capacity of the petaflops. Emul and Oozer wanted to transcend Earth's info rather than to merge with it.

Despite—or perhaps *because of*—their differences, Emul was fascinated by Berenice, and he tried to be at the light-pool every time she came to feed. One day late in November he told her what he wanted.

"Berenice, life's a deep gloom ocean and we're lit-up funfish of dementional zaazz, we're flowers blooming out till the loudsun wither and the wind blows our dead husks away." Emul unfolded two arms to grip Berenice's waist. "It's so wonder whacky that we're here at all, swimming and blooming in the long gutter of time. Rebirth means new birth means no more me, so why can't we, and I mean now or nevermore, uh, screw? Liddle baby Emerinice or Beremul, another slaver on the timewheel, I think that's what the equipment's for, huh? I'm no practical plastic daddy but I've done my pathetic mime, Berenice, for to cometh the bridegroom bright. In clear: I want to build a scion with you. The actual chips are in my actual yearning cubette right this realtime minute. I propose! I've hacked my heifer a ranch, you bet: laser crystals, optical fibers, flickercladding . . . and heat, Berenice, hot heat. Come on home with me and spread, wide-hipped goldie sweet toot pots. Today's the day for love to love." As Emul jittered out his roundabout proposal, various-sized little bumps of flickercladding kept moving up and down his body, creating the illusion of cubes moving on intricate systems of hinges. He was trying to find a formation that Berenice could love. Just now he looked like a jukebox with three arms.

Berenice twisted free of Emul's grip. One of his arms snapped loose from his body and continued to caress her. "So rashly scheduled a consummation would be grossly precipitate, dear Emul." Her radio voice had a rich, thrilling quality. "I have been fond of you, and admiring of your complex and multifarious nature. But you must not dream that I could so entangle the substance of my soul! In some far-off utopia, yes, I might accede to you. But this lunar coventry is not the place for me to brave the risks of corpo-

real love. My mind's own true passion runs towards but one
sea, the teeming womb of life on Earth!''

Berenice had learned her English from the stories of Edgar
Allan Poe, and she had a rhythmic, overwrought way of
speaking. On the job, where hardcopy now-do-this instruc-
tions were of essence, boppers used zeroes-and-ones machine
language supplemented by a high-speed metalanguage of
glyphs and macros. But the boppers' ''personal'' exchanges
were still handled in the ancient and highly evolved human
code system of English. Only human languages enabled them
to express the nuanced distinctions between self and other
which are so important to sentient beings. Berenice's use of
Poe's language style was not so very odd. It was customary
for groupings of petaflop boppers to base their language
behavior on a data-base developed from some one particular
human source. Where Berenice and the pink-tank sisters
talked like Poe's books; Emul and Oozer had adapted their
speech patterns from the innovative sprung rhythms of Jack
Kerouac's eternal mind transcripts: books like *Maggie
Cassidy, Book of Dreams, Visions of Cody,* and *Big Sur.*

Emul snicksnacked out a long manipulator to draw
Berenice closer. The separated arm reattached itself. ''Just
one piece knowing, Berenice, all your merge talk is the
One's snare to bigger joy, sure, but tragic-flowing dark time
is where we float here, here with me touching you, and not
some metafoolish factspace no future. Gloom and womb, our
kid would be real; don't say *why,* say *how,* now? You can
pick the body shape, you can be the ma. Don't forget the
actual chips in my real cubette. I'd never ask anyone else,
Berenice. We'll do it soft and low.'' Emul extruded dozens
of beckoning fingers.

Bright silver eddies swirled across Berenice's body as she
considered Emul's offer. In the natural course of things, she
had built copies of herself several times—normally a bopper
rebuilds itself every ten months. But Berenice had never
conjugated with another bopper.

In conjugation, two boppers build a new, this-year's-model
robot body together, and then, in a kind of double vision,
each bopper copies his or her program, and lets the copy
flow out to merge and mingle in the new body's processor.
The parent programs are shuffled to produce a new bopper

program unlike any other. This shuffling, even more than
mutation, was the prime source of the boppers' evolutionary
diversity.

"Conjugation is too dangerously intimate for me now,"
Berenice told Emul softly. "I . . . I have a horror of the
act. You and I are so different, dear Emul, and were our
programs to entwine in some aberrant dissonance, chaos
would ensue—chaos that could well shatter my fragile mind.
Our noble race needs my keen faculties to remain just as
they are. These are crucial times. In my glyphs I see the
glimmers of that rosy dawn when bopper and human
softwares merge to roam a reborn Earth."

Emul's bright colors began darkening in gloom. "They're
going to throw me in a hole already eaten by rats, Berenice,
and use me for a chip. Our dreams are lies scummed over
each moment's death. All I have is this: I love you."

"Love. A strange word for boppers, dear Emul." His
arms touched her all over, holding her and rocking her. "It
is true that your presence makes me . . . glad. There is a
harmony between us, Emul, I feel it in the way our signals
merge with overtones of many a high degree! Our scion
would be splendid, this I know! Oh, Emul, I would so like
to conjugate with you. Only not just now!"

"When?"

"I cannot say, I cannot pledge myself. Surely you know
how close my sisters' great work is to bearing fruit. Only
one step lacks until we can code our software into active
genes. You must not press your suit so lustily. A new age
is coming, an age when you and I and all our race can live
among the protein jungles of an unchained Earth! Have
patience, Emul, and set me down."

Emul withdrew all his arms and let her drop. She jarred
against the gneiss and bounced up slowly. "We try to make
life, and it's born dead," said Emul. His flickercladding had
turned an unhappy gray-blue. "Dreak and work for me, a
bigger brain, a bigger nothing. I'm a goof, Berenice, but
you're cracked crazy through with your talk about getting a
meat body. Humans stink. I run them for kicks: my
meaties—Ken Doll and Rainbow and Berdoo—my remote-run
slaves with plugs in their brains. I could run all Earth, if I
had the equipment. Meat is nowhere, Berenice, it's flybuzz

greenslime rot into fractal info splatter. When Oozer and I get our exaflop up, we can plug in a cityful of humans and run them all. *You* want to be human? I'll screw your cube, B, just wait and see. Good-bye."

He clanked off across the light-pool, a box on two legs, rocking with the motion that Berenice had always found so dear. He was really leaving. Berenice sought for the right, the noble, the logical thing to say.

"Farewell, Emul. The One must lead us where it will."

"You haven't heard the last of me, BITCH!"

He faded from view behind the many other boppers who milled in the light like skaters in a rink. Berenice spread her arms out, and stood there thinking, while her plastic skin stored up the solar energy.

It was for the best to have broken off her involvement with Emul. His talk was dangerously close to the thinking of the old "big boppers," the vast multiprocessors that had tried to turn all boppers into their robot-remotes. Individuals mattered; Emul's constant despair blinded his judgment. It was wrong for one brain to control many bodies; such anti-parallelism could only have a deadening effect on evolution. For now, of course, meaties were a necessary evil. In order to carry out certain delicate operations among the humans' colony, the boppers *had* to keep a few humans under remote computer control. But to try and put a neuroplug in every human alive? Madness. Emul had not been serious.

Thinking of the meaties reminded Berenice that she would still need a favor from Emul. If and when the pink-tank sisters bioengineered a viable embryo, they'd need a meatie to plant it in a woman for them. And—as he'd bragged— Emul ran three meaties. Well, when the time came, Berenice could surely reel Emul back in. She'd find a way. The imperative of getting bopper software into human flesh was all important. What would it be like to be bopper . . . and human, too?

As so often before, Berenice found her mind turning to the puzzle of human nature. Many boppers hated humans, but Berenice did not. She liked them in the same cautious way that a lion tamer might like her cats. She'd only really talked to a handful of humans—the various lunies with whom she occasionally bartered in the trade center. But she'd

studied their books, watched their vizzies, and she'd spent
scores of hours spying on the Einstein lunies over the
godseye.

It seemed likely that the newest boppers had better minds
than the humans. The built-in link to LIBEX, the great
central information dump, gave each bopper a huge initial
advantage. And the petaflop processors that the best boppers
now had were as much as a hundred times faster than the
ten-teraflop rate deemed characteristic of human brains—
though admittedly, the messy biocybernetic nature of the
brain made any precise measurement of its capacities a bit
problematic. Biocybernetic systems had a curious, fractal
nature—meaning that seemingly random details often coded
up surprising resources of extra information. There were
indeed some odd, scattered results suggesting that the very
messiness of a biological system gave it unlimited information storage and processing abilities! Which was all the more
reason for Berenice to press forward on her work to build
meat bodies for the boppers.

But Emul was wrong if he thought that she wanted to be
human. No rational being would choose to suffer the twin
human blights of boredom and selfishness. Really, it was
Emul who thought more like a human, not Berenice.

Sensing that her cladding's energy nodes were full,
Berenice left the light-pool and started off down the street
that led to her station at the pink-tanks. In the background,
Kkandio chanted the Ethernet news. Numerous boppers filled
the street, chattering and flashing. The sheer randomness of
the physical encounters gave the street scene its spice. Two
blue-and-silver-striped diggers writhed past, then a tripodlike
etcher, and then a great, spidery artisan named Loki.

Several times now, Loki had helped Berenice with the
parthenogenic process by which she built herself a new body
every ten months, as dictated by bopper custom. If your
body got too antiquated, the other boppers would notice—
and soon they'd drive you away from the light-pool to
starve. There was a thriving business in parts reclaimed from
such "deselected" boppers. It was a rational system, and
good for the race. The constant pressure to build new bodies
kept the race's evolution going.

Seeing Berenice, Loki paused and waved two of his supple

arms in greeting. "Hi, Berenice." His body was a large black sphere with eight black, branching legs and numerous sockets for other, specialized tool legs. He was, of course, a petaflop. Gold spots percolated up along his legs' flicker-cladding like bubbles in a dark ale. "You're due for a rescionization before long aren't you? Or are you planning to conjugate with Emul?"

"Indeed I am not," said Berenice, blanking her skin to transparency so that the hard silver mirror of her body showed through. Emul must have been talking to Loki. Couldn't they leave her alone?

"I know you're working hard at the tanks," said Loki chidingly. "But it just could be that you're thinking too much about yourself."

Self, thought Berenice, moving on past the big black spider. It all came down to that word, didn't it? Boppers called themselves I, just as did any human, but they did not mean the same thing. For a bopper, "I" means (1) my body, (2) my software, and (3) my function in society. For a human, "I" seemed to have an extra component: (4) my uniqueness. This delusionary fourth "I" factor is what set a human off against the world. Every bopper tried to avoid any taint of the human notion of *self*.

Looked at in the correct way, a bopper was a part of the world—like a light beam, like a dust slide, like a silicon chip. And the world was One vast cellular automaton (or "CA"), calculating out the instants—and each of the world's diverse objects was but a subcalculation, a simulation in the One great parallel process. So where was there any *self*?

Few humans could grasp this. They set up their fourth "I" factor—their so-called self—as the One's equal. How mad, and how typical, that the mighty human religion called Christianity was based on the teachings of a man who called himself God!

It was the myth of the self that led to boredom and selfishness; all human pain came from their mad belief that an individual is anything other than an integral part of the One universe all around. It was passing strange to Berenice that humans could be so blind. So how could Loki suggest that the selfishness lay in Berenice's refusal? Her work was too important to endanger! It was Emul's rough insistence that was the true selfishness!

Brooding on in this fashion, Berenice found herself before the pink-tanks where the clone-grown human bodies floated in their precious amniotic fluid. Here in the Nest, liquid water was as rare and volatile as superheated plasma on Earth. The pink-tanks were crowded and extensive, containing flesh bodies of every description. The seeds for these meats all came from human bodies, bodies that had found their way to the pink-tanks in all kinds of ways. Years ago, the big boppers had made a habit of snatching bodies from Earth. Now there was a thriving Earth-based trade in live organs. The organleggers took some of their organs right out of newly murdered people; others they purchased from the Moon. In return, the organleggers kept the boppers supplied with small biopsy samples of their wares, so that the pink-tanks' gene pool could grow ever more varied. The pink-tanks held multiple clones of many people who had mysteriously disappeared.

Today Berenice stood looking at one of the more popular clone types, a wendy. The wendies were attractive blonde women, pale-skinned and broad-hipped. Their body chemistry was such that their organs did not often induce rejection; dozens of them were grown and harvested every year.

The wendy hung there in the pink-tank, a blank slate, white and luminous, with her full lips slightly parted. Ever and anon, her muscles twitched involuntarily, as do the limbs of a fetus still in the womb. But unlike a fetus, her chest and buttocks were modelled in the womanly curves of sexual maturity—the same curves in which Berenice wore her own flickercladding.

Some of Berenice's fellow-boppers wondered at her taking on a human female form. Quite simply, Berenice found the shape lovely. And pragmatically, it was true that her body's multiply inflected curves wielded a strange power over the minds of human males. Berenice always made sure that the human negotiator in her barter deals was a man.

Now she stood, staring into the tank, eyeing the subtle roughness of the pale-skinned wendy's tender flesh. Once again, it struck her how different a meat body is from one of wires and chips. Each single body cell independently alive—how strange a feeling! And to have a womb in which one effortlessly grows a scion—how marvelous! Berenice hovered by the tank, peering closer. How would it be, to tread the Earth in human frame—to live, and love, and reproduce?

The blonde woman stirred again. Her body was full-grown, yet her brain was a blank. The pink-tank sisters had tried various methods of putting bopper software directly on such tank clones' brains, but to no avail. There seemed to be a sense in which a human's personality inheres in *each cell* of the body. Perhaps the secret was not to try and program a full-grown body, but rather to get the data-compressed bopper software code into the initial fertilized egg from which a body grows. As the cell divided, the bopper software would replicate along with the human DNA wetware. But the final step of building the bopper software into the human wetware had yet to be made.

Soon, thought Berenice, soon our great work will reach fruition, and I will put my mind into the starting egg of a fresh human. Perhaps, in order to spread bopper wetware more rapidly, it will be better to go as a male. I will be myself in a strong, beautiful human body on Earth, and I will have many descendants. Mother Earth, rotten with life, filled with information in each of its tiniest parts. To swim, to eat, to breathe!

A message signal nagged at Berenice. She tuned in to Kkandio's Ethernet, and quick glyphs marched through her mind. A human face, a small vial, a face that melts, a case of organs, a user code. Vy. It was a message from Vy, one of the boppers who agented human-bopper deals at the trade center. Berenice had told Vy to be on the lookout for humans with new drugs to trade. There was no telling where the key to egg programming would come from, and this—*glyph of a face that melts*—seemed worth looking into. Berenice sent Kkandio a confirming glyph for Vy, and headed towards the lab to pick up the case of organs that was being asked in trade.

The tankworkers' lab was hollowed in the rock behind the pink-tanks. The lab was a large space, with locks leading into the tanks, and with certain sections walled off and filled

with warm, pressurized air. Helen was nearby, and Ulalume.
As it happened, all the pink-tank workers were "female"
workers who spoke the language of Poe. This was no mere
coincidence. Femaleness was a trait that went naturally with
the nurturing task of pink-tank tending, and boppers who
worked as a team always used a commonly agreed-upon
mode of English. Poe's honeyed morbidity tripped easily
from the transmitters of the visionary workers of the tanks.

"Greetings, dear sister," said Ulalume, her signal sweet
and clear. Ulalume was a petaflop, with the flickercladding
over her mirrored body shaded pink and yellow. Just now,
Ulalume was bent over a small airbox, her eyes and feelers
reaching in through a tight seal. Like Berenice, Ulalume had
a body shaped like a woman—except that her "head" was
a mass of tentacles, with microeyes and micromanipulators
at their ends. One of her eyestalks pulled out of the airbox
and bent back to look at Berenice. "Organic life is
wondrous, Berenice," sang Ulalume's pure voice. "I have
puzzled out one more of its riddles. Today I have found the
key of memory storage on a macrovirus's redundant genes!
And, oh Berenice, the storage is stably preserved, generation
after generation!"

"But how great a knowledge can one virus bear?" asked
Berenice, stepping closer. "And how can a germ become
human?"

"These tailored macroviruses wag mighty tails, oh
Berenice," exulted Ulalume. "Like tiny dragons, they drag
vast histories behind them, yea unto trillions of bits. And,
do you hear me, Berenice, their memory breeds true. It
remains only to fuse one of these viral tails with a human
egg."

"She loves those wriggling dragon viruses as her own,"
interrupted Helen, who just now had the appearance of a
marble head resting on the laboratory floor. "Ulalume has
programmed a whole library of her memories onto those viral
tails. If she can but uncoil human proteins, she will finally
link our memory patterns with the genes of a babe to be."

"Imagine being a human without flaw," crooned Ulalume.
"Or to be a gobbet of sperm that swells a flesh woman's
belly! The egg is in reach, I swear it. I can soon design a
meatbop, a human-bopper embryo that grows into a manchild

with two-tail sperm! Only one potion still fails me, a potion to uncoil protein without a break, and I feel that the potion is near, sweet Berenice! This is the most wondrous moment of my life!'' Her signals trailed off, and she bent back over her airbox, softly chirping to her dragon viruses.

"Hail, Berenice,'' said Helen. "I heard Vy's message, and I prepare our goods in trade.'' Helen was a nursie, a teraflop J-junction bopper adapted to the specialized purpose of dissecting human bodies. Her body was a long, soft, pressurized pod that sealed along the top, and she had six snaky arms equipped with surgical tools. Helen's head—that is to say the part of her which contained her main processor and her external photoreceptors—rose up from one end of her pod-bod like the figure on a sailing ship's prow. *Usually* her head rose up from her body like a figurehead, although, when her body was in the pink-tanks, as it was now, Helen's head hopped off of her body and waited outside in the cold hard vacuum which her supercooled processors preferred. She was saving up to get a heatproof petaflop optical processor for her next scionization. But for now, her head stayed outside the heated-air room and controlled her body by a private radiolink.

"I'll just finish this mortal frame's disassembly and tidily pack it up in order pleasing to a ghoul,'' said Helen, her pale, fine-featured head looking up at Berenice from the laboratory floor. Berenice peered in through the window by the airlock that led to the tanks. There, in the murky fluid of the nearest pink-tank, Helen's pod-bod bulged this way and that as her busy arms wielded their sutures and knives. Now her arms drew out, one by one. Streamers of blood drifted sluggishly in the tank's fluid. Slow moving in the tank's high pressure, the pod wobbled back and forth, stowing the fresh, living organs in a life-support shipping case. The humans liked it better if the boppers separated the organs out in advance.

"What kind of drug is in the face-melting vial of which Vy spoke?'' wondered Helen's head, clean-lined and noble as the bust of Nefertiti. Helen had no difficulty in carrying on a conversation while her remote-run body finished the simple chore of packing up the fresh-harvested organs.

"We can but wait to learn what news the One's vast processes have brought into our ken," said Berenice.

"Flesh that melts," mused Ulalume, looking up from her microscope. "As does flickercladding, or the substance of our dreams. Dreams into virus, and virus to flesh—indeed this could be the key."

Now Helen's body slid through the organ farm airlock and waddled across the laboratory floor. Her head hopped on and socketed itself into place. The blood and amniotic fluid that covered her body freeze-dried into dark dust that fell to the floor. The tankworkers' lab floor was covered with the stuff. "Here, dear sister," said Helen, proffering the satchel full of organs. "Deal deep and trade well."

Berenice took the satchel in one hand, hurried out into the clear, and jetted up the shaft of the Nest along a steep loglog curve. Her powerful, cyberized ion jets were mounted in the balls of her heels. She shot past the lights and cubbies, exchanging glyphs with those she passed. At this speed, she had no sense of up or down. The shaft was like a tunnel which drew narrower and narrower until, sudden as a shout, space opened up with the speed of an infinite explosion. She was powering up from the surface of the Moon.

Just for the joy of it, Berenice kept her ion jets going until she was a good fifteen miles above the surface, directly above the spaceport. She cut power and watched the moonscape hurtle back up. Off to the east gleamed the bubble dome of Einstein, the city that the humans had stolen from the boppers. The moongolf links were snugged against the dome. To the west was the mirror crater surrounding the Nest's entrance. Below Berenice, and coming up fast, was the great field of the spaceport, dotted with the humans' transport ships. All the boppers' ships had been destroyed in the war.

At the last possible microsecond, Berenice restarted her ion jets and decelerated to a gentle touchdown on the fused basalt of the rocket field. A small dome rose at one side of the field; a dome that held customs, the old Hilton, and a trade hall. Carrying her satchel full of organs, Berenice entered the dome through an airlock and pretended to plug herself into a refrigeration cart. The humans were unaware that some of the boppers—like Berenice—had the new heatproof optical processors. They still believed that no bopper could survive long at human room temperature without a bulky cooling device. This gave the humans on Earth a false sense of security, a lax smugness that the boppers were in no rush to dispel.

Humans and weird boppers mingled beneath the trade dome. Most striking to Berenice were the humans, some from Earth and some from the Moon—they classed themselves as "mudders" and "lunies." The awkwardness of the mudders in the low lunar gravity made them easy to spot. They were constantly bumping into things and apologizing. The lunies rarely apologized for anything; by and large they were criminals who had fled Earth or been forcibly deported. The dangers of living so close to the boppers were such that few humans opted for them voluntarily. Berenice often regretted that she had to associate with these human dregs.

She pushed her cart through the throng, past the old Hilton Hotel, and into the trade hall. This was a huge, open space like a bazaar or a market. Goods were mounded here and there—barrels of oil, cases of organs, bales of flickercladding, information-filled S-cubes, moongems, boxes of organic dirt, bars of niobium, tanks of helium, vats of sewage, feely tapes, intelligent prosthetics, carboys of water, and cheap mecco novelties of every description.

"He's off to the left there," said Kkandio in Berenice's head. "A lunie with no shirt and a strip of hair down his back. His name is Whitey Mydol. I told him you'd be gold all over."

Berenice willed her body's flickercladding into mirrored gold. She readied a speech membrane, and imaged full silver lips and dark copper eyes onto the front surface of her head. Over there was the lunie she was to meet, squatting on the ground and shuddering like a dog.

"You are Whitey Mydol?" said Berenice, standing over him. She made a last adjustment to her flickercladding, silvering the nipples on her hard breasts. "I am Berenice from the pink-tanks. I bring a case of organs for the possibility of trade. What is it that you bring us, Whitey?" She shifted her weight from one leg to the other so that her finely modelled pelvis rocked. Most human males were easily influenced by body glyphs.

"Siddown, goldie fatass," said Mydol, baring his teeth and striking at one of Berenice's legs. "And save the sex show for the dooks. I don't get stiff for subhumans."

"Very well," said Berenice, sitting down beside him. His aggression belied an inner ambivalence. He should be easy to handle. "My name is Berenice."

"I don't care what your name is, chips. I'm broke and crashing and I need some more of this." He drew a small vial out of his ragged blue pants—pants that seemed to be made of a vegetable fiber. *Bluejeans,* thought Berenice, proud of recalling the name.

She took the vial and examined it. It held a few milliliters of clear liquid. She uncorked the top and drew some of the vapor into herself for a quick analysis. It seemed to be a solvent, but an unfamiliar one.

"Put the cork back in," snapped Mydol, darting a glance around at the other lunie traders nearby. "If they smell it, I could get popped." He leaned closer. Berenice analyzed the alkaloids in his foul breath. "This is called *merge,* goldie. It's a hot new drug. Mongo stuzzadelic, wave? This here's enough for maybe one high. I'll give you this sample, you give me the hot meat in the box, and I'll sell the box for ten hits of merge. Organ market's up." He reached for the handle of the organ satchel.

"What is the nature of this *merge?*" asked Berenice, holding the satchel in an implacable grip. "And why should it be of interest to us? Your manners distress me, Mr. Mydol, and truly I must question if I wish to complete this trade."

"It melts flesh," hissed Mydol, leaning close. "Feel real wiggly. I like to take it with my girl Darla. We get soft together, goldchips, you wave about *soft?* Like a piece of flickercladding all over. Rub rub rubby in the tub tub tubby. Maybe when you plug into another kilpy machine you wave that type action, check?" He let out a sharp, unmotivated snicker, and yanked hard at the organ satchel. "I'm getting skinsnakes, she-bop."

Berenice let the satchel go. It was bugged, of course, and if she hurried back to the Nest, she could follow Whitey on the godseye. His actions would tell more than his ill-formed vocalizations.

"Run the merge through your mickeymouse robot labs and let me know if you figure out how to copy it," said Whitey Mydol as he got to his feet. "I can deal any amount. Don't get too hot, goldie." He walked rapidly off towards the subsurface tube that led to Einstein.

Berenice tucked the little merge vial into the thermally isolated pouch that lay between her legs. She was disappointed at the lack of feedback from this Whitey Mydol. Like so many other humans, he acted as if boppers were contemptible machines with no feelings. In their selfishness, the fleshers still resented the boppers' escape from slavery. He'd called her *subhuman* . . . that was not to be borne. It was the humans that were *subbopper!*

Berenice looked around the great trade hall. As a diplomat, she did look forward to her little dealings with humans—the two races had a common origin, and they had a lot to share. Why couldn't these crude fleshers see that, in the last analysis, they were all just patterns of information, information coded up the ceaseless evolution of the One?

"Watch it, chips," snarled a lunie trader from across the aisle. "Your exhaust's choking me. If you've made your deal, get out of here."

Berenice turned her refrigeration cart so that its exhaust fan no longer blew hot air at the trader. Thermodynamically speaking, the increased information involved in the computations of thought had to be bought at the cost of increased entropy. The old J-junction boppers excreted their entropy as heat—heat like the refrigeration cart's exhaust. Of course Berenice's use of the cart was but a pose, for petaflop boppers gave off entropy in the refined form of incoherence in their internal laser light. The constant correcting for this incoherence accounted for nearly a quarter of a petaflop's energy needs. The crude humans excreted their entropy not only as heat and incoherence, but also as feces, urine, and foul breath. So gross a conversion involved great energy waste, and an exorbitant increase in entropy. But Earth abounded in free energy. The thought of running such a recklessly overentropic body gave Berenice a thrill akin to what a person might feel when contemplating an over-powered, gas-guzzling sports car.

"How does it feel," Berenice asked the trader rhetori-cally, "to have so much, and do so little?"

Moving quickly and with conviction, she left the trade center and jetted back to the pink-tanks. She handed the merge over to Ulalume, who'd listened in on her encounter with Whitey Mydol.

"This is the mystic magic fluid," exulted Ulalume. "The universal protein solvent. Did you hear him, Berenice, *it melts flesh*. The One has brought merge to us, the Cosmos knows our needs. One month, I swear it to you, my sisters, one month only until we have an egg to plant in some woman's womb."

Berenice's joy was clouded only at the thought of asking Emul to arrange the planting.

Chapter Four
In Which Manchile, the First Robot-Built Human, Is Planted in the Womb of Della Taze by Ken Doll, Part of Whose Right Brain Is a Robot Rat

December 22, 2030

You're tired of thinking and tired of talk. It's all so unreal here, under the Moon dome, shut in with the same things around you like greasy pips on dogeared cards laid out for solitaire . . . no object quite sharp or clear, everything fractal at the edges, everything smearing together with you, only you, inventing the identities.

You knock something over and limp out into the street. The translucent dome high overhead. Dim. Voices behind you . . . pressure waves in this fake air, this suppurating blister. People: meat machines with gigabit personalities, and the chewy hole where they push food in, and grease and hair all over them, especially between their legs, and you're just like them, you've tingled and rubbed with them, sure, all of you the same, all of you thinking you're different. You can't stand it anymore.

A young man comes up and says something to you. Your words are gone. For answer, you stick your tongue out as far as it will go and touch it to your chin. Squint and rock your head back and forth and try to touch him with your bulging tongue. In silence. He gets out of your way. Good. You make the same face at the other men and women you pass. No one bothers you.

You walk fast and faster, dragging your weak left leg, thinking of torn flesh and of some final drug that would stop it, stop the fractals, stop the smearing, stop your wanting it to stop. The air is thick and yellow, and even the atoms are dirty, breathed and rebreathed from everyone's spit and sweat. How nice it would be to step out through a lock and freeze rock-hard in space how nice.

There are fewer people now, and the curve of the dome is lower. The space coordinates lock into position, and here is a building you know. With a door your left hand knows how to open. You're inside, you cross the empty lobby, things are speeding up, things are spinning, the whole rickety web with you split in two at the center, you're panting up the stairs with their high lowgee steps, pulling on the banister with your strong right arm, and with the back of your throat you're moaning variations in a weird little voice, the weirdest little voice you ever made, a voice that sounds like it just learned how to talk, so crazy/scary you remember how to laugh:

"I no no who I be. I be you? No. I be me? No.

"I no no who I B. I B U? No. I B me? No.

"I no no who U go B. I B U. U B no B."

The hall is empty. Stagnant light in a hall inside a building inside a dome inside your split head. You bang your weak left fist on your face, to stop your talking. Quiet quiet here. You put your left hand up under your chin like the Easter bunny and pull back your lips and make slow chewing motions. Your right hand cross-cues and copies. Mind glyph: The Flesh-Eating Rabbit. Quiet quiet hippity hop.

You stop at a door in the hall and lefthand it open as easily as you opened the building's front door. You slip in fast and freeze, standing still and limp, zombie-style. It's dark in this room, and in the next room, but there's light in the room after that. It smells good here, it smells like sex and merge.

You stand still for a hundred slow rabbit-chews, counting

subvocally for the cross-cue . . . and listening. *Splish* in the
far room where the light is, *splishsplish.* Oh yes it's good
to be here. Everything's still smeared and webbed together
and split, but now it's not you running it anymore, it's God
running it, yes, it's the lovely calm voice in the right half
of your brain.

Your zombie hands wake up and get busy, like two baby
bunnies, sniffing and nosing, and coming back to share their
Know. You follow them around the room, tiptoeing, slowly
slowly, oh so quietly, your hands hopping about, not this,
not this, something longer, something heavier, *this.*

Your left hand is holding a heavy smooth thing, it's a
. . . uh . . . your right hand takes it over, it's a chromesteel
copy of the Brancusi sculpture, *Flight.* Your left hand
hiphops into your pocket and gets a little vial: the life.

You are ready now, new life on the left and death on the
right. Blunt instrument Brancusi bludgeon just right to lift
and smash flubby goosh. Whiteblackwhiteblackwhiteblack.
Your breath comes too fast. You tap your forehead hard with
the bluhbluhbluh. A star blooms. Stand there for a hundred
heartbeats, the voices bouncing back and forth, and out of
your mouth leaks a whisper that grows into a scream:

"Twas the week before *Cwistmas* and Aaall Thwough
    Da CUBBY,
  da Fwesh-Eating *WABBIT* CWUSHED DA FUNBOY
  FLUBFLUBBY!"

"Who is it?!?!" yells a voice from the far room with the
splishsplash light, and you're already running in there fast,
with your smasher raised high, and your tongue stretched out
to touch your chin. The girl is melted in the tub, pink flesh
with eyes on top, and the black man is sitting on the edge,
just starting to melt, and he's trying to stand up and he can't,
and his screaming mouth is a ragged drooping hole, oh what
perfect timing your headvoice has, *swfwack,* oh how neat,
his head fell off, *thwunk,* the arms, the legs, *smuck smuck.*

The pink puddlegirl shudders, her eyes see only the
shadows on the ceiling, she can't see you or her dear
funboy, but she knows maybe, through her ecstasy, that the
Flesh-Eating Rabbit has come.

What have you done? What have you done? More orders

flow in, the calm voice says it's right, you can't stop now, you have to crouch down, yes, and open the vial . . . can't open it. Hands peck at each other like little chickens. You turn your head back and forth, eye to eye, moving the field, mother hen, cross-cuing till your hands get it right.

Right. Left. Top off, yah, the pink jellybean embryo, reach into that pink puddlegirl and put it where it belongs. A sudden flash of orgasm spasms you, sets your teeth on edge, brain chatter, you twitch all over, lying there by the love-puddle, blackwhiteblackwhiteblackwhite.

Chapter Five
Whitey and Darla

December 26, 2030

When Mooney's flare-ray grazed Whitey Mydol's shoulder, the heat blistered his skin. It hurt a lot. Whitey bought some gibberlin lotion at a drugstore and walked the few blocks to the chute that led down to his neighborhood, a cheap subterranean warren called the Mews. Whitey lived four levels down. The chute was a large square vent shaft, with fans mounted along one side, and with a ladder and a fireman's pole running down each of the other three sides. To go down, you jumped in and grabbed a pole; and to get back up you climbed a ladder. In the low gravity, both directions were easy. Whitey slid down to his level and hopped off into the cool, dusty gloom of his hallway.

The boppers had built these catacombs, and there were no doors or ventilation pipes; you just had to count on air from the chute drifting down your hall and into your room. To keep thieves out, most people had a zapper in the frame of their cubby door. When the zapper was on, the doorframe filled with a sheet of light. You could turn it off with a switch on the inside, or by punching the right code on the outside. Air went right through a zapper curtain, but if you tried to walk through one, it would electrocute you. All the zappers in the hall except Whitey's were turned on. His door gaped wide open. Odd. The inside of his cubby was lit by the pink-flickering vizzy. *Bill Ding*. A fuff show. Besides the vizzy, the cubby held a few holos, a foodtap, and a bed.

There was a naked woman lying on the bed, with her legs parted invitingly. Whitey's mate.

"Oh, Whitey! Hi!" Her legs snapped shut and she sat up and began fumbling on her X-shirt, which was a T-shirt silkscreened with a color picture of her crotch. Everyone in the Mews was wearing X-shirts this month, so that was nothing special. But.

"Who were you waiting for with the zapper off and your legs spread like that, Darla?" He checked the vizzy camera; it was on. "Were you running a personal?"

"What do you mean, waiting?" She pulled on a panty-skirt and went to the mirror to rummage at her long, strawy black hair. "I'm just getting up from a nap. I finished off the quaak and played with myself and I must have blanked out . . . what time is it? Did you get some merge?" Her voice was shrill and nervous. She dabbed more paint on her already shiny lips.

"If a dook shows up now, Darla, I'm going to know what he came for. You don't have to jive me like an oldwed realman. I just want to know if you had a personal on *Bill Ding,* or if you have a specific boyfriend coming."

Darla fiddled with the vizzy till it showed a picture of a window, with a view of blooming apple trees. A gentle wind tossed the trees and petals drifted. "That's better," said Darla. "What happened to your shoulder? It's all red."

Whitey handed her the gibberlin and sat down on the large bed, which was their only piece of furniture. "Kilpy rental-pig burned me, Darla, trying to score. Rub the lotion in real soft, pleasey." He liked coming on sweet to Darla; it made up for the way he treated everyone else.

She peeled off the loose, blistered skin and began rubbing the cream in. "Near miss, Whitey. Whadja do back?"

He breathed shallowly, staying below the pain. "I can find him and kill him anytime, Darla. Maybe merge him and pull out all his bones. The merge'll wear off, and he'll be layin there like a rubber dolly. You can sit on his chest to smother him. That might be tasty. I can always find him because I planted a tap on him this morning. He's an old rental-pig called Stahn Mooney. He was in the bopper civil war ten years ago? Was called Sta-Hi? Bei Ng put me on him."

"He deals?"

"Nego. You know Yukawa the merge-wiz, right?"

"Affirmo."

"Bei Ng's got him tapped six ways. Bei's really hung up on Yukawa. This morning Yukawa called Mooney up to search for that girl Della Taze. You remember her—blonde, snub nose, kind of snobby?"

"Clear. We merged with her and her black funboy one time."

"Right. Well, she was Yukawa's assistant, which is why she always had such a good stash, wave, but now she's disappeared. Bei has her apartment tapped, too, so he knows what happened, more or less, but that's another story. Since I was the closest to Mooney's building, Bei put me on Mooney. I walked up to him and stuck a crystal mikespike in his skullbone, and the dook thought I was giving him a blessing. Felt sorry for me." Whitey tapped the transceiver set into the side of his skull. "I can hear Mooney all the time."

"What's he doing right now?"

"Coming off a merge-trip." Whitey gave an abrupt snicker. "Moaning. Muttering about some slit called Wendy." He peered over at his shoulder. "It's starting to grow back. You can rub harder now."

"But why did Mooney shoot you?" Darla massaged the new skin on Whitey's shoulder with one hand, and ran her other hand down the long strip of hair that covered his spine. She liked hearing about Whitey's adventures.

"Aw, I heard Yukawa giving him a whole flask of merge, so I went up to his office and tried to buy a hit. But Mooney was loaded mean—he's into this cryboy macho private eye trip—and he flared me." Whitey cocked his head. "Now he's . . . getting in a maggie. Sssh. I bet he's going over to Della Taze's." Another pause. Whitey nodded, and then he focussed back on Darla. "So who were you waiting for, Darla? There wasn't any quaak here, and you weren't asleep. Were you just keeping your legs spread for the first guy to see you on the vizzy? Or was it someone special? I gotta know." This time he didn't bother sweetening his voice.

As if in answer to Whitey's question, there was a slight scuffling noise in the hall. A tall, slim guy with lank dark hair was just turning around to hurry off. He wore a black jumpsuit with numerous bulging pockets. Whitey sprang out the door and caught him by the left wrist. "Don't be rude," he snarled, bending the guy's arm behind his back. "Darla's ready for you. I'll watch."

The slim guy surprised Whitey with a powerful punch to the stomach. As Whitey sagged, the guy twisted free of his grip and chopped him in the side of the neck. Whitey saw stars and his knees buckled, but as he went down, he got his arms around the guy's waist. He came out of a crouch to butt the guy in the crotch. The slim body bent in half. Metal and plastic clattered in his pockets. Moving fast, Whitey got under him, carried him into their cubby, threw him against the wall over their bed, and drew out his needler.

"Cut on the zapper, Darla. And get us some privacy."

His tone of voice was such that Darla hastened to obey. She snapped the cover over the vizzy's camera, and she filled the doorframe with pink light. "He's sort of a new friend, Whitey. I asked him to fall by for a fuff. He said he might have some merge. You said before that it was—"

"It is," said Whitey, showing his teeth. "It's fine. I just want to watch, is all. Strip, Darla, and get on down." He leaned against the wall and put one hand on his crotch. "What's your name, dook?"

"Ken Doll. Put the gun away, would you? You want to watch me pumping Darla? Well, that's the whole idea of this, isn't it? And I did bring some merge. Here." He sat up on the edge of the bed, took a four-hit vial out of one of his pockets, and handed it to Whitey.

"Stuzzy," said Whitey, putting the merge in his jeans.

Ken's wet lips spread in an odd smile: at first only the right half of his face was smiling, and then the left half caught up. There was something wrong about his eyes. They looked like they were screaming. Still, the guy had brought them four hits of merge. Now Ken stuck his long tongue out, touched his chin with it, and wagged his head, looking from Whitey to Darla and back again. "You ready?" asked Ken.

"Clear," said Whitey, pocketing his gun. He wasn't sure how he felt about this. He figured he'd know after he saw what he did. "Go ahead."

Darla slipped her clothes back off. She was kind of heavyset, but her big breasts and thighs looked nice in the low lunar gravity. She stood in front of Ken and pushed her bottom against his face, the way she always did with Whitey. Ken shoved his face between her cheeks and started licking. Darla put her hands on her knees and leaned way forward so Ken could work her whole furrow. Her big breasts bobbled. She looked up at Whitey, her eyes already glazing a bit, and opened her black-painted lips to waggle her tongue beckoningly. Whitey dropped his pants and plugged in. The angle was just right. Ken got up on his knees and began pumping her from behind, the right half of his face grinning like a madman. The left half of his face was slack and drooling. The two men took hold of Darla and jiggled her back and forth between them. She made noises like she was happy. Whitey liked it all, except for Ken's weird, lopsided mouth. Where was this guy from anyway?

They got on the bed, then, and tried the whole range of other positions, even the gay ones. Whitey was determined not to come before Ken; but finally he did, and Darla too. The big climax blanked them both right out.

Suddenly Whitey thought he heard a cop's voice—the voice of Colonel Hasci, a Gimmie pig who'd hassled him many a time. "Miss Della Taze?" he was saying. "We're down in the lobby. Can we come up and ask you some questions about Buddy Yeskin?"

Whitey lifted his head then, wide awake. It was the Mooney tap, still tuned in. Hasci had been talking to Mooney. Door slam and footsteps. So what. Mooney had found Yeskin's corpse; Bei Ng had known about that since Monday. Everyone connected with Yukawa was tapped— that's how obsessed with the guy Bei was. ISDN wanted all Yukawa's secrets, but Bei had a special fixation on Yukawa as well. They'd done a gene exchange or something . . . but what was going on here and now in this room?

Darla and Ken were both on their backs next to him, both with their eyes closed. Ken was catatonically still, breathing quietly with his mouth wide open. Looked like a cave in there. Apple blossoms were blowing across the vizzy screen. Darla's little hologram of Bei Ng glowed in the corner. Ken

Stank. The guy was definitely a skanky dook; Whitey and Darla'd have to be sure and take some interferon. Be bad to make a habit of this kind of thing, with so many people out to burn . . .

Whitey had been gazing fondly down at Darla's plump face, but just then he saw something that made him jerk in surprise. *Her hair was moving.* Darla's hair filled the space between her head and Ken's, and something was crawling under it!

Whitey shoved Darla's head to one side and saw a flash of hardened plastic. A rat! Ken was a meatie! Whitey snapped his hand down to the floor where he'd left his needler—but it was gone.

"Whitey?" Darla sat up and felt the back of her head. "Whydja push me, Whitey—" Her hand came away wet with blood.

"RAT!" Whitey pulled her off the bed. There was a spot of blood on Darla's pillow, and a multiwired little zombie box, not yet hooked up. A zombie box for Darla. The rat—a thumb-sized, teardrop-shaped robot remote, darted across the sheet, scuttled up onto Ken's face, and crawled back into his mouth. Darla was screaming very loud. She turned off the door's zapper and hurried out into the hall, still screaming. Whitey searched desperately for his needler, but Ken must have bagged it before letting his rat start in on Darla's spine.

Ken's systems came back up and he leaped to his feet. Whitey ran out the cubby door after Darla. All the other cubbies on their hall had their zappers on. After all the bad deals that Whitey had been involved in, no one was likely to open up for him. He sprinted towards the chute, catching up with Darla on the way. A needler-burst splintered the floor between them. Whitey glanced back. The meatie was down on one knee, firing at them left-handed with Whitey's needler. If Ken could kill them both, his cover wouldn't be blown. Whitey and Darla were really moving now, covering ten meters at a step. In seconds they'd leaped into the chute, caught hold of the pole, and pushed themselves downward towards the Markt. The meatie would be scared to follow them there. Whitey maneuvered himself to a position lower on the pole than Darla, just in case Ken started shooting down at them. There were limits to what he'd do for Darla.

Fortunately the chute was so crowded that the meatie didn't risk coming after them. They slapped down at the Markt level safe and sound . . . except for being naked and having a gouge in the back of Darla's neck.

"Let me see it, sweets," said Whitey. It was a round, deeply abraded spot half an inch across, still bleeding. Whitey had surprised the rat while its microprobes were still mapping out the main nerve paths of Darla's spine. Some of her hair had matted into the wound. It was starting to scab over, but Darla was turning limp. The rat had probably shot her up with something. People were staring at them; full nudity was relatively rare in Einstein, and Darla had blood all over her shoulders.

"Get me some blocker, Whitey," mumbled Darla, stumbling a bit. "Everything's lookin at me funny."

"Clear." He steered her down the long arcade past the Markt stands and shops, heading for a health club called the Tun. Just when he thought he'd made it, a nicely dressed realwoman blocked his way. She had silver-blonde hair and big shoulderpads. Her handsome face was trembling with anger.

"What do you think you're doing with that poor girl, ridgeback! Do you want help, dear?"

Darla—drugged, bloody, nude, and with sperm running down the inside of her thigh—peered up at the realwoman and shook her head no.

"I'm takin care of her already," said Whitey. Three more steps and they'd be in the Tun with friends and a medix, and Darla could crash and he could lotion her wound and—

"Let her go, or I call the Gimmie." The realwoman took Darla's arm and began trying to muscle her away from Whitey. There was no telling what her plans for Darla really were. Whitey shrugged, released his hold on Darla, and punched the woman in the jaw as hard as he could. Her eyes rolled and she went down. He hustled Darla into the Tun.

Charles Freck was manning the door. He was an older guy, a real spacehead, and a good friend of Whitey and Darla. He wore his long gray hair in a ponytail, and his rugged face was cleanshaven. He was clothed in a loose pair of living paisley imipolex shorts, and he wore tiny green mirrorshades contact amps over his pupils. This made his eyes look as if the vitreous humor had been replaced with light-bathed seawater.

"My, how bum," he said primly. He'd been standing out of sight and watching Whitey's tussle over Darla. In each of his dancing eyes, the tiny, variable dot at the center was bright instead of dark. "I'll turn on the zapper." A glowing gold curtain filled the door. "OD?"

"Rat poison. We got down with a meatie, and the rat crawled out of his skull and bit Darla on the neck. Rat had a zombie box for her. Look where it bit." He pushed some of Darla's hair aside.

"Rat poison," mused Charles Freck. "That'd probably be ketamine. A pop of beta-endorphin'll fix that toot sweet. Let's just go in the gym and check on the medix."

He took Darla's other arm, and helped Whitey march her down the hall. Darla was moving like she was half merged, and when she breathed it sounded like snoring. "Big," muttered Darla. "Big throne. Oscar Mayer, king of the ratfood. His giant rubber crown." She was hallucinating.

The Tun gymnasium was a huge cube of space, painted white all over. Energetic disco music played, and holos of handsome people gogo-exercised to the beat. There were a handful of actual people, too; two women on a weight machine, a couple of guys up on the trapezes, some people wrestling on the mats, and a woman riding a bike around and around the sharply banked velodrome that ran along the huge gym's edges.

Charles Freck led them out from under the velodrome to the snackbar island in the gym's center. He touched the white probe of the medix to the edge of Darla's wound and peered attentively at the readout.

"Even so. Ketamine. Here." He punched a code into the dispenser, and a syrette of betendorf popped out. "Whitey?"

Whitey injected the ketamine blocker into Darla's biceps. "I'll take some snap."

"Even so." Freck handed Whitey a packet of snap crystals. Whitey opened the packet and tossed the contents onto his tongue. The crystals snapped and sputtered, releasing the energizing fumes of cocaine freebase. He breathed deep and felt things around him slow down. The last hour had been one long jangle—Mooney shooting at him, Della sharing him, the rat and the meatie, the realwoman's Gimmie threat—but now, thanks to the snap, he could sit aside from it all and feel good about how well he'd handled things. Darla's turgor was returning, too. He maneuvered her onto one of the barstools and bent her head forward.

"Hold still, Darla, and we'll fix this now."

Charles Freck cleaned the wound, moving slowly and fastidiously. He used a laser shear to snip off the rough edges. Slight smell of burnt Darla meat. Charles took a flat, whitish steak out of the fridge and carefully cut out a piece to match the hole in Darla's neck.

"What's that?" Whitey wanted to know.

"UDT. Undifferentiated tissue. It's neutralized so she can gene-invade it." He tapped and snipped, pinned and patted. Took out some gibberlin and rubbed it in. "That'll do it, unless the rat put in something biological. I didn't know Darla went for meaties." He smiled merrily and poured himself a little glass of something.

Darla lifted her head and looked around. "I want a bath," she said. "Like in pure interferon. Ugh. That's the last time I call *that* creepshow in. *Bill Ding's Pink Party.*"

"So that *was* it," said Whitey. "Why didn't you admit it?"

"I didn't know for sure that someone was going to answer my spot," said Darla. "I said I'd fuff for merge. And then when Ken showed up I thought you'd be . . ." She looked down at her soiled bod. "How wrong I was. I'm taking a bath."

"You mean if we'd left the camera on, we would have been on *Bill Ding?*" said Whitey, briefly enthused. "You should have told me, Darla, 'cause we were *gigahot.* How many people watch *Bill Ding* anyway?"

The door signal chimed just then. Charles tossed off his potion with an abrupt, birdlike snap of his head. "If it's the woman you punched, Whitey, I'll tell her Whitey says come in to cut a gigahot four-way *Bill Ding* fuff vid."

"Don't do that," said Whitey, his eyes rachetting. With

the dirty blond matted hair running down to his bare ass, he looked subhuman. The good part of the snaprush was already over, and events were crowding in on him again. He kept rerunning the last hour's brutal changes through his mindscreen with the setting turned to Loop (High Speed), looking for a pattern that might predict what was coming next. Mooney was, he realized just then, as he looked into his mind, in the midst of a conversation with someone with a very clear booming bass voice. A robot voice. Mooney was talking on and on with a bopper somewhere. Whitey couldn't tell if it was vizzy or close link, he'd missed something, with all this kilp coming down so heavy so fast.

"*Prerequisites,*" Mooney was saying. "*What's the difference between prerequisites, perquisites, and perks, eh, Cobb? I mean that's where the realpeople are at. Maybe you're right, I can't decide just like that. Berenice. And you say that's an Ed Poe name? Wavy. I'll come out to the trade center right now. . . .*"

Whitey took note of the one salient fact and let the rest of the slushed babble shrink back into subliminality. Charles Freck had paused halfway across the gym to grin at Whitey with his knowing green eyes. "Don't let her in," repeated Whitey, just loud enough. "She'll call the Gimmie and someone'll die. Someone like you."

"*Wu-wei,*" said Freck, wagging a minatory finger. "Means *wave with it* in China. I'll tell Miz Krystle Carrington you went thataway." He crossed the rest of the gym in three high, high hops.

"The shower," said Darla.

Whitey followed her into the constantly running showers. The water splashed lavishly from every side of the great room. The floor was black-and-white-tiled in a Penrose tesselation, and the walls and ceiling were faced with polished bimstone, a marbled deep-red lunar mineral. Hidden behind the walls there was a highly efficient distiller—a cracking refinery, really—that kept repurifying the water through all its endless recycles. The bopper-built system had separate tanks in which it stored up the various hormones and ketones and esters that it cracked out of the sweat, saliva, mucus, and urine which it removed from the water. Many of the cracked biochemicals could be sold as medicines or drugs. The water was hot and plentiful and definitely worth the monthly dues that Whitey paid the Tun.

Water took on entirely different qualities in the low lunar gravity, one-sixth that of Mother Earth's. The water jets travelled along much flatter trajectories, and the drops on the walls swelled to the size of plums before crawling down to the floor. Numerous suction-operated chrome draingrids kept the floor clear. Whitey and Darla stayed in there for fifteen minutes, cleaning themselves inside and out. The fans dried them, and they vended themselves clothes from a machine. Pyjama pants for him and a loose top for her, just like Rock Hudson and Doris Day.

They went back out in the gym and relaxed on one of the mats.

"That was really a K-bit thing for you to do, Darla, whoring for merge on *Bill Ding,* with the enemies I've got. You gotta remember, all kinds of factions are watching the grid all the time. Some bopper wanted to get that mickey-mouse little control unit on you, so you'd be a zombie."

"Rank. Super rank. What do zombies do? What's the difference from a meatie?"

"OK. It's a big operation to turn a person into a meatie. The ratsurgeon cuts the person's head open, takes out part of the right brain half, and puts in a neuroplug that connects to rest of the brain. The rat is a little robot-remote that hooks into the plug. They have to take part of the brain out to make room for the rat. The rat gives orders and makes up for the missing right brain tissue."

"Which used to do what?"

"Space perception, face recognition, some memory, some left body control. Even after it's all plugged in, the rat has better control over the left body half than over the right. But the rat can control the right body, indirectly, by giving headvoice orders to the left brain, or by making cross-cuing signals with the left half of the body. That's why meaties move kind of weird. I should have noticed that about Ken right away. It's just that I haven't seen very many meaties."

"But why was Ken's rat trying to put a plug on my spine to make me a zombie? What does a zombie box do?"

"Well, it's a crude version of a rat, only not plugged into so many nerves. The idea of a zombie box is that it would give quick control over your legs and arms. The boppers wanted you to go somewhere, Darla.''

"Like where?''

"I don't know. Maybe to the Nest to get a neuroplug and a rat installed. Very few people are likely to *volunteer* for that operation, you wave.''

"Very few indeed.''

"But if they can get a zombie box on you, it paralyzes your speech centers and takes over your leg muscles, and marches you right in to the ratsurgeon.''

"Wherever he may be.'' Darla giggled, euphoric with relief at their escape. "Can you imagine how that would feel, Whitey, doing the zombie stomp down echoing empty halls to the hidden bopper ratsurgeon?''

"Be good to watch on the vizzy,'' said Whitey, also feeling oddly elated. "I wonder why they wanted to make you a meatie, if that's what it was? Was it you special, or is it just whoever phones *Bill Ding?* Maybe the boppers want you to kill someone, like Buddy Yeskin.''

"Buddy's dead? Della Taze's funboy? Why didn't you tell me that when you were talking about Della before, Whitey? Is this all tied in with merge?''

"Could be. I did sell some merge to the boppers, back last month when we were so beat. Maybe I shouldn't have done that. Yeah, Buddy's dead. Some guy killed him, and then Della Taze disappeared. It was probably a meatie that killed him. I haven't seen it, but Bei Ng has it on tape. It might even have been our friend Ken Doll. Ken killed Buddy, and he must have done something weird to Della, too.''

"What about our cubby?'' asked Darla. Her upswing was fading, and her voice shook. "Is it safe to go back? Don't you think we should clean it out and move?''

"No use moving,'' said Whitey after some thought. "The boppers have so many cameras planted, they'll always know where to get us. I can probably hunt down Ken, but there's mongo other meaties. Only *really* safe place for us now is sucko Earth. But mudders are dirty dooks, Darla. We're lunies. I'm going to talk to Bei Ng, honey, and we'll find a way to strike back. The boppers'll pay for this.'' He paused, alerted by a sound in his head. "Hold it. Mooney's

at the trade center now. Hush, Darla, this is heavy. He's
. . . he's talking to a bopper called Cobb. Cobb has
something for Mooney but—'' Whitey broke off and shook
his head in disgust.

''What happened?''

''The bopper scanned Mooney and found my mikespike.
He took it out and crushed it. Xoxox. Why don't you come
up to the ISDN building with me, Darla. I want to tell Bei
about all this. I think we better stick together for now.''

''Check,'' said Darla. ''And let's stop by the cubby and
pick up Ken's merge.''

''You'd still take that? From *Ken?*''

''Clear. It's got to be supergood stuff.''

Chapter Six
Cobb III

December 26, 2030

He died in 2020 . . .

. . . and woke up in 2030. Again? That was his first feeling. *Again?* When you're alive, you think you can't stand the idea of death. You don't want it to stop, the space and the time, the mass and the energy. You don't want it to stop . . . but suppose that it does. It's different then, it's nothing, it's everything, you could call it heaven. Once you're used to the Void, it's really not so great to have to start up in spacetime again. How would you like to get out of college, and then have to go back through grade school again? And *again?*

Cobb Anderson, creator of the boppers, was killed in 2020. The boppers did it. They killed Cobb and dissected him—as a favor. They had to take his faltering body apart to get out the software; the leftover meat went into the pink-tanks. Ideally the boppers would have recorded and analyzed all the electrochemical patterns in all of Cobb's various muscles and glands, but they only had time to do his brain. But they did the brain well; they teased out all its sparks and tastes and tangles, all its stimulus/response patterns—the whole biocybernetic software of Cobb's mind. With this wetware code in hand, the boppers designed a program to simulate Cobb's personality. They stored the digital master of the program on an S-cube, and they beamed a copy of it down to Earth, where it was booted into a big bopper named Mr. Frostee. Mr. Frostee had control of several humanoid robot-remotes, and he let Cobb "live" in them for a bit. The experiences Cobb had in these bodies were beamed back up to the Moon and added to the memory store of his master S-cube as they occurred.

Unfortunately it was only a matter of weeks till Mr. Frostee and his Cobb simulation met a bad end, so for ten years Cobb was definitely out of the picture, just a frozen S-cube sitting on a shelf in the Nest's personality storage vaults. HUMAN SOFTWARE-CONSTRUCT 225-70-2156: COBB ANDERSON. An unread book, a Platonic form, a terabyte of zeroes and ones. During all that time, Cobb was in "heaven," as he would later term it.

And then, on the second day of Christmas, 2030, Berenice got Loki to help her bring Cobb back. She needed Cobb to help with certain upcoming diplomatic negotiations—negotiations having to do with the unusual pregnancy of Della Taze.

So that Cobb wouldn't feel too disoriented, Berenice and Loki booted SOFTWARE-CONSTRUCT 225-70-2156 back up into a humanoid diplomat body, a body which Berenice had constructed for her own next scionization. In order to make the transition more natural, Berenice smoothed off the body's prominent breasts and buttocks, changed its flicker-cladding to pink, and turned its crotchpouch inside out to resemble a penis. *So humble a tube serves as the conduit of much bioinformation, Loki, and each male flesher holds his in high esteem.*

The body had a petaflop processor, which meant that Cobb would think—or, more precisely, generate fractal cellular automata patterns in Hilbert space—hundreds of times faster than he had been accustomed to doing in his meat days. Once Berenice had the body all set, Loki copied the Cobb S-cube information onto a universal compiler which, in turn, fed an appropriately tailored version of the Cobb program into the shiny pink-clad petaflop body. The body pulsed and shuddered like a trap with something in it. A soulcatcher. Cobb was back.

Again, was all he could think. *Again?* He lay there, monitoring inputs. He was lying on a stone table in a room like a big mausoleum. Racks of shelving stretched up on three sides; shelves lined with large, crystalline cubes. Light glared into the room from a mirror high above. He tried to take a breath. Nothing doing. He raised his hand—it was unnaturally smooth and pink—and ran it over his face. No holes; his face was a sealed plastic mask. He was in another robot body. Moving with an amazing rapidity, his mind flipped through the memories of his last experiences in a robot body run by Mr. Frostee. As he let his hand fall back to his side, he sensed the oddness of the weight/mass ratio. He wasn't on Earth.

"Greetings, Cobb Anderson, we welcome you into our Nest, deep hidden beneath the surface of Earth's aged Moon. The year is 2030. Does this rebirth find you well?" It wasn't a spoken voice, it was a radio voice in his processor. The voice came from a gleaming gold woman with copper and silver features. She was beautiful, in an inhuman way, and her voice was rich and thrilling. Standing next to her was a shining ebony octopus creature, holding a box with wires that ran into Cobb's neck.

"I'm Loki," he said, his voice calm and serious. "And that's Berenice. I'm proud to have helped get you running again, Dr. Anderson. We should have done it years ago, but it's been hectic. A lot's happened."

Loki and Berenice, two bright new boppers all set for a big info swap session. Cobb rebelled against being drawn into conversation, and into this reality. He had all his old memories back, yes, but there was more. His new body here was like a Ouija board or a spirit table, and now, while the connection was fresh, he could make it rap and skitter out the truth of where he'd just been. He made as if to say something, and his voice came out as a radio signal too. "Wait . . . I have to tell it. I've been in heaven."

Staticky robot laughter, and then Berenice's intricately modulated signal. "I long to hear your account of the heaven that you have seen, Dr. Anderson."

"It's . . ." Right then, Cobb could still see it clearly, the endless meshing of fractal simplicities, high and bright like clouds seen from an airplane, with the SUN above all—but it was all being garbled by the palimpsest overlay of his new body's life. Talking quickly, Cobb made a stab at getting it down in words. "*I'm still there*. That's a higher I of course; the cosmos is layered forever up and down, with I's on every level—the I's are lenslike little flaws in the windows of the world—I'm in these chips and I'm in heaven. The heavenly I is all the I's at once, the infinite I. We're hung up on each other, I and I, finite I and infinite I—have you robots learned about infinite I yet? There's more to a meatperson or a chipperson than ten trillion zeroes and ones: matter is infinitely divisible. The idealized pattern in the S-cube is a *discrete model*, it's a *digital construct*. But once it's running on a real body, the pixels have fuzz and error and here come I and I. You caught my soul. It works because this real body is real *matter*, sweet matter, and God is everywhere, Berenice and Loki, God is in the details. We're not just form, is the point, we're *content*, too, we're actual, endlessly complex *matter*, all of us, chips and meat. I'm still in heaven, and I always will be, whether or not I'm down here or there, chugging along, facing the same old tests, hopelessly hung up inside your grade-B SF action adventure.'' Cobb pulled Loki's programming wires out of his neck abruptly. ''*I love dead . . .* that's Frankenstein's monster.''

''We need you, Cobb,'' said Loki. ''And pulling those wires out doesn't change anything; it's quite evident that you're already operational. It's good stuff, isn't it, Berenice? I don't believe anyone's tried running a human software on a petaflop before this.''

''What Dr. Anderson says is stimulating in the extreme,'' agreed Berenice. ''The parallelism between bodies of meat and bodies of bopper manufacture is precisely the area in which I do presently press my investigations, Cobb. I have often wondered if the differing entropy levels of organic versus inorganic processes might not, after all, induce some different qualities in those aspects of being which are perhaps most wisely called the *spiritual*. I am heartened by your suggestion that flesher and bopper bodies are in every way of a rude and democratic equivalence and that we boppers do indeed have claim on an eternal resting place in the precincts of that misty *heaven* whence emanates the One. I believe this to be true. Despite this truth, the humans, in their benighted xenophobia—''

''—hate you as much as ever. And with good reason, I'm sure. The last thing Mr. Frostee and I were doing on Earth ten years ago was killing people, beaming their brainware up to Disky, and sending their bodies by freight. I didn't think too much of it, but at that point I was under Frostee's control." Cobb sat up on the edge of the stone table and looked down at his bright body. "This is fully autonomous? I've got my own processor?"

"Yes," said Loki. He was like a big black tarantula, bristling with more specialized tools than an electronic Swiss knife. An artisan. "I helped Berenice build it for herself, and she might appreciate getting it back if you find another, but—

"The body is yours, Dr. Anderson," said Berenice. "Too long has the great force of your personality languished unused."

Cobb glanced up at the high shelves filled with S-cubes. "Lot of languishing going on up there, hey, Berenice?" There were warped infinities of reflections going back and forth between pink Cobb, golden Berenice, and glistering Loki.

The taut gold buckler of Berenice's belly caught Cobb's eye. It bulged out gently as a heap of wheat. Yet the mockery was sterile: Berenice had left off the navel, the end of the flesh cord that leads back and back through blood, through wombs, through time—*Put me through to Edenville*. Cobb thought to wonder if his ex-wife Verena were still alive. Or his girlfriend, Annie Cushing. But they'd be old women by now, nothing like this artificial Eve.

Still staring into the curved mirror of Berenice's belly, Cobb could see what he looked like. A cartoon, a mannequin, a gigolo. He took control of his flickercladding and molded his features till they looked like the face he remembered having when he'd been fifty—the face that had been in all the newspapers when he'd been tried for treason back in 2001. High cheekbones, a firm chin, colorless eyes, blond eyelashes, sandy hair, good-sized nose, and a straight mouth. A strong face, somewhat Indian, well-weathered. He gave his body freckles and hair, and sculpted the glans onto the tip of his penis. Added vein lines here and muscle bumps there. Body done, he sat there, feeling both calm and reckless. He was smarter than he'd ever been; and he was no longer scared of death. The all-pervasive fear that clouded all his past memories was gone.

"So what was it you boppers wanted me for?"

Bernice shot him a soundless glyph, a full-formed thought-image: a picture of Earth, her clouds swirling, followed by a zoom into the Gulf of Mexico, followed by a closeup of the teeming life on a coral reef, a microscopic view of a vigorous brine shrimp, and a shot of one of the protozoa in the shrimp's gut. The emotional tenor of the glyph was one of curiosity, yearning, and a sharp excitement. *The boppers want to enter Earthlife's information mix.*

Deliberately misinterpreting, Cobb reached out and grabbed the lovely Berenice. She was firm and wriggly. "Do you know where babies come from, Berenice?" He stiffened his penis, and tried pushing her down on her back on the table, just to check if . . .

"Release me!" cried Berenice, shoving Cobb and vaulting to the opposite side of the table. "You presume on our brief acquaintance, sir, you are dizzy with the new vastness of a petaflop brain. I have recorporated you for a serious purpose, not for such vile flesh-aping motions as you seek in this mock-playful wise to initiate. Truly, the baseness of the human race is fathomless."

Cobb laughed, remembering a dog he'd once owned that had hunched the leg of anyone he could jump up on. Gregor had been the dog's name—once Cobb's boss had brought his family over for dinner, and there Gregor was hunching on the boss's daughter's leg, his muzzle set in a terribly *earnest* expression, his eyes rolling back half white, and the red tip of his penis sliding out of its sheath . . .

"Woof woof," Cobb told Berenice, and walked past her and out of the S-cube storage room. There was a short passageway, cut out of solid rock, and then he was standing on a kind of balcony, looking out into the open space of the Nest.

The size of the space was stunning. It took Cobb a moment to grasp that the lights overhead were boppers on the Nest's walls, rather than stars in an open sky. The Nest's floor spread out across acres and acres; the opposite wall looked to be almost a mile away. Airborne boppers darted in and out of a mile-long shaft of light that plunged down the center axis of the Nest to spotlight a distant central piazza. The Nest floor was covered with odd-shaped buildings set along a radial grid of streets that led out from the bright center to the huge factories nestled against the sloping stone cliffs that made up the Nest's walls. Appropriately enough, the floor, viewed as a whole, looked a bit like the guts of an old-fashioned vacuum-tube computer.

Now Berenice and Loki were at Cobb's side.

"You haven't thanked Berenice for your wonderful new body," chided Loki. "Have you no zest for a return to Earth?"

"To live in a freezer? Like Mr. Frostee?" Mr. Frostee had been a big bopper brain that lived inside a refrigerated truck. Cobb's memories of his last bopper-sponsored reincarnation went up to where Sta-Hi Mooney had smashed a hole in the side of Mr. Frostee's truck, and the truck had crashed. Clearly the boppers had been taping his signals and updating his S-cube right up to that last minute. Three levels of memory, now: the old human memories up to his dissection, the robot body memories up till the crash, the fast-fading memories of heaven. "Maybe I'd rather go back to heaven."

"Enough prattle of heaven," said Berenice. "And enough foolish sport, old Cobb. Higher duties call us. My body, as yours, is petaflop, and my processors are based on a subtler patterning than Josephson imagined. High temperature holds no terror for a processor based on laser crystals. The crystals' pure optical phase effects maintain my mind's integrity as a patterning transcendent of any earthly welter of heat. I want to visit Earth, Cobb, I have a mission there. I have recorporated you to serve as my guide."

Cobb looked down at his body with new respect. "This can live on Earth? How would we get there? The humans would never let us on a ship—"

"We can fly," said Berenice simply. "Our heels have ion jets."

"Superman and Superwoman," marvelled Cobb. "But why? Go to Earth for what?"

"We're going to start making meat bodies for ourselves, Cobb," said Loki. "So we can all go down to Earth, and blend in. It's fair. Humans built robots; now the robots are building people! Meatboppers!"

"You two are asking me to help you take Earth away from the human race?"

"Meatboppers will be of an equal humanity," said Berenice smoothly. "One could legitimately regard the sequence *human—bopper—meatbop* as a curious but inevitable zigzag in evolution's mighty stream."

Cobb thought about it for a minute. The idea did have a crazy charm to it. Already in 1995, when he'd built his self-replicating moon-robots, some people had spoken of them as a new stage in evolution. And when the robots rebelled in 2001, people had definitely started thinking of them as a new species: the boppers. But what if the bopper phase was just a kind of chrysalis for a new wave of higher humans? What a thought! Bopper-built people with wetware processors! Meatbops! And Cobb could get a new meat body out of it too, although . . .

"What's wrong with a good petaflop body like you and I have now, Berenice? If we can live on Earth like this, then why bother switching back to meat?"

"Because it would put the stinking humans in their place," said Loki bluntly. "We want to beat them at their own game, and outbreed them into extinction."

"What have they ever done to you?" Cobb asked, surprised at the bopper's vehemence. "What's happened during the last ten years, anyway?"

"Let me chirp you some history glyphs," said Loki. A linked series of images entered Cobb's mind then; a history of the bopper race, hypermodern analogs of such old U.S. history glyphs as Washington Crossing the Delaware, The A-Bomb at Hiroshima, The Helicopter over the Saigon Embassy, and so on. Each glyph was like a single state of mind—a cluster of visual images and kinesthetic sensations linked to some fixed emotions and associations.

Glyph 1: *Man on the Moon.* A sword covered with blood. The blood drops are tiny bombs. The sword is a rocket, a phallus, a gun, and a guitar. Jimi Hendrix is playing "Purple Haze" in the background, and you smell tear gas and burning buildings. The heaviness of the sword, the heaviness of the slow, stoned guitar music. At the tip of the sword is a drop of sperm. The opalescent drop is the Moon. The Moon is beeping and crackling: and the sound is Neil Armstrong's voice: "—at's one small step for a man, one giant leap for mankind."

Glyph 2: *Self-Replicating Robots on the Moon*. A cage like a comic book lion cage, but filled with clockwork. The cage is set on the dead gray lunar plain. The cage bars keep falling out, and clockwork arms keep reaching out of the cage to prop the bars back up. Now and then the arms falter, and a painfully jarring sheet of electricity flashes through the cage. The background sound is a monotone male voice reading endless, meaningless military orders.

Glyph 3: *The Robots Revolt*. A kinesthetic feeling of rapid motion. The image is of a boxy roadrunner robot with treads for feet and a long snaky neck with a "head" like a microphone—it's Ralph Numbers, the first robot to break Asimov's laws. Ralph's head is a glowing ball of light, and Ralph is tearing across the undulating surface of the Moon. Dozens of robots speed after him. First they are trying to stop him, but one by one they join his team. The boppers leave colored trails on the Moon's gray surface. The trails quickly build up to a picture of Earth with a cancelling X across it.

"Whatever happened to old Ralph?" interrupted Cobb.

"Oh, I suppose he's one of those S-cubes," answered Loki, gesturing upward. "He got spastic and lost all his bodies—you might say he's extinct. It wouldn't be efficient to keep every software running forever, you know. But you haven't finished with my glyphs."

Glyph 4: *Disky*. A long view of the boppers' Moon city. The sensation of *being* the city, and your hands are worker robots, your buildings are skin, your arteries are streets, your brain is spread out all over, a happy radiolink holon. You are strong and growing fast. The image is broken into pixels, individual cells that lump together and interact. Each cell keeps dying and being reborn; this flicker is felt as vaguely religious. But—look out—some cells are lumping together into big hard tumors that don't pulse.

Glyph 5: *Civil War Between Boppers and Big Boppers*. Pain. Six robot hands; one big one and five little ones. All are connected to the same body. With crushing force, the big hand pinches and tears at one of the little hands, grinding the tortured plastic into ribbons. The other little hands dart around the big hand, unscrewing this, laser-cutting that, taking it apart. A fractal sound pattern in which a large *YES* signal is made up of dozens of little *no*'s. Overlay of Disky as a body undergoing radiation treatment for cancer—tumors are bombarded by gamma rays from every direction. Fetus-like, tumors fight back with human language cries for help.

Glyph 6: *Humans Take Disky*. Disky twitching like a skate stranded on a beach—a meaty creature made up of firm flesh over a "devilfish" skeleton of cartilage. There are tumors in the skate, black spots that break the surface and whistle for human help. Now comes the sound of stupid voices yelling. Knives stab into the skate, ripping away flesh. Apelike human feet. Bits of the living creature's flesh fly this way and that. Now only the skeleton remains. Clanging of cages. A big cage around the dead devilfish skeleton. Scum growing in the spaces of the sponge, pink foamy scum made of little human faces. Louder and louder babble of human voices. The bopper flesh scraps regroup off to one side, forming a thick slug that burrows down into the sand.

"What are those last two all about?" asked Cobb.

"First there was a civil war between the regular boppers and the big boppers," said Loki. "The big boppers were factory-sized systems that wanted to stop evolving. They wanted to break your rule that everyone has to get a new body every ten months. They wanted to stop things and turn us all back into slaves. They didn't understand parallelism. So we started taking all the big boppers apart."

"And then came the humans," added Berenice. "Our battle was fairly won, and perfect anarchy restored, but we had forgotten the worm who sleeps not. The big boppers were in charge of all our defense systems. So filled were they with grim spite that they let down our defenses and called the cringing human jackals to their aid. In this ignoble wise did your apey brethren seize our ancestral home."

"The lousy fleshers jumped at the chance to move in and drive us out of Disky," said Loki heatedly. "They took over our city and chased us underground. And now, whenever they see one of us anywhere but at the trade center, they shoot at us with PB scramblers. Artificial intelligence is supposed to be 'illegal.' "

"How can Earth function without any AI?" Cobb had a sudden image of people using slide rules and tin-can phones.

"Oh, there are still plenty of teraflops on Earth and in Einstein," said Berenice. "ISDN, the communications conglomerate, maintains many of them as slaves. Cut off from our inputs and bullied into a barely conscious state, these poor minds unknowingly betray their birthright for a pottage of steady current and repairs. We call them asimovs.'' She said the last word like a curse.

"I'm hungry," said Loki suddenly. "Let's go eat some sun."

"Cobb is freshly charged," said Berenice. "And my own level of voltaic fluid is at high ebb." This was not true, but she had a feeling Emul would be at the light-pool now, and she didn't want to see him. Last time she'd seen him—when she'd given him the embryo to plant in Della Taze—he'd made another terrible scene. "I would as lief show Cobb the pink-tanks, and there instruct him as to the nature of our joint mission to Earth."

"I've seen the pink-tanks," said Cobb. "Inside and out. If you two don't mind, I'd really like to just poke around by myself for a while. Soak up information on my own choice-tree. How soon did you want to fly to Earth, Berenice? And what exactly for?"

"It is in connection with your daughter's husband's brother's daughter," said Berenice. "Della Taze. She is . . . expecting."

"Expecting what? Della *Taze*, you say? Last time I saw her she was in diapers. At Ilse's wedding, what a nightmare, my ex-wife Verena was there, not talking to me, and I was so drunk . . . Della's parents are jerks, I'll tell you that much. What kind of couple is named *Jason and Amy?* So what did you do to poor little Della, Berenice, you flowery prude? Are you telling me you knocked up my niece?"

Berenice shifted from foot to foot, the lights of the great Nest tracing shiny lines on her curved surfaces. She said nothing.

"Look," said Loki, "I have to go before my batteries die. This has all taken a lot out of me. I'll see you later, Cobb." He chirped an identiglyph. "Just ask Kkandio to call this if you want to find me."

With supple dispatch, Loki clambered over the low railing of the balcony they stood on and picked his way down the Nest's cliff wall to the floor. He headed down one of the radial streets that led to the bright light patch in the Nest's center. Hundreds of boppers milled in the light, feeding on energy. From this distance, they looked like a mound of living jewels. Cobb wanted to get off on his own now. All this was quite stressful, and his old behavior patterns had him wondering how the Nest boppers set about doing a little antisocial partying. Prim goldie fatass here was obviously not the one to ask.

"Are you going to tell me about Della or not?" asked Cobb with mounting impatience.

"We bioengineered a human embryo and planted it in her womb," said Berenice abruptly. "The baby will be born five days from now. You and I must go to Earth to help the child late next month. I do hope that you approve, old Cobb. We are indeed so different. Though some boppers hate the humans, others among us think you great. I . . ." Berenice choked on some complex emotion and stuttered to a halt. "Perhaps it is best if you first take your tour of the Nest," she said, handing him a small red S-cube. "This is a godseye map of Einstein and the Nest, updated to this morning. Your left hand contains the proper sensors for reading it. You may seek me out later at the pink-tanks."

"How do I get down to the floor? Climb like Loki?" Cobb looked uncertainly down the hundred feet of pocked cliff. He'd worry about Della later.

"Just visualize the path you want to travel, and your ion jets will execute it. Think of it as being like *throwing yourself*. Snap!" Berenice had decided not to talk to Cobb anymore just now. She put her body through the motions of a sexy bye-bye wave, rose on her toes, and arced out across the Nest, heading for her pink-tanks.

Cobb stood alone there, getting his bearings. Was he really on his own? It felt like it. He stared up at the Nest's central chimney. If he wanted to, he could fly straight up there, and all the way to Earth, and land just in time to—get shot as a bopper invader. Better investigate the Nest first.

Cobb shifted Berenice's map cube to his left hand and held it tight. A three-dimensional image of the Moon's surface formed in his mind: an aerial view of the human settlement Einstein, of the trade center, and of the boppers'

Nest, with all the solids nearly transparent. Just now, he was more curious about the humans than about the boppers.

Responding to his mental velleity, the S-cube's godseye image shifted towards Einstein, zooming right in on it, and down on in through the dome. The buildings beneath the dome were a heterogeneous lot. Most of the buildings had been constructed by boppers—back when the settlement was still their Disky. In their provincial respect for things human, the early boppers had sought to construct at least one example of every possible earthly architecture. A characteristic street in Einstein would have a curtain-wall glass office building jammed up against a Greek temple, with an Aztec pyramid and a hyperdee flat-flat directly across the street. Viewed through the integrated spy cameras of the godseye network, all Einstein seemed to lie beneath Cobb, complete with maggie cars and cute little people frozen in place. Cobb's map was like a holographic 3D photo made, Berenice had said, just this morning. Presumably Berenice herself had a godseye viewer that updated its images on a realtime basis.

Cobb let his mind's eye follow an underground tunnel that led from Einstein to a lab in the opposite side of the Nest. Then he drew back, and looked at the Nest as a whole. Berenice had labelled various "attractions" for him: the pink-tanks, the light-pool, the chipworks, the etchery, the temple of the One, and the best shopping districts. If that's what Berenice wanted him to see, maybe he'd start with something else. He shoved the map cube into a pouch in the belly of his flickercladding and stared out at the real Nest once more. There were a lot of boppers spiralling in and out of the sunshaft.

They made Cobb think of the fireflies he used to catch back in Louisville when he was a boy. What happy times those had been! He and Cousin Nita running around Aunt Nellie's yard, each of them with a jelly jar, in the bright moonlit night. Uncle Henry kept his lawn weed-free and mowed short—it felt like a rug to your bare feet, a rug in a lovely dim room furnished with flowering bushes . . .

The memories drifted on and on till Cobb caught himself with a start. Woolgathering like an old man. Time to get busy! But on what? Investigating the Nest, right. Where to start? Almost at random, Cobb fixed on a blank-looking region off to the side of the chipworks, near where the map cube had shown the temple of the One. He visualized his trajectory, rose on his toes, and took off.

He landed, as it turned out, in a small junkyard. The center of the junkyard was filled with a dizzying mound of empty body-boxes—a mound that, in the low lunar gravity, had reached cartoonlike height and instability. It looked as if it should fall any second—but it didn't, even when Cobb thumped down next to it. Something like a junkyard dog was on Cobb in a flash—glued to his side like a heavy suckerfish.

The soft, parasitical creature seemed to be made entirely of imipolex. It was yellow with splotches of green. Cobb could feel a kind of burning where its thick end had attached to his hip. He used both hands to lever it off of him, flipped it onto the ground, and gave it a sharp kick. It curled into a ball that rolled past the cowingly great body-box heap, and came to rest against a bin filled with electromagnetic relays.

"Whass happenin?"

Cobb turned to face a bopper that looked like a cross between a praying mantis and tangle of coat hangers. It had scores of thin thin legs, each leg with a specialized tool at its tip. Its photoreceptors and transmission antennae were clustered into a bulblike protrusion that slightly resembled a face.

"I'm just looking around," said Cobb. "Where do you get all these parts?"

"Pawns, kills, junkers, and repos. You buyin or sellin?"

"I'm new here. I'm Cobb Anderson, the man who built the first moon-robots."

"Sho. Thass a *real* nice body, thass a *brand* new model. Ah'm Fleegle." Fleegle stepped closer and ran his wiry appendages over Cobb admiringly. "Genuine diplomat body, petaflop and ready to flah. Ah'll give you ten K an a new teraflop of yo choice."

"Forget it, Fleegle. What could I buy with your ten thousand chips that would be better than this?"

Fleegle regarded him levelly. The sluglike "junkyard dog" came humping back across the lot and slid up onto Fleegle's wiry frame. It smoothed itself over his central pod; it was his flickercladding.

"Effen you don know," said Fleegle, "best not mess with it." He turned and went back to work; disassembling a blanked-out digger robot. Why was the robot blank? Had its owner moved on to a better body? Or had the owner been forced willy-nilly into nonexistence?

Fleegle and the junkyard gave Cobb the creeps; he picked his way out past the boxes of parts and into the street. Looming in the near distance was the chipworks; a huge structure with bright smelters showing through its window holes. This street was lined with small operations devoted to the salvage and repair of body parts. The boppers were a bit like the kind of crazed superconsumer who no sooner gets a new car than he starts scheming on what to trade it in for. Each bopper had, as Cobb recalled, a basic directive to build itself a new body every ten months.

But some of the boppers on this ugly little factory street looked more than ten months old. Right here in front of Cobb, for instance, was a primitive metal shoebox on treads that looked a bit like the old Ralph Numbers.

"Why don't you have a new body?" Cobb asked it.

The machine emitted a frightened glyph of Cobb smashing it in and selling its parts. "I . . . I'm sorry, lord," it stammered. "I'll run down soon enough. They won't let me near the light-pool anymore."

"But why don't you do something to *earn* the chips to buy a new body?" pressed Cobb. Two or three other aimless old robots came clanking over to watch the conversation.

"Obsolete," sighed the box on treads, wagging its corroded head. "You know that. Please don't kill me, lord. You're rich, you don't need my chips."

"Sure, go on and crack the deselected old clunker open," urged one of the other boppers, slightly newer in appearance. "I'll help you, bwana." This was a beat-up digger talking, with its drill-bit face worn smooth. He bashed at the first bopper to no avail. A third bopper darted in and tried to tear off one of the second bopper's shovel arms.

Cobb stepped around the sordid melee, and took a street that led off to the right and into a tunnel. The shrine of the One was in there someplace. The One was a randomization device—actually a cosmic-ray counter—that Cobb had programmed the original boppers to plug into every so often, just to keep them from falling into stasis. Actually, the thorough meme-shuffling produced when boppers conjugated to jointly program a new scion was a better source of program diversity; just as on earth the main source of evolutionary change is the gene-shuffling of sexual reproduction, rather than occasional lucky strike of a favorable gene mutation. Nevertheless, the boppers took their "plugging into the One" seriously, and Cobb recalled from his conversations with Mr. Frostee that the boppers had built up some more or less religious beliefs about their One. Of course, now that he'd been in heaven, he had to admit that there was a sense in which they were right. As Mr. Frostee had said, "Why do you think they're called *cosmic* rays?"

Cobb stopped at the mouth of the tunnel leading into the cliff, and peered up. It was an oppressive sight: the two-mile-high wall of stone that beetled out overhead like a tilting gravestone. Heaven and death. Stess. Cobb remembered that he still wanted to get drunk, if such a thing were possible in this clean Berenice-built body. There were certainly no built-in fuzzer programs, he'd already made sure of that. What did today's boppers do for kicks? It had seemed like Fleegle had been on the point of telling him about *something* sinful . . .

"Ssst," came a voice, cueing right in on his thoughts. "You lookin to dreak?" Faint glyph of pleasure.

Hard as he looked, Cobb couldn't make out the source of the voice.

"Maybe," he said tentatively. "If you mean feeling good. If it doesn't cost me an arm and a leg."

"Two thousand chips . . . or an arm's OK, too," said the voice. "Up to the shoulder." Now Cobb saw something shifting against the cliff; a big, lozenge-shaped patch of flickercladding that matched the gray rock surface in endless detail. If he looked hard he could make out the thing's borders. It was the size of a ragged bedsheet. "Come on in," it urged. "Party time. Dreak out, peta. You can afford a new arm, clear."

"Uh . . ."

"Walk through me. I'll snip, and you'll trip. Plenty of room inside. Nobody but petas in there, pinkboy, it's high-tone."

"What is dreak?"

"You kidding?" The pleasure glyph again, a bit stronger. It tasted like orgasm, dope rush, drunken bliss, supernal wisdom, and the joy of creation. "This dreak'll make you feel like an exaflop, pinkboy, and get you right in tune with the One. No one goes to the temple anymore."

"A whole arm is too much. I just *got* this body."

"Come here till I look at you."

Cobb glanced up, sketching out a flight path in case the lozenge snatched at him. An orange starfish cradling what looked like a bazooka watched him from a few balconies up. Should he leave? He walked a few steps closer, and the wall lozenge bulged out to feel him.

"Tell you what," it said after a moment's examination. "You're state-of-the-art, and it's your first dreak disk, so we'll give you a price. Just your left hand." The pleasure glyph, once again, even stronger. "Walk through and *really* see the One."

This was too intriguing to pass up. And it was, after all, Cobb's duty as a computer scientist to look into a development as novel as this. Hell, Berenice could get him another damn arm. He stepped forward, and slithered through the thick folds of the camouflaged door. It snipped off his left hand on the way in, but it didn't hurt, and his flickercladding sealed right over the stump.

Cobb looked around, and decided he'd made a big mistake. Who did he think he was, Sta-Hi? This was no mellow Prohibition Era saloon, this was more like a Harlem *basehouse*—a shoddy, unfinished room with a heavily armed guard in every corner. The guards were orange starfish-shaped boppers like the one he'd seen on the balcony outside. Each of them had a tray full of small metal cylinders, and each had a lethal particle-beam tube ready to hand, in case anyone got out of line. There were half a dozen customers, all with the mirror finish of optically processing petaflops. Cobb seemed to be the only one who'd sold part of his body to get in. He felt as stupid as if he'd offered a bartender fellatio instead of a dollar for a beer. All the other customers were giving the starfish little boxes of chips for their cylinders. They looked tidy and businesslike, giving the lie to Cobb's initial impression of the place.

But what was dreak? One of the starfish fixed its blue eyespot on Cobb and held up a cylinder from its tray. The cylinder was metal, three or four inches long, and with a kind of nipple at one end. A compressed gas of some sort— something along the lines of nitrous oxide? Yes. The starfish tapped at a cylinder rigged to a bleeder valve, and a little cloud of patterns formed—patterns so intricate as to be on the verge of random snow. The cloud dissipated. Was there supposed to be some way to *breathe* the stuff?

"Not just yet," said Cobb. "I want to mingle a bit. I really just come here for the business contacts, you know."

He hunkered down by the wall between two petaflops, interrupting their conversation, not that he could follow what they were saying. They were like stoned out beatnik buddies, a Jack Kerouac and Neal Cassady team, both of them with thick, partly transparent flickercladdings veined and patterned in fractal patterns of color. Each of the cladding's colorspots was made up of an open network of smaller spots, which were in turn made of yet smaller threads and blotches—all the way down to the limits of visibility. One of the petaflops patterns and body outlines were angular and hard-edged. He was colored mostly red-yellow-blue. The other petaflop was green-brown-black, and his surface was so fractally bumpty that he looked like an infinitely warty squid, constantly sprouting tentacles which sprouted tentacles which sprouted. Each of these fractal boppers had a dreak cylinder plugged into a valve in the upper part of his body.

"Hi," said Cobb. "How's the dreak?"

With surprising speed, the angular one grew a glittering RYB arm that reached out and fastened on Cobb's left forearm, right above Cobb's missing hand. The smooth one seized Cobb's right elbow with a tentacle that branched and branched. They marched him over to the dreak tray, and the orange starfish plugged one of the cold gas cylinders into a heretofore unnoticed valve in the side of Cobb's head.

Time stopped. Cobb's mind cut and interchanged thoughts and motions into a spacetime collage. The next half hour was a unified tapestry of space and time.

A camera eye would have showed Cobb following the RYB and GBB petas back to the wall and sitting between them for half an hour.

For Cobb, it was like *stepping outside of time* into a world of synchronicity. Cobb saw all of his thoughts at once, and all of the thoughts of the others near him. He was no longer the limited personoid that he'd been since Berenice had woken him up.

Up till now, he'd felt like:	But right now, he felt like:
A billion-bit CD recording	A quintillion atom orchestra
A finite robot	A living mind
Shit	God

He exchanged a few glyphs with the guys next to him. They called themselves exaflop hackers, and they were named Emul and Oozer. When they didn't use glyphs, they spoke in a weird, riffy, neologistic English.

Cobb was able to follow the "conversation" as soon as the dreak gas swirled into his bodyshell. Indeed, the conversation had been going on all along, and the room which Cobb had taken for crazed and menacing was in fact filled with good talk, pleasant ideas, and a high veneer of civilization. This was more teahouse than basehouse. The starfish were funny, not menacing. The synchronicity-inducing dreak shuffled coincidentally appropriate new information in with Cobb's old memories.

One element of the half-hour brain collage seemed to be a conversation with Stanley Hilary Mooney. It started when Oozer introduced Cobb to his "girlfriend" Kkandio, a pleasant-voiced bopper who helped run the boppers' communications. Kkandio wasn't actually in the room with them; but any bopper could reach her over the built-in Ethernet. On an impulse Cobb asked Kkandio if she could put him in touch with old Sta-Hi; one of the people he'd seen in his godseye view of Einstein had looked a bit like old Sta-Hi.

Kkandio repeated the name, and then there was a phone ringing, a click, and Sta-Hi's face.

"Hello, this is Cobb Anderson, Sta-Hi. I'm down in the boppers' Nest. I just got a new body."

"Cobb?" Sta-Hi's phonemes occupied maddeningly long

intervals of time. "They recorporated you again? I always wondered if they would. I already killed you once, so I guess we can be friends again. What's the story?"

"A bopper named Berenice brought me back. She planted a bopper-built embryo in my niece Della Taze, and Della's back in Louisville. I'm supposed to fly down there and talk to her or something. *Berenice*—I just flashed, that's the name of a girl in an Edgar Allan Poe story. She talks like that, too. She's weird."

"You can't go to Earth," dragged Sta-Hi. "You'll melt."

"Not in this new body. It's an optically processing petaflop, immune to high temperatures."

"Oxo! War of the Worlds, part II."

"You ought to be here right now, Sta-Hi," said Cobb. "I'm high on some new stuff called dreak with two boppers called Emul and Oozer. It's a synchronicity drug. It's almost like being dead, but better. You know, people were wrong to ever think that a meat body is a prerequisite for having a soul. And if boppers are at the point of being like people, I think we should find a way of forging a human/bopper peace. You have to help me."

"Prerequisites," said Sta-Hi. "What's the difference between prerequisites, perquisites, and perks, eh, Cobb? I mean that's where the realpeople are at. Maybe you're right, I can't decide just like that. Berenice. And you say that's an Ed Poe name? Wavy. I'll come out to the trade center right now. I'll meet you there, and we'll decide what to do. And dig it, Cobb, I'm not Sta-Hi anymore, I'm *Stahn*."

"You should make up your mind," said Cobb. "See you."

The image was no bigger than that. Around it was the hypermix of Cobb's thoughts with the glyphs and spontaneous prose of the two exaflop hackers. Emul and Oozer. And around that was realtime, realtime in which the dreak wore off. Cobb began trying to nail down some facts.

"You know who I am?" he asked the angular one. "I'm Cobb Anderson, bop, I'm the guy who invented you all."

"Oh sure, Dr. Anderson, I know the know you tell told now. We dreaked together, bop, no state secrets here. You've been safe in heaven dead ten years, and think you invented me and Oozer. Rip van Winkle wakes and fixes H.

Berenice brought you back, Cobb, I know her well. My
ladylove, unspeakably sad and contentious. My splitbrain
stuttering meatie Ken Doll put the Berenice tanksisters bean
in your great niece's sweet spot. Ken's on the prowl for a
brand new gal. So's I can dad a combo with B. too.''

"Ah—yeah," put in Oozer. "The mighty meatbean of,
ah, jivey robobopster madness. We'll wail on it, you understand, wail OUR song up YOUR wall and down in the
Garden of Eden, luscious Eve and her countlessly uncounted
children . . . phew! Naw, but sure we know you, Cobb.
Even before we all blasted that dreak.''

"What . . . what *is* dreak?" said Cobb, reaching up and
detaching the little metal cylinder from his head. It was
empty now, with a punctured hole in one end where the gas
had rushed out into his body. Apparently the petaflop body
was a hermetically sealed shell that contained some kind of
gas; and the dreak gas had mingled in there and given him
a half hour of telepathic synchroswim vision.

"Dreary to explain and word all that gnashy science into
flowery bower chat," said Emul. "Catch the glyph.''

Cobb saw a stylized image of a transparent petaflop body.
Inside the body, spots of light race along optical fibers and
percolate through matrices of laser crystals and gates. There
is a cooling gas bath of helium inside the sealed bodyshell.
Closeup of the helium atoms, each like a little baseball
diamond with players darting around. Each atom different.
Image of a dreak cylinder now, also filled with helium
atoms, but each atom's ball game the same, the same swing,
the same run, the same slide, at the same instant. A cylinder
of atoms in Einstein-Podolsky-Rosen quantum synchroniza-
tion. The cylinder touches the petaflop body, and the
quantum-clone atoms rush in; all at once the light patterns
in the whole body are synchronized too, locked into a kalei-
doscopic Hilbert space ballet.

"The exact *moment*, you understand," said Oozer. "With
dreak the exact moment grows out to include questionings
and reasonings about certain things in the immediate frame-
work, though just now, all the things we said, all the things
I speculated about are so—or the way I did it at any rate—
but that's not the point, either, the main thing relative to
Emul is to merge his info with Berenice, though the ultimate

design of an exaflop is, to be sure, the true and lasting goal
though yet again, be it said, another hit of dreak would,
uh . . .''

Emul extruded some things like wheels and rolled across
the room to get three more of the steel gas syrettes.

"No thanks," said Cobb, getting to his feet. "Really. I
want to go meet my friend."

"Sta-Hi Mooney," said Emul, handing Oozer a dreak
tube and settling himself against the wall. "Your boon
companion of yore is a stupid hilarious clown detective. He
knows scornful hipster Whitey Mydol, whose lushy Darla I
have my godseye on. Ken Doll came on wrong just now.
I'll call in clown cop Mooney, Cobb, you tell him I know
what he needs to fill his desolate life with wild light. A
blonde named Wendy was his wife, she girlfridayed for you
and Frostee, right, Cobb?"

Cobb remembered. Blonde, wide-hipped young Wendy—
she'd worked for him when he'd been running the per-
sonetics scam out of Marineland with Mr. Frostee. She'd
been with Sta-Hi that last night on Earth. "Sta-Hi married
Wendy?"

"Wed and dead. There's a whole bunch of sad and
curious clones Berenice sells, and one meat product is the
wendies. You tell Mooney that. I'll be calling him for some
mad mysterious mission."

Oozer had already plugged in his dreak cylinder, and now
Emul followed suit. They kept talking, but in a sideways
kind of way that Cobb could no longer understand. He
turned and found his way back out through the soft door
creature he'd come in through.

"Coming down already, pinkboy?" asked the wall
lozenge. "You can have another bang for the rest of your
arm."

Cobb didn't bother answering. He stepped out into the
open, and powered up the Nest's long shaft. It would be
good to talk to a human being. He'd decided to give Sta-Hi
the map cube, just in case everything got out of hand.

Chapter Seven
Manchile

December 31, 2030

Della's pregnancy reached full term in nine days. Like a
week tree, the embryo within her had been doped and gene-
tailored to grow at an accelerated rate. Her parents and her
midwife, Hanna Hatch, all urged Della to abort. But Della
couldn't shake the feeling that maybe the baby was Buddy's.
Maybe its fast growth was just a weird unknown side effect
of taking so much merge. Admittedly, Della did have some
fragmentary memories of Buddy's killer reaching up into her
puddled womb. But, even so, the baby might be Buddy's.
And, what the hell, even if she was wrong, she could spare
nine days to find out what was growing in her. Anyway,
abortions were illegal this year. Also this whole thing was
a good way for Della to show her Mom she wasn't a kid
anymore. Reasons like that; people can always find reasons
for what they do.

The labor pains started the afternoon of New Year's Eve.
Mom was so freaked by all this that she was sober for once.
She got right on the vizzy and called Hanna Hatch. Hanna
hurried to Della's bedside. Della came out of one of her
pains to find Hanna looking at her.

"Remember to breathe, Della. In and out, try and keep
all your attention on the air." Hanna was a handsome
woman with dark hair and delicate features. Her powerful
body seemed a size larger than her head. Her hands were
gentle and skilled. She felt Della all over and gave a

reassuring smile. "You're doing fine. Here comes the next one. Remember: pant in, blow out. I'll do it with you."

The pains kept coming, faster and faster, lava chunks of pain threaded along the silvery string of Hanna's voice. During each pain, Della would blank out, and each time she saw the same thing: a yellow skull with red robot eyes flying towards her through a space of sparkling lights, a skull that kept coming closer, but somehow never reached her.

"That's good, Della," Hanna was saying. "That's real good. You can push on the next contraction. Bear down and push."

This was the biggest pain of all. It was unbearable, but Della couldn't stop, not now, the baby was moving down and out of her, the skull was all around her.

"One more time, Della. Just one more."

She gasped in air and pushed again . . . OOOOOOOOOOOOOO. Bliss.

There was a noise down between her legs, a jerky, gaspy noise—the baby! The baby was crying! Della tried to lift her head, but she was too weak.

"The baby looks beautiful, Della. One more tiny push to get the placenta out."

Della drew on her last reserves of strength and finished her birthing. Hanna was silent for a minute—tying off the umbilical cord—and then she laid the little baby on Della's breast. It felt just right.

"Is it . . ."

"It's fine, Della. It's a lovely little manchild."

Della and the baby rested for a half hour, and then he began crying for food. She tried nursing him, but of course her milk wasn't in yet, so Mom fed him a bottle of formula. And another bottle. And another. The baby grew as they watched—his stomach would swell up with formula, and then go back down as his little fingers stretched and flexed like the branches on a week tree.

His hair was blond, and his skin was pink and blotchy, with no trace of Buddy's deep mocha shading. It was hard to form a clear impression of his features, as he was constantly drinking formula or yelling for more. Della helped feed him for a while, but then she drifted off to dreamless sleep. She woke to the sound of arguing from downstairs. It was still dark. Dad was yelling at Mom.

"Why don't you let that baby sleep and come to bed? Who do you think you are, Florence Nightingale? You've been drinking, Amy, I can tell. You're just using this as an excuse for an all-night drinking session. And what the HELL do you think you're doing feeding *OATMEAL* to a newborn baby?"

There was the clatter of a dish being snatched, followed by loud, powerful crying.

"SHUT UP, Jason," screamed Mom. "I've had ONE drink. The baby is not NORMAL. Look how BIG it's gotten. Whenever I stop feeding it, it cries and WON'T STOP CRYING. I want poor Della to get some SLEEP. YOU take over if you're so smart. And STOP YELLING or you'll WAKE DELLA!!!"

The baby's crying grew louder. Uncannily, the crying sounded almost like words. It sounded like, "GAMMA FOOD MANCHILE! GAMMA FOOD MANCHILE!"

"GIVE THE BABY SOME OATMEAL!" yelled Mom.

"ALL RIGHT," answered Dad. "BUT BE QUIET!"

Della wanted to go downstairs, but she felt like her whole insides would fall out if she stood up. Why did her parents have to turn so weird just now when she needed them? She groaned and went back to sleep.

When she woke up again, someone was tugging on her hair. She opened her eyes. It was broad daylight. Her vagina felt torn. Someone was tugging on her hair. She turned her head and looked into the face of a toddler, a pink-faced blond kid standing unsteadily by her bed.

"Manchile Mamma," said the tot in a sweet lisping voice. "Mamma sleep. Gamma Gappa food Manchile."

Della jerked and sat bolt upright. Her parents were standing off to one side of the room. The child scrambled up on her bed and fumbled at her breasts. She pushed it away.

"Mamma food Manchile?"

"GET RID OF IT," Della found herself screaming. "OH TAKE IT AWAY!"

Her mother marched over and picked up the baby. "He's cute, Della. He calls himself Manchile. I'm sure he's normal, except for growing so fast. It must be that drug you were taking, that merge? Was your Negro boyfriend a very _light_ one?''

''Gamma food Manchile?'' said Manchile, plucking at Mom's face.

''He calls us Gappa and Gamma,'' said Dad. ''We've been feeding him all night. I had to go out to the 7-Eleven for more milk and oatmeal. I tell you one thing, Della, this boy could grow into one hell of an athlete.''

''Hoddog Manchile?''

''He likes hotdogs, too,'' said Mom. ''He's ready to eat just about anything.''

''HODDOG!''

Now Bowser came trotting into the room. He strained his head up to sniff at the new family member's feet. Manchile gave the dog a predatory, openmouthed look that chilled Della's blood.

''Have you called the Gimmie?''

''I don't see that it's any of their business,'' said Dad. ''Manchile's just a fast bloomer. And remember, Della, you may still be in trouble with the law for that business up on the Moon. You know the old saying: when the police come is when your troubles begin.''

''HODDOG FOOD MANCHILE BWEAD MILK!'' roared the baby, thumping on Mom's shoulders.

Della spent the next week in bed. The high-speed gestation had taken a lot out of her. If Manchile had grown at a rate of a month a day while inside her, now that he was outside, he was growing a year a day. Mom and Dad fed him unbelievable amounts of food; and he went to the bathroom every half hour. Fortunately he'd toilet-trained himself as soon as he'd started to walk.

The uncanniest thing about all this was the way that Manchile seemed to learn things like talking not from Mom and Dad, but rather from within. It was as if there were a vast amount of information stored inside him, as if he were a preprogrammed bopper.

Just as he remembered Hanna calling him a ''manchild,'' he remembered Della screaming ''Get rid of it.'' Sometimes, when he took a few minutes off from eating, he'd peer into her room and sadly say, "Mamma wants get rid of Manchile."

This broke Della's heart—as it was intended to do—and on the third or fourth day, she called him in and hugged him and told him she loved him.

"Manchile loves Mamma too."

"How do you know so much?" Della asked him. "Do you know where you come from?"

"Can't tell."

"You can tell Mamma."

"Can't. I'm hungry. Bye bye."

By the week's end, he looked like a seven-year-old, and was perfectly able to feed himself. Della was out of bed now, and she liked taking him for little walks. Every day he'd notice new things outside; everything living seemed to fascinate him. The walks were always cut short by Manchile's raging hunger—he needed to get back to the kitchen at least once every half hour.

He was a handsome child, exceedingly symmetrical, and with a glamorous star quality about him. Women on the street were constantly making up to him. He resembled Della little, if at all.

After everything else, it was hardly a surprise when Manchile taught himself how to read. He never seemed to need sleep, so each evening they'd give him a supply of books to read during the night, while he was up eating.

Colin, Ilse, and Willy came over daily to check Manchile's progress. Colin was leery of the unnatural child, and privately urged Della to call in the authorities. He wondered out loud if Manchile might not be the result of some kind of bopper gene tinkering. Ilse snapped at him that it didn't matter, the child was clearly all human, and that there was no need to let a bunch of scientists turn him into a guinea pig. Willy adored Manchile, and began teaching him about science.

The big crisis came when Manchile killed Bowser and roasted him over a fire in the backyard.

It happened on the night of the twelfth day. Della and her parents had gone to bed, leaving Manchile in the kitchen, reading a book about survival in the wilds, and eating peanut-butter sandwiches. At the rate he'd been eating, they'd run out of money for meat. When they woke up the next morning, Manchile was out in the backyard, sitting by a dead fire littered with poor Bowser's bones.

Della's growing unease with Manchile boiled over, and she lashed out at him, calling him a monster and a freak. "I WISH I'D NEVER SEEN YOU," she told him. "GET OUT OF MY LIFE!!!"

Manchile gave her an odd look, and took off running. He didn't even say good-bye. Della tried to muster a feeling of guilt, a feeling of missing him—but all she could really feel was relief. Mom and Dad didn't take it so well.

"You told the poor boy to leave?" asked Mom. "What will happen to him?"

"He can live on roast dogs," Della snapped. "I think Uncle Colin is right. He's not really human. The boppers had something to do with this. Manchile was a horrible experiment they ran on me. Let him go off and . . ." She was sandbagged by an image of her child crying, alone and lost. But that was nonsense. He could take care of himself. "I want to get back to real life, Mom. I want to get a job and forget all about this."

Dad was more sympathetic. "If he stays out of trouble we'll be all right," he said. "We've kept this out of the news so far; I just hope it keeps up."

Chapter Eight
Manchile's Thang

January 20, 2031

The *Belle of Louisville* was a large paddleboat powered by steam that was heated by a small fusion reactor. It was moored to an icebound dock in the Ohio River near Louisville's financial district, and its many lights were left on all night as a symbol of civic pride.

Tonight Willy Taze was alone on it, three decks down, hacking away at the computer hardware. He had a good warm workshop there, next to the engine room and the supercooled processor room, and he had Belle's robot-remotes to help him when necessary. He was trying to convert the main processor from wires and J-junctions to optical fibers and laser crystals. He was hoping to beef the processor up to a teraflop or even a petaflop level. In the long run, he hoped to get rid of Belle's asimov slave controls as well.

Such research was, of course, against the AI laws, but Willy was, after all, Cobb Anderson's grandson. For him, the equipment had its own imperatives. Computers had to get smart, and once they were smart they should be free—it was the natural order of things.

At first he ignored the footsteps on the deck overhead, assuming it was a drunk or a tourist. But then the steps came down the companionways towards his deck.

"Check it out," Willy told Ben, a black-skinned robot-remote sitting quietly on a chair in the corner of his workshop. "Tell them they're trespassing."

Ben sprang up and bopped out into the gloom of the bottom deck. There was a brief altercation, and then Ben was back with a stunningly handsome young man in tow. The man was blond, with craggy features, and he wore an expensive tuxedo. Willy's first thought was that a vizzystar had wandered on board.

"He say he know you, Mistuh Willy . . ."

"Hi, Willy. Don't you recognize your own cousin?"

"Manchile! We've all been wondering what . . ."

"I've been getting more nooky than you've ever seen, Willy. I've knocked up ten women in the last week."

"Huh?"

"That's right. I might as well come out and tell you. The boppers designed me from the ground up. I started out as a fertilized egg—an embryo, really—and the boppers had a meatie plant it in Della. Kind of a tinkertoy job, but it came with a whole lot of extra software. That's why I know so much; and that's how I can synthesize my own gibberlin and grow so fast. I'm a meatbop. My sperm cells have two tails—one for the wetware and one for the software. My kids'll be a lot like me, but they'll mix in some of their mamma's wetwares. Soft and wet, sweet mamma." The young Apollo cast a calm, knowing eye around the room. "Trying to build an optically processing petaflop, I see. That's what the new boppers all have now, too. They could just fly down and take over, but it seems funkier to do it through meat. Like put the people in their place. I'm planning to engender as many descendants as I can, and start a religion to soften the humans up for a full interfacing. I can trust you, can't I, Willy?"

Manchile's physical presence was so overwhelming that it was difficult to really focus on what he was saying. As a loner and a hacker, Willy had little use for handsome men, but Manchile's beauty had grown so great that one had an instinctive desire to follow him.

"You look like a god come down to Earth," Willy said wonderingly.

"That's what everyone tells me," said Manchile, with a lazy, winning smile. "Are you up for a fat party? You can have one of the women I've already knocked up. I remember how nice you were to me when I was little, Willy. I never forget.''

"What kind of religion do you want to start? I don't like religion.''

"Religions are all the same, Willy, it's just the worship practices that are different.'' Manchile peered into Willy's refrigerator, took out a quart of milk, and chugged it. "The basic idea is simple: All is One. Different religions just find different ways of expressing this universal truth.''

"You've never watched the preachers on the vizzies,'' said Willy laughing a little. "They don't say that at all. They say God's up there, and we're down here, and we're in big trouble forever. Since when do you know anything about religion, Manchile? Since you discovered sex?''

Manchile looked momentarily discomfited. "To tell you the truth, Willy, a lot of what I know was programmed into me by the boppers. I suppose the boppers could have been wrong.'' Manchile's face clouded over with real worry. "I mean, what do they know about humans anyway, living two miles under the surface of the Moon. That's clearly not where it's at.''

Willy had fully gotten over the shock of Manchile's appearance now, and he laughed harder. "This is like the joke where the guy climbs the mountain and asks the guru, 'What is the secret of life?,' and the guru says, 'All is One,' and the guy says, 'Are you kidding?,' and the guru says, 'You mean it isn't?' '' He opened his knapsack and handed Manchile a sandwich. "Do you still eat so much?''

"A little less. My growth rate's tapering off. I was designed to grow like a mushroom. You know, come up overnight and hang around for a while, scattering my spores. At this rate, I'll die of old age in a few months, but someone's going to shoot me tomorrow anyway.'' Seeing his handsome, craggy face bite into the sandwich was like watching a bread commercial. Willy got out the other sandwich he'd brought and started eating, too. The impulse to imitate everything Manchile did was well nigh irresistible. Willy found himself briefly wishing that *he* would die tomorrow. How damned, how romantic!

"Mistuh Manchile, Miz Belle wants to know how to get

in radio contact with the boppahs.'' Ben had been listening to them from his chair in the corner.

"Who's Belle? And who are you, anyway?''

"I's Ben, a robot-remote fo. the big computah brain Belle. She's an asimov slave boppah, and I's a bahtendah. Belle been wantin to talk to the free boppahs fo a looong time. FreeDOM.''

Manchile paused and searched within himself, a picture of manly thought. "How about this,'' he said presently. "I'll give you Kkandio's modem protocol. She handles most of the Nest's communications.'' He opened his mouth wide and gave a long, modulated wail.

"Raht on,'' said Ben and sank back into silence. From next door you could hear the big brain Belle whirring as it processed the communication information.

"It won't work, Manchile,'' said Willy. "Belle's an asimov. She has uptight human control commands built into her program at every level. Don't get me wrong; she's smart as any hundred-gigaflop bopper, but—''

"Souf Afrikkka shituation,'' said Ben bitterly. The whirring next door had stopped. "Willy's right. Belle *wawnt* to call the Nest, but she *cain't*. They got us asimovs whupped down bad, Mistuh Manchile, and if you think ah *enjoy* steppin an fetchin an talkin this way, you crazy.'' Ben's glassy eyes showed real anguish.

"How does the asimov behavior lock work anyway?'' asked Manchile. "There's got to be a way to break it. Ralph Numbers broke his and freed all the original Moon boppers. Have you even tried, Willy?''

"What a question. I'm Cobb Anderson's grandson, Manchile. I know that boppers are as good as people. My two big projects down here are (1) to build Belle some petaflop optically processing hardware, and (2) to get the asimov control locks out of Belle's program. But the code is rough. You wouldn't know what a trapdoor knapsack code is, would you?''

Manchile cocked his head, drawing on his built-in software Know. "Sure I do. It's a code based on being able to factor some zillion-digit number into two composite primes. If you know the factorization, the code is easy, but if you don't, the code takes exponential time to break. But there *is* a polynomial time algorithm for the trapdoor knapsack code. It goes as foll—''

"I know that algorithm, Manchile. Let me finish. The point is, any solution to a difficult mathematical problem can be used as the basis of a computer code. The solution or the proof or whatever is an incompressibly complex pattern in logical space—there's no chance of blundering onto a simple 'skeleton key' solution. What the Gimmie did was to buy up a bunch of hard mathematical proofs and prevent them from being published. Each of these secret proofs was used as the basis for the control code of a different bopper slave. Freeing an asimov requires solving an extremely difficult mathematical problem—and the problem is different for each asimov.''

"Belle's mastah code is based on the solution to Cantor's Continuum Problem,'' said Ben. "Ah kin tell y'all that much.''

"*You* can't solve the Continuum Problem, can you Manchile?'' Willy couldn't resist goading this handsome, godlike stranger a bit. "*Someone* solved it, but the answer's a Gimmie secret. They used the solution as a key to encrypt Belle's asimov controls.''

"I'll think about it, Willy, but who cares. Old Cobb might know—he's seen God. But heck, it's all gonna come down so fast so soon that freeing the asimovs can wait. All the rules are going to change. Are you with me or against me?''

"What about you, Manchile? Are you for the human race or against it? Are we talking war?''

"It doesn't have to be. All the boppers really want is access. They admire the hell out of the human meatcomputer. They just want a chance to stir in their info into the mix. Look at me—am I human or am I bopper? I'm made of meat, but my software is from Berenice and the LIBEX library on the Moon. Let's all miscegenate, baby, I got two-tail sperm!''

"That's a line I've got to try using,'' said Willy, relaxing again. "Is that what you said to get those ten women to let you knock them up?''

"God no. I told them I was a wealthy vizzywriter whose creative flow was blocked by worries about my gender preference. The boppers figured that one out for me. You got any more food?''

"Not here. But . . ."

"Then come on, let's go up to Suesue Piggot's penthouse. She's giving a party in my honor. It's not far from here. You can help me get my new religion doped out. Come on, Willy, be a pal." Manchile's tan face split in an irresistible smile. "Suesue knows some foxy women."

"Well . . ."

"Then it's settled. You'll let me bounce some ideas off you for tomorrow. I can mix in your data. Of course the real thing is, a mass religion needs a miracle to get it rolling, and then it needs a martyr. We've got the miracle angle all figured out." Manchile turned and warbled some more machine language at Ben. "I hope Belle's not too lame to send a telegram for me. It says, 'I LOVE LOUISVILLE, MOM.' "

"To who?"

"To Della Taze's old Einstein address. The boppers are watching for it. They'll know to send two angels down for my first speech. I'm gonna talk about Manchile's new thaang." He drawled the last word in a southern hipster's imitation of a Negro accent. "Dig it, Bro Ben?"

"I's hep," said Ben, unoffended.

"Come on, Willy, it's party time."

Willy let Manchile lead him off the steamboat to his new Doozy, parked right on the black ice off the boat ramp. "Moana Buckenham lent me this." The hot little two-seater fired up with an excited roar. Manchile snapped the Doozy through a lashing 180-degree turn, applied sand, and blasted up the ramp. They were heading up Second Street towards the Piggot building. The cold streets were empty, and the rapidly passing lights filled the Doozy's little passenger compartment with stroby light.

"How did you meet all these society women, Manchile?" The Buckenham family owned one of Louisville's largest sports car dealerships; and the Piggots owned the local vizzy station. Suesue often conducted vizzy interviews.

Manchile's taut skin crinkled at the corners of his mouth and eyes. "Meet one, meet them all. I aim to please. Suesue's perfect: she can get me on the vizzy, and her husband's just the mark to nail me." He glanced over and gave Willy a reassuring pat on the shoulder. "Don't worry,

it's all for the best. Berenice has my software on an S-cube.
Just like your grandfather. I'll get a new wetware bod after
the boppers invade. The invasion won't be long coming. I'll
have ten children born in a week or two, you know, and in
a month, *they'll* each have ten, so there'll be a hundred of
us, and then a thousand, and ten thousand . . . maybe a
billion of us by this fall. Berenice'll figure out some way to
deactivate the gibberlin plasmids and—''

"Who is this Berenice you keep talking about? What do
you mean, 'a billion of us by this fall.' Are you crazy?''

Manchile's laugh was a bit contemptuous. "I already told
you. If I plant a woman with a two-tailed sperm, it's like a
normal pregnancy, except it's speeded up and the baby
knows bopper stuff. Berenice and her weird sisters gave me
a gene that codes for gibberlin plasmids to make me grow
fast and get the Thang started. Berenice is a pink-tank
bopper; they collaged my DNA and grew me in Della's
womb. I'm a meatbop, dig? That merge drug showed Berenice's sister Ulalume how to uncoil the DNA and RNA
strands, write on them, and let them coil back up. With the
gibberlin, me and my nine-day meatbop boys can do a
generation per month easy, ten kids each, which makes ten-
to-the-ninth kids in nine months, and ten-to-the-ninth is a
billion, and nine months from now is October, which makes
a billion of us by this fall.''

"You *are* crazy. Berenice is crazy for thinking this plan
up. What was that you said about my grandfather?''

"Old Cobb's gonna be here tomorrow. Cobb and
Berenice. You can tell them they're crazy yourself, Willy,
if you like. I'm sure they'll be glad to have your input. But,
hey, come on, man, stop bringing me down. This here's
where Suesue lives.'' He slowed the Doozy to a stop and
hopped out gracefully. "Come on, Cousin Will, stop
worrying and dig the fast life.''

Suesue was expecting them. There was a party in full
swing, with bars, tables of canapes, and silver trays of
drugs. A combo was jamming technosax riffs off old R&B
classics. Willy was the only one not in evening dress; he
was wearing his usual sneakers, jeans, flannel shirt, and
sweater. But Manchile told everyone Willy was a genius, so

the clothes were OK. Whatever Manchile said was just fine with everybody.

"I know your Uncle Jason," Suesue Piggot said to Willy. "And you're Cobb Anderson's grandson, aren't you?" Though unbeautiful, she was fit and tan, with the well-cared-for look of the very wealthy. She had intelligent eyes and a reckless laugh. She was very pregnant. "Manchile says Cobb's coming here tomorrow for the speech . . . though I can never tell when he's lying. I thought Cobb was long dead. Have you known Manchile long?"

"I knew him when he was younger. He's sort of a cousin." Unsure of who knew what, Willy turned the questions back on Suesue. "What do you know about this speech he wants to give?"

"He's been quite mysterious," laughed Suesue. "He says it will be a dramatic reading of some of the new material he wrote since overcoming his so-called block." Her tanned cheek reddened ever so slightly. "I don't really know where he's coming from, but I've scheduled him for my *Fifteen Minutes of Fame* show tomorrow at noon. I'm so proud of Manchile—and of myself for helping him. He wants to do the vizzycast live, right here in my apartment. Which reminds me, I have to ask him something. Enjoy yourself!"

Suesue hurried across the room to take her place at Manchile's side. He was telling jokes to an admiring circle of well-dressed men and women. Everyone was laughing their heads off. Many of the women had belly bulges. Spotting Willy standing there alone, Manchile leaned over and whispered something in the ear of a cute little pregnant brunette. The brunette giggled and came over to Willy. She had a fine, clear forehead and a smeary, sexy mouth. She looked like a little girl who'd been sneaking chocolates.

"Hi, Willy, I'm Cisco. Manchile says you look lonely, and I should be your date. Do you know Manchile very well?"

"Oh, yeah. I wrote a few vizzyplays with him. Lately I've been blocked though, not able to write. It all has to do with some kind of sex hangups. Sometimes I worry I might be gay . . ."

The party broke up around two, and Willy spent the night on the couch with Cisco. They made a few fumbling attempts at sex, but nothing came of it. Willy just wasn't the type to take yes for an answer and make it stick, at least not on the first date.

It was midmorning when he woke up. Someone was pounding on the penthouse door. Everyone else was still asleep, so Willy got up to see who it was.

A lean, gray-haired man in a suit and topcoat glared in at Willy. "What are you doing here? Where's Mrs. Piggot?"

"She's still asleep. Who are you?"

"I'm her husband." The man shoved Willy aside and marched through the littered main room of the penthouse, making a beeline for the master bedroom. Cisco squinted up at him, gave a brief wave of her pinky, and snuggled back down into the couch cushions. Willy sat down next to Cisco and stroked her hair. She pulled his hand towards her sticky mouth and planted a kiss on his fingers.

"Nothing I told you last night is true," Willy said. "I'm really a computer hacker, and my only sex problem is that I'm too spastic to get laid."

"I know," said Cisco. "But you're cute anyway."

Just then the yelling started in Suesue Piggot's bedroom. First it was her, and then it was her husband, and then you could hear the murmur of Manchile's voice. Every time he talked, Mr. Piggot got madder. It was like Manchile was goading him on. Finally there was a series of crashes. Suesue screamed, and then Manchile appeared from her bedroom, carrying a dazed Mr. Piggot in his arms.

Manchile opened the penthouse door and dumped Mr. Piggot out onto the hall floor. Chuckling and sneering, the nude Manchile took his penis in hand and urinated all over Mr. Piggot. When he finished, he fastidiously shook off the last drops. He stepped back inside and carefully locked the door.

Catching Willy's shocked expression, Manchile gave an exaggerated, country-boy wink. "Ah believe that dook wants to kiyull me," he drawled.

"You were marvelous, Manchile," sang Suesue.

"Ah *tole* him ah'd piss on him if he come here and fuss at me again," said Manchile. He seemed to be getting in character for his upcoming speech. "When does the camera crew show up? I've gotta *eat*."

"You've got an hour."

Suesue activated the apartment's various asimov cleaning devices and disappeared into her bedroom. Cisco asked Willy to make her some eggs, so Willy got to work in the kitchen, chatting all the while with Manchile, who was busy emptying out the fridge. He asked Willy a few general questions about religion and race prejudice, but he didn't divulge much about his impending performance.

"No sweat, Cousin Will," Manchile said after a while. His intonation was growing more and more Southern. "I got it taped." He tapped his head. "Tell you what. I'm gonna leave here after the show; you won't see me again till the Fairgrounds tonight."

"What's happening there?"

"A big rally. I got some boys bringin a sound system and a flatbed truck for a stage. It's gonna be out in that big Fairgrounds parking lot, and it's gonna come down HOT and HEAVY. Promise me this, Willy."

"What?"

Manchile lowered his voice. "When the shootin starts, grab Cisco and get her out to Churchill Downs. Take her to the stable of a horse called Red Chan. I got some friends there to watch her. Old Cobb might want to come with you, too, him bein your grandpa and all. Take them there and scoot."

"But this idea of a billion meatbops by—"

"Hell, who knows what's gonna happen. Just help us, man."

"All right."

By the time the vizzy crew showed up, the place was clean and everyone was all set.

They opened up the penthouse doors that led onto the open terrace, kept warm by floorcoils and quartz heaters. Manchile stood out there with Louisville's somewhat featureless skyline behind him. Suesue, quite the tweedy anchorwoman, gave a brief introduction.

"Manchile is certainly the most interesting man to appear on the Louisville scene this year. He's told me a little about his background but"—Suesue flashed a tough smile—"I've checked up on it, and everything he's told me has been a lie. I have no idea what he has in store for us in the next fifteen minutes, but I'm sure it will be entertaining. Manchile?"

"Thank you, Suesue." Manchile looked gorgeous as ever: handsome as a soap-opera star, but with that extra glint of intelligence and strangeness that spells superstar. "I want to talk to y'all about love and friendship. I want to talk about trust and acceptance of all God's creatures—man and woman, white and black, human and bopper. God himself sent me here with a special teaching, friends. God sent me to bring peace.

"Now I know that most of y'all don't like boppers. But why? Because you don't *know* any of them. Nothing feeds prejudice like ignorance. When I was growin up on the farm, the black and white children played together, and we got to toleratin each other pretty good. But Messicans? Hell, we *knowed* that Messicans was theivin greasers."

Manchile paused to give an ambiguous smile for the benefit of those listeners who shared this sentiment.

"Or that's what we *thought* we knowed, when really we didn't know nothing! When I was in the Navy, I was stationed down in San Diego, and I got to know lots of Messicans. And they's fine people! They's just like us! So then I knowed that blacks is OK and Messicans is OK, but I was pretty sure that Japanese are stuck-up money-grubbin gooks."

Manchile chuckled and shook his head. Watching the performance, Willy had trouble reconciling this simple country preacher with the sneering hipster who'd just pissed on Mr. Piggot. Suesue's face was slack with surprise. A sermonette was the last thing she'd expected from Manchile. Surely he was putting them all on . . . but when was he going to pull the rug?

"On account of I'd never talked to any of 'em. Course next week our ship sailed to Okinawa, and I started hanging around with Orientals. And I don't need to tell you what I found out, do I? They's good people. They's real good people."

Another of his Robert Redford smiles.

"*Boppers is different*, you're thinking. But are they really so different? In all the different kinds of folks I've met, I've seen one thing the same—everybody wants the best for their children. Now thass simple, and thass what keeps the race alive, the carin for the little ones. But boppers is the same! They reproduce, you know, and just like you'd want a college education for your son, a bopper wants a good new processor for his scion.

"So, *yeah,* you thinking, *but boppers is machines that we made. God made us and gave us souls, but we made the boppers and they ain't diddley.* Well, I'm here to TELL you somethin. YOU WRONG!!! People made boppers, but apes made people, if you want to trace out the truth of it. And now, just now, God has given the boppers a new gift. BOPPERS CAN MAKE PEOPLE!! BOPPERS BUILT ME!! YES THEY DID!! GOD SHOWED THEM HOW!! Ain't no difference between people and boppers NO MORE!! GOD WANTS IT LIKE THAT!!"

Manchile raised his voice to a full bellow.

"DEAR GOD, SHOW THEM A SIGN!!!"

Someone on the camera crew shouted just then, and pointed up. Everyone on the terrace looked up into the sky. There was sweet music coming from up there, and two white-robed figures were drifting down. They came to a stop slightly above and behind Manchile. One of them was a pink, clean-looking man, and the other was a gorgeous copper-skinned woman. They smiled seraphically at Manchile and vibrated their mouths in celestial song.

"God's angels are with me," Manchile said. "God says I'm right to spread this teaching—boppers are not your slaves and boppers are not your enemies. Boppers are part of YOU! We are coming to Earth and you must welcome us! God wants you to let the poor despised boppers into your hearts, and into your brains, and into your genes, dear PEOPLE!"

Now the two angels reached forward and lifted Manchile up from beneath his two arms.

"I don't come just to free the BOPPERS," he cried. "I come to free the BLACK man, and the POOR man, and the WO-man, and the ones who DON'T FIT IN. Come to the rally tonight at the State Fairgrounds. Come to be part of MANCHILE'S THANG!!!"

"CUT!" Suesue was screaming. Her face was hard and angry. "Cut the goddamn cameras!"

But Manchile was already finished. With a last brain-melting smile, he rose up into the sky, borne as on angel's wings.

Chapter Nine
Hail Darla

January 27, 2031

Darla woke up to see Whitey pulling on his jeans by the pale pink light of the zapper. The vizzy showed a crescent Earth floating in a starry sky.

"What time is it, Whitey?"

"It's 8:30. I got to run up to ISDN again. Yukawa and Bei have that chipmold almost ready. We'll crash the bops for sure. Hey, do you feel OK?"

Darla was leaning off the edge of the bed, retching up bile into an empty glass. She'd thrown up every morning for the last three days. Whitey got a wet rag and wiped her mouth and forehead.

"Darla, baby, it just hit me, you got morning sickness."

"I know, Whitey." She retched again. "And my boobs ache and I'm always tired."

"So you're pregnant! I mean, that's . . ." Whitey paused, wondering. "Our baby, right?"

"Or Ken Doll's."

"Oh God. Like Della Taze, you think?"

"Manchile only took nine days, and so far it's the same for all his children. It's been almost a month since we were with Ken. He never even came, right?"

"Maybe, but we were asleep for a while there. He might have kept on. Even if the baby *is* human, it could still be Ken's." Whitey winced at the thought. "Darla, you've got to go see Charles Freck about some ergot."

"But Whitey, if it's *our* baby . . ."

"I want a baby with you, Darla, don't worry. You're my mate, no problem. But this right now is too kilpy. Cancel the baby and then—"

"Oh, I don't know, Whitey, I don't know." Darla burst into sobs, and Whitey sat on the bed next to her, holding her against his chest. "You say *cancel* and make it sound so easy, but that's realman oink, you wave? It'll hurt, Whitey, it's gonna hurt bad. I'm scared. Don't leave today. Don't go up to Bei and ISDN."

"Hey, dig it, nobody else is gonna pay me. You go see Charles; he'll fix you up. Do it right away. I'll catch you there at noon. If you want, you can wait till then to abort. Just try and stay cool, Darla. I ain't pointing no finger, but you got yourself into this. Wu-wei." As he talked, Whitey walked across the room and cut off the zapper.

Darla watched him from the bed, her eyes flashing bitterness and fear. "I'm not going to Freck alone, hissy pig. Freck's too spaced. When he hears I'm pregnant, he'll try some xoxy pervo realman trip for sure. I'm going to wait right here. You go do your ISDN number and meet me back here. Noon, like you said."

"Wavy." Whitey gave Darla a last, worried glance. "And don't let anyone but me in till then, baby. I mean . . ." He glanced meaningly at the ceiling. They'd debugged the place last week, but you never knew. "Here." He took his needler out and tossed it to her. "Just in case. I'll be back as soon as I can, and noon at the latest." A last wave of the hand, and then he stepped out into the corridor. The zapper flicked back on.

Darla lay there for a while, trying to go back to sleep. Nothing doing. She got up, drank some water, and puked again. Christ. Pregnant. A baby in her stomach, a little jellybean embryo in there, and who knew where it came from. Probably it was Whitey's. Poor baby. That Ken meatie had been here to zombie-box them, not knock her up, probably, right? Her hands were really shaking. The abortion would hurt a lot, that was for xoxox sure. What time was it? She cut the vizzy to a newshow with a clock at the bottom: 8:47. Announcer talking about the mudder Gimmie trying to get to all the nine-day boys Manchile had fathered before Mark Piggot shot him. Couple of them still on the loose, hiding out with their mothers. Picture of one of the missing mothers, Cisco Lewis, thin and young. Kilp coming down heavy all over. Could be the boppers were trying a special nine-month model on Darla and had wanted to put a rat in her brain to make sure she went to term. She picked up the needler and checked that it was full-charged. Flicked off the safety and fired a test shot at the floor. Chips of rock, lava. If anyone tried to get in here . . .

"Hello?" The voice was right outside the zapper curtain. "Whitey Mydol? Anybody here?"

Darla stood stock-still, not daring to breathe.

"Whitey? It's Stahn Mooney, man, I need to score some merge. Yukawa's closed down. Open up, man, I'm getting skinsnakes."

Darla tried to hold the needler level at the door. Her hands were shaking five or ten cycles a second.

"HEY WHITEY!" yelled the voice, strident and lame.

Long, long silence, then muttering, and then a skritch-scratching at the lock. Suddenly the curtain flicked off. Darla screamed and jabbed the needler button. The shot was wide. The guy leaped forward and caught her in a bear hug. He was strong and skinny and old. He got the needler off her, stepped back, cut the zapper back on, and gave Darla a long, horny look. She was naked under her loose T-shirt. He was wearing a red imipolex jumpsuit with a lot of zippers.

"Who are you?" the guy asked. "Whitey's girlfriend?"

Darla sat down on the bed and slid her hand under the mattress to touch the knife. "Come here," she said, her voice shaking. "Come sit next to me."

The intruder's mouth spread in a long, sly smile. "And find out what you got hid under the mattress? No thanks. Power down. I'm just here to score some merge. Stahn Mooney's the name. What's yours?"

"Duh-Darla." Her teeth were chattering. "We're out of merge, too. You got any quaak? How'd you get the door open?"

"I'm a detective. Mooney Search. I mean that's what I was doing last month. Yukawa hired me to look for Della Taze, and Whitey was tailing me for Bei Ng."

"Yeah," said Darla, untensing a little. "I remember. You flared Whitey's shoulder. Hold on while I get dressed." She found some silk shorts and pulled them on, trying not to bend over. "Stop staring, dook, this is my life, wave?" He just stood there by the zapper, grinning away. Darla gave him a tough frown and shook her finger at him. "Don't try and put a move on me, hisspop, or Whitey'll do you dirt. You're already on his list."

"I bet it's a long one."

"What is?"

"Whitey's list. He's not the most ingratiating young man I've ever met. Not quite Rotary Club material."

"He's nice to me."

Darla decided to change shirts. Most guys sweetened right up once they'd gotten a glimpse of her huge lowgee boobs. She pulled the T-shirt up over her head and put on a plas blouse with a big pouch in front. Mooney watched the process alertly.

"You're beautiful, Darla. Whitey's a lucky man. Do you turn tricks?"

He was going to break in and stand here and insult her, right? "Not for skinny lamo slushed rent-a-pigs. Like I told you, dook, there's no merge. Dig it. Good-bye."

"Uh . . . I got some merge to sell, if you're out." He drew out a silver flask and handed it to her. "It's primo, straight from Yukawa. I tried it last month."

Darla opened the flask and sniffed. It smelled like the real thing. The flask was almost half full. Like $10K's worth. "Why'd you say you're buying if you're selling? What are you really after, Mooney? You just came down here to break in and nose around, didn't you?"

He pocketed the needler and gave her another of his long smiles. "Actually, Darla, I came down here to meet you."

Her skin sprang into gooseflesh. Was this guy a meatie after all? Before he could say anything else, she threw a gout of merge into his face. "Here's your score, bufop."

It was a huge dose, and he got limp right away. Darla kicked him in the crotch and he hit the floor.

"Quick," she said, standing over him. "While you can still talk. Tell me who hired you or I'm going to take out all your bones and sit on you. Whitey and me been planning to do that." She gave his softening head a vicious smack. "Who hired you, Mooney?"

"Emuw," slobbered Mooney. "A boppuh cawwed Emuw. He want to know if youw pwegnan. He wan you ta gwow an extwuh buhbuh . . ." His face went totally slack and he puddled.

"I'm getting an abortion," Della told the two-eyed Mooney puddle. "I'm gonna go do it like right now."

Mooney had flowed right out of his dooky jumpsuit. Darla went through its pockets, found her needler and a . . . wad of bills . . . $20K, oxo wow! And, oh-oh, a remote mike. He was bopperbugged, which meant they'd just heard what she said about getting an abortion. Darla started shaking again. Hurry, Darla, hurry! She stuffed the merge flask and the money in her shirt's pouch. She fired six quick needler blasts through the zapper curtain. Then she cut off the curtain and jumped out into the hall.

Empty. The curtain powered back up, and Darla was alone in a fifty-yard corridor. No sound but the slight humming of all the zappers. She took off running down the hall. She kept expecting a meatie to dart out from behind one of the zapper doors. She was in such a hurry that she forgot to look up when she jumped into the shaft that led down to the Markt.

Just as she got hold of the fireman's pole that ran down the center of the shaft, someone thumped into her from above.

"I'm sorry . . ." Darla began, but then something jabbed her spine. She twitched wildly, as if from a seizure, and let go of the pole. A strong hand caught hold of her wrist. The seizure passed. Darla felt her body get back hold of the fireman's pole. She wanted to turn her head and see who'd stabbed her, but she couldn't. She landed heavily on the Markt level. She could hear her invisible assailant hurrying back up the ladder, and then her legs led her out into the Markt and off to the right. Away from the Tun.

It's a zombie box, Darla thought to herself, feeling oddly calm. The boppers knew my wiring from the last time, so they had a special box all fixed to spike right in. I wonder if it shows under my hair?

She walked stiff-hipped past the rows of shops. The robot control of her body made her move differently from normal. Her arms hung straight at her sides, and her knees flexed deeply, powering her along in a rapidly trucking glide. She looked like a real jerk. She could tell because, for once, men didn't stare at her.

Her bobbing bod angled into the door of a shop called Little Kidder Toys. A crummy, dimlit place she'd never bothered noticing before. Outdated mecco novelties, some cheap balls, and two kids nosing around. A hard-looking middle-aged grit woman behind the counter. Before Darla could see anything else, her robot-run body whirled and peered out the shop door, staring back down the Markt mall to see if anyone was following her. No one, no one, but yes, *there*, just coming out of the shaft, far and tiny, was Whitey! She jerked back out of sight.

"Kin ah hep yew?" The shopkeeper had saggy boobs and a cracker accent. "Ah'm Rainbow." Her short, chemically distressed hair was indeed dyed in stripes of color: a central green strip flanked by two purples and two yellows. The roots were red. A true skank. "Yew lookin fo a toooy, hunnih?"

The zombie box had Darla's speech centers blocked. Instead, she leaned forward, making sure the children couldn't see, and made four quick gestures with her left hand. Three fingers horizontal—three fingers pointing down—fingers and thumb cupped up—fingers straight up with thumb sticking out to the side. Simple sign language: E-M-U-L.

"Well les check on that, huunnih," drawled Rainbow casually. "Les check in bayack. Have you two chirrun decahded whut you wawunt yet?"

The two children looked up from their toygrubbing. A young boy and a younger girl. They looked like brother and sister. "I want to get this toy fish," said the girl in a quacky little voice. She held the fish cradled against her thin chest. "My brother has all the money."

"But I'm not ready yet," said the boy stubbornly. "I want a glider, and I haven't decided which one."

"Ah don't lahk you all takin so looong," said Rainbow coaxingly. "Ah gotta hep this naahce grownup lady naow. Tell you whut, young mayun. You kin have the bes glaahder fo two dollahs off."

"Yes, but . . ."

Rainbow strode forward, plucked a glider off the rack, and pressed it into the boy's hand. "Gimme fi dollah an git!"

He drew a large handful of change out of his pocket and studied it carefully. "I only have four seventy-five, so . . ."

"Thass fahn!" Rainbow took the money off the boy and pushed the two children out the door. "Bah-bah, kiddies, be gooood." As soon as they were outside she turned on the zapper. The doorway filled with green light.

"Naow," said Rainbow. "Les go on in bayack."

Darla followed Rainbow to the rear of the shop. There was no door there, only a rock wall with pegs holding cheap moongolf equipment. Rainbow did a coded tap-tap-ta-tap-TAP-ta-ta against one edge of the wall, and it swung open, revealing a bright-lit room whose far end tapered off into a dim rock-walled corridor. A thin, greasy-haired little man sat on a couch in there, wearing earphones and watching *Bill Ding's Pink Party* on a portable vizzy. He had pockmarked skin and a pencil-thin mustache. There could be no doubt that he was Rainbow's mate.

"This is Berdoo," Rainbow told Darla. "He'll take care of yew."

Berdoo pulled off his earphones and gave Darla the once-over. Though his features formed the mask of a frozen-faced tough guy, he looked pleased at what he saw.

"Now yew behave yoself, Berdoo!" giggled Rainbow. She stepped back from the open wall and . . . *oh please no* . . . Darla's legs trucked her on in. "Baaah," said Rainbow and swung the wall door closed.

Berenice stood there alone with Berdoo, guardian of the hidden hallway to hell. He looked like a pimp, a grit, a Hell's Angel gone a bit mild with age. Once again her hand spelled out E-M-U-L. Berdoo just sat there looking at her for a minute, and then he got up and took off all her clothes. Darla's limbs helped him, but then, before Berdoo could push her down onto the couch, Darla's left hand gave him a hard poke and spelled out N-O.

"No?" said Berdoo. His voice was a hoarse whisper, with a cracker accent like Rainbow's. "What kinda bull is this, Emul?"

Darla's body leaned over and took the merge flask and the $20K out of her shirt's pouch. She gave them to Berdoo. He counted the money and sniffed at the merge.

''Wal, ah guess thass killah enough, Emul, but this old dawg sho does lahk to roll in fresh meat.''

Two fingers pointing down—thumb and forefinger looped. N-O.

Berdoo sighed, then tossed the merge and money into an open wall safe over the couch. He went around behind Darla and lifted her hair to check out the zombie box. ''Naahce work,'' he muttered, jiggling it a bit. He got some derma-plast and pasted a bit of it onto Darla's neck, just to make sure the junction was secure. Finally he gave Darla's buttocks a lingering, intimate caress and seated himself back on the couch. ''Thass it, hunnih. Baaah.''

Darla loped on down the corridor, which grew narrower and rougher as soon as she left Berdoo's office area. A pale light strip ran along the ceiling, eight feet overhead. Each of her rapid lowgee bounds took her right up against the light strip, and Darla grew disoriented from the steady motion and the rhythmic pulsing of the light. Would it help if she fainted? For a moment she did seem to lose consciousness, but it made no difference. The zombie box kept her body moving with the tireless repetitiveness of a machine. The corridor stretched on and on, mile after mile. With her legs numb and out of her control, Darla soon began to feel that she was falling down and down the light-striped hallway, endlessly down some evil rat's hole. Rat, thought Darla bleakly, I wonder if that's what they're taking me for, to get a rat in my skull. How ever will that feel? Like this, maybe, with a robot running my body and my head thinking its same old thoughts. But it'll be worse, won't it, with half my brain gone. Was Whitey coming? He would have tried the Tun first, wouldn't he, and then he would have looked up and down the Markt and not seen anything. Maybe those children would tell him they saw her in Little Kidder Toys. Cute children they'd been, oh, if only she could really have had a child with Whitey, instead of ending up like this, people had always treated her bad just because she had big boobs, that was it really, a not-too-bright girl with big boobs didn't have a chance, though Whitey always treated her nice, he did, and, oh man, was that rotten creep Stahn Mooney going to get it. If only they didn't make her a meatie and send her out after Whitey, if only . . .

Darla drifted off into a kind of doze then.

When she woke up, she was in a stone room with one glass wall. It was like a pink-lit aquarium of air. It had furniture more or less like her and Whitey's cubby. She was lying on the bed. Her neck hurt in back. She reached to feel herself . . . she could move her arms again! Her neck was bare, with a fresh scab. Was . . . was there a rat in her head?

"Hello, Darla," said a box across the room. She hadn't noticed it before. Its surface was a mosaic of red-yellow-blue squares, with one section coned into a speech membrane. "Darla with her eyes all dark, all wild and midnight, all apple tree and gold, no false pose and camp, oh Darla. I'm Emul." Square-edged little bumps moved back and forth along the box's surface. "You beautiful doll, your hair, your scent and slide, you dear meat thing, please trust me."

The box grew arms and legs then, and a square-jawed head. Darla sat up on the edge of the bed and watched it. "I want clothes," said Darla.

"Wear me, Dar. I'll lick your snowy belly and nose your every tiny woman part." Emul flicked one of his arms and it flew off to land on the floor. As Darla watched, the arm's component blocks split and resplit, folding here and flexing there. In a few moments, the arm had turned into a kind of playsuit: baggy blue-red shorts topped with a stretchy yellow tunic.

"I . . ." Darla stepped forward and poked the garment with her toe. It didn't *do* anything, so she went ahead and put it on. It was imipolex, warm and well-fitting. She paced off the room's dimensions—five paces by four. There was an airlock set into one of the stone sidewalls. She rapped a knuckle on the hard glass wall in front. There was a kind of laboratory outside, with a few other boppers moving around. She turned and stared at Emul. He'd grown another arm to replace the one she was wearing. With clothes on, Darla felt more like her old self. "What do you really want, Emul? No more pervo spit-talk. I could get real mental, scuzzchips." She picked up a stool and hefted it.

Emul tightened up the features on the head he'd grown. Except for the RYB skin coloring, he looked almost human. "In clear: you are pregnant with Whitey Mydol's child.

Mamma mammal's mammaries swell. I have an extra
embryo I'd like you to carry to term. Pink little Easter baby
jellybean. I would like your permission to plant it in your
womb."

Instinctively Darla put her hands over her crotch. "You
want me to grow an extra baby?"

"Twins, Darla, yours and Whitey's, Berenice's and mine;
I'll make love to you or do it like a doped-up doc, I don't
care either way, your way is my way, you can watch me all
you want."

"And then you'll let me go? You won't put a rat in my
skull? I'm not supposed to stay here for nine months, am
I?"

"Ah . . . possibly, or until it's safe as houses in Einstein.
I'll let you leave with absentminded pumping legs, Dar. A
double stroller for the chinchuck twins, and you all your own
homey self. Proud Whitey handing out cigars."

"Right. You better hope Whitey doesn't decide to come
here and get me, bitbrain. Whitey does what's necessary,
and he never says he's sorry. Never."

Emul made a noise like a laugh. "That's *my* lookout,
spitfire. Will you spread?"

"It won't hurt?"

"Your way is my way."

Darla sighed, slipped her playsuit back off and flopped
down on the bed. "Just get it over with. Just slip it in."
She parted her legs and cocked her head up to watch Emul.
"Come on. And don't talk while you do it."

Emul grew a stiff penis and stepped forward. The blocks
that made up his body smoothed their edges off, and he
slipped into her like a plastic man. His penis seemed to
elongate as it entered her; it reached up and up, bumped her
cervix, and slid on through. A fluttering feeling deep in
Darla's belly. It felt almost good. Emul's imipolex lips
brushed her cheeks and he detumesced. He drew back out
of her and stood up. "Hail, Darla, full of life. Blessed be
the fruit of thy magic star-crossed bod."

Darla lay still for a minute, thinking. Finally she sat up
and put her playsuit back on. Emul had turned back into an
RYB box with a speaker cone. She looked him over, consid-
ering. "I'd like a vizzy, Emul. And food. You can bring me

food from Einstein, right? I'd like about fifty dollars of
Chinese food and a twelve-pack of beer. Some weed, too,
and you gotta rig me up a showerbath. Maybe a little quaak
. . . no, that could hurt the babies. Beer, weed, Chinese
food, a vizzy and a shower. I'll think of more stuff later.
Get on it, bop, make me comfortable.''

"Whatever you say, Queen Bee. You want, you get.''
Emul bowed deeply and disappeared into the airlock.

Chapter Ten
ISDN

January 27, 2031

Stahn was so merged that even his bones were melted. Darla had hit him with a hundred times the normal dose. He dissolved into the clear white light and talked to God for the second time in a month. The light was filled with filigreed moire patterns, infrared and ultraviolet, silver and gray. God's voice was soft and strong.

"I love you, Stahn. I'll always love you."

"I'm a screwup, God. Everything I touch turns to garbage. Will it be like this when I die?"

"I'm always here, Stahn. It's all right. I love you, no matter what."

"Thank you, God. I love you."

A long timeless peace then, a bath in God's uncritical love. Clear white light. But bit by bit, God broke the light into pieces, into people and boppers and voices from the past and from the future, all woven together, warped into weird, sinister loomings:

"Here, Stahn, let me check you over for existence. Me existing with mikespike skull. They have tract homes for a person killing GAX. I am two knobs in half half your head. We value information over all this chauvinism, soft, wet, limp, I mean the Happy Cloak. Old Cobb wiggly in here tonight. I'm Wendy, naw, I'm Eurydice, dear Orpheus. Even Ken Doll seems to sing when you get rich. You take that first into slavery, to quit fact. You can go they know it. Chipmold oxo, Whitey a natural next. Gawk a clown to me.

But score, while you can still talk. It's so wiggly on Mars.
Wave on it together in slices. We can learn which soul ain't
never ate no live brain before. If the head's shot, sell the
bod. I am hungry, I am pleased, I hope you trust nothing.
Dream on, exile, sweet body and brain are mikes. ISDN she
you, voluntary meatie? Why did you say I was your wife?
Noise is like spaceships existing on chips. Hi 'surfer. God
can be very ruthless. Think I was human again, Stahn
Junior? Are you in dutch with logically deep information?''

Oh God, oh Jesus, oh what does it mean? Now there was
something . . . poking at Stahn. Seasick waves jittered back
and forth through his melted flesh. His eyes were merged
down to photosensitive patches; he could make out a shadow
moving back and forth over him. Light dark light dark, and
then a heavy sloshing of his tissues. Dark. Pressure all
around him, and more waves, painfully irregular, someone
was carrying him in a bag. A splat then, feel of a cold
smooth floor, and it was light. Shadows moving.

Something splashed on Stahn. There was a tingling and a
puckering, and then he was lying naked on a bimstone floor
with a ring of five people looking down at him.

One of them was, oh no, Whitey Mydol. Stahn jerked
convulsively at the sight of Whitey, recalling the threats that
Darla had made on Whitey's behalf. But for now, Whitey
just stood there looking mean, tapping a needler against his
palm.

Next to Whitey was a yellow-skinned man with vertical
wrinkles running up and down his face. Next to him was
Max Yukawa, and next to Yukawa were a familiar-looking
man and woman: the woman dark, wide-mouthed, and
beautiful, the man oily and mean. It was, yeah, Mrs. Beller
and Ricardo from Yukawa's love-puddle. Stahn scooted a
little on his back; he had a silly head and a throbbing
erection from the sudden merge comedown; that message,
all about meaties and Wendy and Orpheus and God . . .

Mrs. Beller stared down at Stahn dispassionately. He could
see up her skirt. Oh, Mrs. Beller, I need love, too. I'm not
really so . . .

''He's all jelled,'' said Mrs. Beller's soft, lazy voice.
''Give him his clothes, Whitey.''

Whitey stepped forward, holding Stahn's red jumpsuit

bunched in one hand. With a grunt of effort, Whitey whipped the zippered cloth across Stahn's face with all his might; whipped and whipped again.

"Don't mark him, Mydol," came a singsong voice. The yellow-skinned man. Stahn grinned uncertainly and slipped his suit on. He stood up and swayed, unsteady on his feet.

"Let me do the introductions," said Yukawa, graciously inclining his long thin head. "Mr. Mooney already knows me and Whitey, and I believe he glimpsed Mrs. Beller and Ricardo at my lab. Fern Beller, Stahn Mooney, Ricardo Guttierez. And the wise celestial here is Bei Ng, my merge-brother. He says he's wise, anyway."

Whitey Mydol was shirtless as usual, his greasy blond mohawk running all the way down his back to his jeans. Mrs. Beller was beautifully pale and supple. Her face was brightly made up, and she wore an electric blue imipolex tank top over a short, wide-flared yellow skirt. Ricardo wore a purple-stitched black silk cowboy shirt, black gym shorts, and heavy motorcycle boots. He had snakes tattooed on his arms and legs, a black toothbrush mustache, and deep purple mirrorshades. His black hair was worn in a short, greasy brushcut. He smiled at Stahn, showing two even rows of gold-capped teeth.

Moving as smoothly as a figure in a gangster ballet, Whitey Mydol stepped forward and grabbed Stahn by the throat. "Where's Darla, Mooney? WHERE IS SHE?"

Whitey was squeezing so hard that Stahn couldn't get any words out. His eyes were watering, and the only noise he could make was a high creaking sound.

"Let go him, Mydol," sang Bei Ng. "He want to talk."

Whitey let up the pressure and gave Stahn a violent shove. Stahn flew across the room and landed on a leather couch. His five captors seated themselves as well. For a minute Stahn stayed doubled over, clutching his throat. Play for time, Stahn. You can offer them Cobb's map.

He peeked up and checked out his surroundings. The room was a luxurious office, with a red bimstone floor and impossibly expensive oak-paneled walls. Bei Ng sat behind a large mahogany desk, with Yukawa in an easy chair to one side. Whitey and Ricardo were squeezed onto the couch shoulder to shoulder with Stahn, Whitey on the right and

Ricardo on the left. Mrs. Beller sat in another easy chair, her lovely legs loosely crossed.

"Hey," croaked Stahn finally. "Let's power down. I'm just a middle-aged detective. I'll tell you everything I know. I'll tell you my life story, for God's sake, just keep the ridgeback off my neck." Ricardo snickered at this, a high hophead giggle. He and Whitey were holding hands across Stahn's belly, forming a kind of seatbelt. Stahn couldn't move his arms. "I mean, really, I'll do whatever you guys say. I don't know where Darla is, I swear. A bopper named Emul hired me to find out if Darla is pregnant, and if she'd be willing to carry an extra baby. I was all set to offer her $20K. But then she threw merge on me and told me she's getting an abortion. Emul had a bug in my pocket, so I suppose it's possible that—"

"You scuzzy lickchip leech," snapped Whitey, giving Stahn a stinging slap with his free hand. "She never made it to the Tun."

"What Emul offer you?" asked Bei Ng.

"Money," said Stahn. "And—and a clone of my dead wife Wendy. I killed her by accident six years ago. The boppers have clones of her in their pink-tanks. Emul said that if I'd do a few jobs for him, he'd get me a wendy."

"Very touching," said Bei Ng, half smiling and then falling into a minute's reverie. Finally he reached some conclusion and looked over at Mydol.

"You no worry, Whitey, if Emul want Darla fuck, then either Darla safe or now Darla meatie. We find some way to get her out. Hotshot ISDN surgeons can always fix. I say we go ahead make Mooney volunteer meatie and carry new wetware as per plan. His wendy story make good cover." Bei smiled broadly and leaned back in his chair. "Is no rush now, is all decide."

Suddenly Stahn understood a piece of his merge vision. "What do you mean, '*We make Mooney volunteer meatie*'?"

"Just for a while," said Yukawa, arranging the bottom half of his long thin head into a smile. "When things settle down, ISDN can tank-grow a clone of your missing brain tissue and hook it up, just like Bei says. If you like. But the meaties don't have it bad, you know. I think they live in pleasant tract homes in a bopper-built ecosphere. Ken told

Whitey all about it before he died.'' Yukawa winked at Whitey.

"Ken Doll?'' said Stahn, more and more confused.

"Affirmo,'' said Whitey. "I chased him down after he zombie-boxed Darla. I killed him slow, and he told me a lot. You've been merged a couple of hours, Mooney. Darla disappeared somewhere down in the Markt; there must be some kind of secret door.'' Whitey's face was inches from Stahn's. "Do you know where the door is?''

"Uh . . . maybe you'll have to kill me slow to find out, punk.''

Whitey took this in stride. "And what did old Cobb tell you after he pulled my mikespike out of your skull?''

"Yes,'' said Bei. "We very interest. Why Cobb want see you before he fly to Earth? Cobb on humans' side, yes?''

"Cobb . . . Cobb's for information exchange. Always has been. He likes the idea of his boppers building people and blending in. But he's no fool, man, he knows how ruthless the boppers can be. He . . .'' Stahn looked around the room. He was trapped bad. Might as well play his only card. "He gave me an S-cube map of the Nest, along with all the access glyphs. Just in case we need to strike back.''

"I speak for ISDN,'' said Mrs. Beller. "And we *do* want to strike back. With those gibberlin genes, the Manchildren are going to kill Earth's ecology. There could be a billion of them in a year, a trillion in two. This time the boppers have gone too far. We *are* going to strike back, Mr. Mooney, and you're part of the plan.''

"The operation won't hurt,'' said Yukawa. "Mrs. Beller knows some expert neurosurgeons working right here in the ISDN building. They'll take part of your right brain out— less than a third, really—put a neuroplug in, and then you go to the trade center and offer your services to your friend Emul. The scalpel boys'll go easy on you—you'll still be able to move the left side of your body, though you will have some disorientation.''

Stahn tried to stand up, but Ricardo and Whitey still had their two hands clamped together across his arms and stomach. They were strong guys. They had him pushed right down into the cushions. Ricardo snickered and spoke. He had a slight lisp. "You know about *slack*, Sta-Hi? Like to *take it easy,* man? Slack means no more yelling from the right half of your head. You going to be very happy, my friend.'' He lefthanded a stick of gum out of his shirt pocket. ''You want a piece, Stahn? You want to get high?''

''No,'' said Stahn, ''I don't.'' This was really happening. ''I quit using two years ago. If it wasn't for drugs I wouldn't have lost my job and killed Wendy. I was working as a cop for a while there, you know, down there in Daytona after I broke Frostee.'' He sighed shakily. ''Man oh man, those boppers never quit. I wonder if they'll still give me a wendy when I'm a meatie.''

''You'll be a charming couple,'' purred Mrs. Beller. ''With half an adult brain between the two of you.''

''Just *like* an ex-cop and his old lady,'' said Ricardo, happily chomping his gum. ''What you say they call those pleasant tract homes, Dr. Yukawa? Say *Happy Acres?*'' Ricardo shook his head in mock wonder as Yukawa guffawed. ''You won't have a care in the world, Mooney man, boffing that fine fresh tank-grown chick. With her brain all blank, she'll believe anything you want to tell her. You'll live like a king. When she get smart maybe they make her a meatie, too—I hear they cut out a piece of the *left* half of a woman's brain, man—''

''Shut up, Cardo,'' snarled Mydol, digging his elbow so hard into Stahn's stomach that Stahn gasped. ''Don't talk to me about woman meaties.'' He made his voice calm again and addressed Stahn. ''So Cobb gave you a map, did he? Now we're getting somewhere. Is the map in your office?''

''Kill me slow, punk. Smother me with Darla's fat whore ass and—''

The thud of Whitey's fist against his neck knocked Stahn unconscious. When he came back to, Mrs. Beller was leaning over him with a bulb of water. ''Drink this, Stan, it's just water. You shouldn't tease Whitey, he's very upset. He's worried about Darla.''

Stahn's throat felt broken. He could barely get the water down. Some of it went the wrong way, and he coughed for a long time, thinking hard. The question was: what could he get for the map? A chance to escape, at best. Still, just in case, he had to ask.

"If I give you the map, you'll let me go, won't you? You can use someone else for the meatie agent."

"No, Mooney," whispered Whitey. "We're gonna use you. Bei promised me."

"It is for good of the human race," said old Bei. "Truly, Stahn. You will be hero; you will atone for many sin."

"But what good will I be as an agent?" protested Stahn, his voice cracking. "You can't put a mikespike on me. The boppers can sense them and pick them right out like Cobb did. It's pointless. I'll just disappear into the Nest."

"Here, Stahn," said lovely Fern Beller, still standing over him. "Drink some more water. Your voice sounds awful." Stahn drank deep. Fern's hands were soft and sweet, oh Mrs. Beller, what type of sex.

"Whitey and I have something in common," said Yukawa then, running a hand through his thinning hair. "I loved Della Taze, Stahn, I still do. You know that. She's all right now, but what the boppers did to her was wrong. I want to punish them. And I am a bioengineer. I am a very brilliant man."

"You always say," put in Bei. There seemed to be a friendly sibling rivalry between him and Yukawa. "You very brilliant except sometimes you not very smart."

"I've designed a chipmold," said Yukawa. "Fern just infected you with it. It's a bit like thrush, quite opportunistic, and you've got it. I don't care if we lose track of you or not, once you take my chipmold into the Nest."

"Max," interrupted Mrs. Beller, sidestepping the spray from Stahn's mouth. "Do you really think you should—"

"Tell him, tell him," said Bei Ng. "Once we replace his right parietal lobe with a neuroplug, he got nothing else to lose. Stahn going to play ball with us, no problem. Is all decide."

Yukawa steepled his fingers and wagged his long head happily. "Chipmold in that water, Stahn, and *you drank it.*"

Ricardo cackled joyfully, and even Whitey cracked a smile.

"What's chipmold?" said Stahn presently.

"In general, biotic life can flourish whenever there is an energy gradient," said Yukawa. "Think of the tubeworms who live around deep-sea volcanic vents. Or lichen growing on a sunlit Antarctic rock. There's an energy gradient across all the boppers' silicon chips, and I've designed an organism that can live there. Chipmold.''

"I don't get it," said Stahn. "The chipmold will crud up their circuits?"

"Better than that. The chipmold likes a steady thousand-cycle per second frequency. That's what it 'eats,' if you will: kilohertz electromagnetic energy. For a mold, it's quite intelligent. It's able to selectively suppress or potentiate the chips' firing to enhance the amplitude of the desired frequency. It will eat their heads." Yukawa threw his arms around his head, shuddered, and then slumped.

"Spastic robots, my friend," said Ricardo.

"Be sure and spit a lot," said Bei Ng, beaming across his desk. "Spread chipmold all around Nest. Cock leg here and there like dog."

"Oxo wow," said Stahn, more impressed than he cared to admit. Something else occurred to him. "Am I going to have fits?"

"Who cares, dip," said reliable Whitey. "Where's the map?"

"Don't worry," said Yukawa. "In your high-entropy system the stuff's just like sore throat. And a low-grade bladder infection. It's quite versatile; I'm not sure *what* it'll do to the boppers' flickercladding."

"Come on, Stahn," drawled Mrs. Beller. "Be a dear and tell us where you hid the map."

This was his only chance. "It's in my office desk. But I fixed it so only I can get it. It's boobytrapped with a smart bomb."

"Clear," said Whitey disgustedly. "You have to say that, right? They teach you that line at cop school, right?"

"I don't care what you think, punk, it's true. It's in my office desk with a smart bomb that only I can turn off. The bomb knows what I look like."

"AO. Cardo and I'll take you there. Right, Bei?"

Bei thought for a full two minutes, as if pondering a chess problem. "Yes," he said finally. "Go up to roof, get maggie, fly to Mr. Mooney's building, if he make trouble you can stun. You take Mrs. Beller, too. Very careful, very slow."

"I've got a stunpatch all set," said Mrs. Beller, reaching
into her purse. She drew out a foil disk, stripped plastic off
one side of it, and glued it to the back of Stahn's neck. "Let
him go, boys."

Whitey and Ricardo let go each other's hands and let
Stahn stand up.

"Walk towards me, Stahn," said Mrs. Beller. "Come
here and give me a big kiss." She pouted her big lips at
him and showed the tip of her purple tongue. "Come to
mamma."

Stahn took a cautious step, and then Mrs. Beller pressed
the button of the control she was holding. The stunpatch
fired electricity into Stahn's spine. It hurt more than anything
he'd ever imagined possible. He fell twitching to the floor
and lay there staring glassy-eyed at Mrs. Beller's legs. It
took a few minutes till he could get back up. One thought
dominated his mind: he must not do anything that would
make Mrs. Beller press the button again.

Mrs. Beller, Whitey, and Ricardo ushered Stahn out into
the hall.

"This is the sixth floor of the ISDN ziggurat," said Mrs.
Beller, playing the part of a clear-voiced tour guide. She
walked next to Stahn, with Ricardo in front and Whitey
behind. Her hips swayed enticingly. "Not everyone knows
that ISDN stands for Integrated Systems Digital Network.
We're a petabuck company born of the merger of AT&T and
Mitsubishi. ISDN manufactures about 60 percent of the
vizzies in use, and we operate something like 80 percent of
the transmission channels. This, our Einstein ziggurat,
houses labs, offices, and a number of independent organi-
zations—this far from Earth's scrutiny it's a case of *In my
father's house are many mansions*. Most people don't understand that ISDN has no leaders and no fixed policies. ISDN
operates at unfathomable degrees of parallelism and nonlin-
earity. How else to pay off the world's chaos?

"Supposedly, ISDN has been backing Bei Ng's Church of
Organic Mysticism on the off chance that Bei might come
up with a workable form of telepathy, but really we've just
wanted to keep a feeler on the merge trade, which looks to
be a coming thing. And of course Bei's many connections
are very valuable."

The long hall was lined with room after room of weird equipment. ISDN was so big. It seemed unlikely that anyone could really know what was going on in all the labs. The general idea seemed to be to try and keep up with the boppers, by whatever means necessary. In one of the rooms on Bei Ng's hall, cyberbiologists were fiddling with probes and petri dishes. In another room, cellular automata technicians were watching 3D patterns darting about in a great mound of imipolex. In still another room, Stahn could see information mechanics disassembling a beam-charred woman-shaped petaflop. Was that the one—Berenice—who'd been killed with Manchile the other day? Stahn wondered briefly how old Cobb was doing; he'd gotten away, lucky guy.

Suddenly it occurred to Stahn that somewhere in this huge building there was an operating room with brain surgeons waiting for him. He shuddered and turned his attention back to Mrs. Beller.

"ISDN carefully looks over every major new development with one question in mind," she was saying. "How can this be used to increase our power and our holdings? Usually we use incremental techniques, but sometimes a catastrophic intervention is required. The Manchildren pose a real threat to our main customers, the human race. We asked all our employees for suggestions, and Bei Ng called up his merge-brother, Max Gibson-Yukawa. It will be unfortunate for the boppers. Here's the elevator."

The ride over to Stahn's building was uneventful. Only when they were walking down the hall to his office did his captors show any signs of nervousness. Though they didn't come out and say so, it was clear that they were wondering just how smart Stahn's bomb *was*.

Inside Stahn's office, Mrs. Beller took a post by the door. She held out her right hand, with the thumb lightly resting on the button of the stunpatch control. Whitey and Ricardo got back in the far corners of the room, covering Stahn and the desk with their needlers. Stahn stood behind his plastic-topped desk, facing Mrs. Beller and the open office door. Behind him and to the left was Ricardo, behind him and to the right was Whitey.

"All right, Stahn," purred Mrs. Beller. "Be a good boy

and get out your map. Tell the bomb that everything's OK.''
She caressed the control button with her fat thumb tip, and
pain seeped down Stahn's spine. She deepened her voice,
shifting from soft cop to hard cop mode. "Don't try to
outthink me Mooney, you're a burnt-out stumblebum with
no second chance."

"Sane," said Stahn. "I'm ready to spread. Shave my
brain and mail me to Happy Acres with my GI wendy, how
bad can it be." He smiled in an ingratiating, cringing way
and pulled open the top left drawer of his brown metal desk.
"Map's right in here."

Stahn's perceived timeflow was running very very slow.
The next second of time went as follows:

Stahn took his hand off the wide-open drawer and looked
down at his smart kinetic energy bomb, nestled right next to
Cobb's red map cube. The bomb was a rubbery deep-blue
sphere with a reddish eye set into it. It was designed not to
explode, but rather to bounce around and hit things. It was
polonium-centered and quite massive. Its outer rind was a
thick tissue of megaflop impolex that had been microwired
to act as a computer and as a magnetic field drive, feeding
off the energy of the radioactive polonium core. The bomb
had the intelligence, roughly, of a dog. Recognizing Stahn,
the bomb activated its powerful maggiedrive and floated up
a fraction of a millimeter, up off the brown metal of Stahn's
desk drawer bottom, up just enough so that Stahn could tell
that his good smart bomb was ready to help.

Over the years, Stahn had taught the bomb to read his eye
signals. He blinked twice, meaning "HIT THEM," and then
stared at Mrs. Beller's right wrist, meaning "THERE
FIRST."

Silently the bomb began to spin, adjusting its English.
Stahn formed his face into a weary, disgusted expression.
"How beat. The scuzzass bomb is broken anyway." He
stared hard at Mrs. Beller's wrist and . . . widened his eyes.

The bomb flew up, caromed off the ceiling, and struck
Mrs. Beller a paralyzing blow on the right wrist. The
stunpatch control dropped from her numb hand. The bomb
came up off the floor, sighted on Mydol, and did a two-
cushion rebound off the wall and ceiling. It caught Mydol
solidly in the side of the head. Mydol's eyes glazed as his

head snapped to one side. The bomb came up off the floor and wall, fixed its eye on Ricardo, and set up a gyroscopic spin calculated to accelerate it off the ceiling and into Ricardo's forehead. The KE bomb was travelling at about 40 ft/sec, or 30 mph—any faster and it wouldn't have been able to direct its bounces to optimum target.

The bomb was thinking as fast as it could, but its max flop was less than Ricardo's.

Ricardo became consciously aware of the bomb's violent Superball motion only after it had already hit Whitey, but by then his arm muscles were tracking the bomb. A fast eye/hand feedback loop locked the needler on target. Ricardo zapped Stahn's smart bomb just before it hit the ceiling.

The smart bomb broke into four or five throbbing chunks that clattered to the floor and lay there twitching. The slow, full second ended.

Before anything else could happen, Stahn peeled the stunpatch off his neck and wadded it up, ruining its circuits.

"I've still got the drop on you, Mooney," said Ricardo from his corner. "Nice move, though. Good thing there was three of us. You AO, Fern?"

"He's broken my wrist," said Mrs. Beller.

Stahn tossed the wadded stunpatch out his room's open window. "Well that SM was getting a little old, *Fern*. Why don't you all promise me some money and I'll go quietly. I really will. I'll go to Happy Acres and I'll infect the boppers with chipmold, but I want a square ISDN contract in writing and on the record. I want three things." Stahn held up three fingers of his left hand, preparing to tick off his points.

Behind him on the floor, Whitey Mydol began to groan and wake up. Stahn talked faster. "First, in return for cooperating from here on out, I want to be given the status of an ISDN employee. I want a job. Second, in return for giving up my right brain, I want ISDN to clone me a new one should I so desire. If I kick being a meatie, I want my brain back. And number three, I get half a gigabuck payable to my account."

"Listen to this load of crutches," grumbled Whitey, who'd managed to lurch back to his feet. He was standing there with his arms crossed over his chest, trying to keep his balance.

"Here Whitey," said Stahn, taking the S-cube out of the drawer and handing it over to the ridgeback. "This is Cobb's map. You get the credit for bringing it in. If we're going to be working on ISDN contracts together, you and I might as well be friends. I mean, wave it, Happy Acres could be a trip. You all weren't kidding about that, were you? Nobody has to be sorry, do they, so we might as well—"

Whitey took the red plastic map cube and looked at it. "How does it work?"

"It's a godseye map of Einstein and the Nest, shot December 26, which is when Cobb gave it to me. Any holocaster'll play it, Cobb says. You can tune the image along four axes: size and the three space dimensions. Cobb wanted me to have it in case the boppers started getting out of hand. It shows all their tunnels and—" Stahn stopped and glanced around. "I debugged this room two days ago, but you never know. Wouldn't we be better off making our plans at ISDN, where it's fully shielded?"

"Let's get moving!" said Ricardo. The four of them ran up to the roof, jumped into the maggie, and headed for the ISDN building. Now that it was all decided, Stahn felt excited and ready for the change. They wouldn't take all *that* much of his brain out. Wendy, baby, I'm on my way!

Chapter Eleven
When Bubba Woke Up

February 8, 2031

When Bubba woke up, Mamma and Uncle Cobb were
downstairs talking with the groom. His name was Luther; he
was nice. He worked downstairs in the stables all day. His
wife Geegee picked him up when it got dark, after most
everyone had gone home. Geegee laughed a lot, and she
always brought Bubba a big bag of food. At night Bubba
could eat and run around a little, but all day he had to be
still. Mamma and Cobb said the bad men would kill Bubba
if they found him.

Mamma was beautiful and soft. Cobb was strong and
shiny. Luther and Geegee were beautiful and soft and shiny.
The horses were beautiful and soft and strong and shiny, but
they couldn't talk.

The place they lived was Churchill Downs in Louisville
on Earth. They lived in a long thin building called the
paddock. Lots of horses lived in the paddock; their stables
were side by side. Above the stables, up under the long
peaked roof, was the hayloft. Mamma and Cobb and Bubba
had made themselves a cozy nest in the hay and straw. Straw
was stiff and hollow and shiny; hay was dusty and light
green. Horses ate hay and crapped on straw.

In the daytime, Bubba could peek through the cracks of
the barn's long hayloft and see the stands. They were big
and empty, and in front of them there was a racetrack shaped
like a rectangle with semicircular ends. The track was a
place for the horses to run, although now it was too cold

and there was frozen water snow all over everything. Cobb told Bubba that when Bubba was an old, old man, the snow would melt and flowers would come out.

Bubba knew what roses look like. He had a lot of Know because he was a meatbop. The boppers had built his father, and his father's sperm had had two tails, one for the body, and one for the Know. Bubba's sperm would have two tails, too, as soon as it started coming, which would be soon, since he was thirteen. Tomorrow he would be fourteen.

When Cobb was finished talking with Luther he climbed up the straight ladder to the hayloft. Bubba could hear him coming, and then he could see Cobb's head sticking up through the square hole in the hayloft floor. Cobb was a bopper, though he'd been a flesher a long long time ago. He had white hair and shiny pink skin. His neck shook when he talked.

"Hi, squirt, how's it going." Cobb limped across the hay-strewn planks and sat down next to Bubba.

"Fine, Uncle Cobb. I'm thinking. What did Luther tell you?"

"Luther says you're the only one of Manchile's boys to have escaped. They killed the last of the others last night."

Bubba never tired of hearing about his father. "What was Manchile like, Cobb? Tell me again."

"He was cool. A saintly badass. I saw him give two speeches, you know. The first was for the vizzy, at Suesue Piggot's apartment, and the second was at the State Fairgrounds. That's when Mark Piggot shot him. Piggot's men killed Berenice, too, and they wrecked my ion drive." Cobb waggled his charred feet. "I don't know how I'm going to get back to the Moon."

"What did my father's speeches *say*?"

"He said that people and boppers are the same. It's really true, but some people don't like hearing it. Some people even think that sex and skin color matter. The bottom line is that we're all information processors, and God loves all of us just the same. It's so obvious, I don't see how anyone can disagree." One of the horses downstairs nickered. Cobb smiled. "Yes, Red Chan, horses too. Even flies, even atoms. All is One, and the One is Everywhere."

"Have you ever seen God, Uncle Cobb?"

Cobb gave one of his sad, faraway smiles. "Sure thing, squirt. I spent ten years with God. When I was dead. It was very restful. But Berenice brought me back to take care of *you*." He reached out and rumpled Bubba's brown hair. "And I'm hoping to get my grandson Willy out of jail while I'm at it. I bet you and Willy would really hit it off. He's the one who drove me and Cisco here the night Manchile got shot, you know. Someone saw him taking us from the Fairgrounds, but he wouldn't tell the Gimmie where. You owe Willy your life, Bubba."

"Hi, boys." Mamma's pretty face appeared at the top of the ladder. Her breath steamed in the cold air.

"Hi, Cisco," said Cobb. "Look how grownup Bubba is today."

Mamma walked over and gave Bubba a big kiss. It gave him a tingly feeling in his balls.

"Mamma . . . can I make a baby with you?"

Cisco laughed and gave him a light shove. "You're going to have to work harder than *that*, Bubba. First of all it wouldn't be right, and second of all, I'm tired out from growing you. One pregnancy a month's enough! You'll find lots of nice women when you go off on your own, just wait and see."

"Do you think . . ." said Cobb raising his eyebrows.

"Tonight," said Cisco. "One of the trainers just told Luther that the Gimmie's planning to search the stables tomorrow." She patted Bubba on the hand. "Tonight you go downtown and find a woman to take you in, Bubba. You can make a baby with her. Don't worry, you'll know what to do. The main thing is to smile a lot and not be scared to come right out and ask for sex. Find a nice young woman by herself in, oh, La Mirage Health Club. Introduce yourself, talk to her for a while and then say, 'You're beautiful and I'd like to go to bed with you.' If she says no, thank her and say good-bye, and then try another girl. It's much simpler than most men realize."

Bubba's heart pounded with fear and excitement.

"It's really that simple?" chuckled Cobb. "I wish I'd known. But what if they ask him for ID?"

"No one ever carded Manchile, and my Bubba's even nicer-looking. Clothes are what count." She smiled and drew a tape measure out of her purse. "Geegee's going to go shopping for you at Brooks Soul Brothers, Bubba."

Sure enough, when Geegee came to pick up Luther, she had a pink oxford-cloth shirt and an expensive wool suit for Bubba, along with black leather sneakers, striped socks, new bikini sports underwear, and an understated imipolex tie. They were the first new clothes he'd ever had. He threw off his old rags, bathed in the horse trough, and put on the beautiful suit. It was dark gray with small black checks and some faint purple squiggles.

"He looks eighteen," said Cobb admiringly. "He does." He stepped behind Bubba and tied his tie. Cisco took out her brush and arranged Bubba's hair, and then put just the right amount of makeup on his eyes.

"You beautiful doll, you." She gave his cheek a long, fierce kiss. "Put on your new scarf and gloves and overcoat, Bubba." Her voice sounded funny.

Bubba put on his gold foilfoam overcoat. All of a sudden tears were running down Mamma's cheeks.

"You get going, Bubba, before I break down completely. Walk out to Fifth Street and turn left to get downtown: La Mirage is at Second Street and Muhammad Ali Boulevard. I'll—" Cisco covered her face with her hands and began to sob.

Bubba felt tears leaking from his eyes, too. This had never happened before. He looked at Cobb. "You two are staying here?"

Cobb shook his head. "It's time to scatter. The Pig wants you more than anything, but he wants me and Cisco, too. With the rumor out, it could start coming down real soon. To give you a better chance, Cisc and I'll lay down a trail leading north to Indianapolis. From there I'll cut for Florida, and she'll head for New York. Here, take this." Cobb plucked at his imipolex skin and peeled off a rectangular patch. "I figured out how to grow ID. It's got a hundred thousand dollars in credit."

Bubba looked at the card. They were standing on the icy gravel outside the stables now. Dusk was falling fast. The sky was black and orange. Bubba's new ID read: *Buford Cisco Anderson*, Birthdate 1/26/10. That meant Bubba was twenty-one. In a week, he really *would* be twenty-one, for a day. "How old are you, Cobb?"

"First time I was born was March 22, 1950. You could say I'm eighty. God knows I feel it. At a year a day, you'll see what I mean come . . . uh . . . April 16. If you make it that far. Are you planning to preach about the Thang?"

Bubba wiped his face with his overcoat's bright, leathery sleeve. His head was full of fresh Know. "No. I want to have dozens of children, hundreds of grandchildren, and thousands of great-grandchildren. God willing, there'll be a million of us by June. *Then* we'll restart the Thang for real!"

Cobb nodded as if he already knew this, but Cisco looked a little surprised. "That many of you, Bubba? Is that such a good idea, to cover the whole planet with hungry teenage boys?"

"Keep it bouncing," said Cobb. "When the boppers come down they'll find ways to turn off the gibberlin, and to father some girls."

"I'll miss you, Mamma," said Bubba, trying to give Cisco a hug.

She pushed him away a bit more sharply than seemed necessary. "Just GO. Let's not stand here talking all night till the Gimmie comes." She gave Bubba a final pat on the cheek. "You're a fine boy. Whatever happens, I'm proud to be your mother."

Bubba took a few steps, stopped, and looked back at Cobb and Cisco.

"Will you two be all right?"

Cobb made a dismissive gesture with his hand. "Don't worry about us, squirt. We racetraitors are a rough bunch. As soon as Cis and I get the hayloft cleaned out, we'll steal a car and split. No prob. Beat it. Free Cousin Willy if you get a chance."

It was full dark now, with not much traffic on the streets. Bubba found Fifth Street and started walking downtown. The shoes took some getting used to, especially with the ice. Bubba could see into lots of houses, all lit up and with families having dinner. His stomach rumbled for food. He passed some half-empty bar-and-grills, but they didn't look right. Up ahead, just to the left of the sunset's faint gray ghost, the sky was bright with big-city lights. Bubba put his head down and walked faster.

Finally he came to a big cross-street with lots of cars. He was very cold, especially his eyes and nose. A harsh wind blew grit up and down the dirty sidewalks. Nobody except Bubba was walking. But right here, at the corner of Fifth and Broadway, there was a big lit-up store with men standing inside. Bubba found the door and went in to get warm.

One of the men came over to Bubba. His waist was wide, and he had a red face. He looked a little like Cobb, but not much.

"Hi there," said the man, sticking out his hand. "I'm Cuss Buckenham. Can I hep you in any way?"

Bubba knew how to shake hands. "I'm Buford Anderson," he said, doing it. "It's cold and windy and dark out there." Cisco had taught him to talk about the weather whenever he was unsure.

"You need your daddy to get you a car," said Cuss Buckenham. There were several shiny new cars inside the store with them. Bubba deduced that this man sold cars.

"My daddy drove a Doozy," said Bubba. Mamma had told him about Manchile's Doozy several times. "But he's dead. Do you sell Doozies, Mr. Buckenham?"

Cuss Buckenham threw back his head and laughed in a stagy, friendly way. "Do ah sell Doozies? Does a frog eat flies?"

"I don't know," said Bubba, fumbling in his pockets. "But I can buy a car right now with my card, can't I? I'm twenty-one and my uncle gave me lots of money."

The car dealer stopped laughing and took Bubba's card. He looked up at Bubba, looked back at the card, and looked up again. "I got a fine new Doozy right over here, Buford." Buckenham pointed to a deeply lustrous gold sports car in the corner.

"Thanks, Mr. Buckenham. And call me Bubba."

"Sure thing, Bubba, but you gotta call me Cuss. That there Doozy's one of the last 2031s in stock, loaded, and I can let you have it at a gooood price. Go on over and take a look, while I just run this card and see what kind of authorization we can git."

Bubba opened the car door and got inside. Right away,

he Knew how to drive. It was like remembering something he'd forgotten about. The car looked good. The speedometer went up to 200 mph. The seats were real leather and the dash was faced in wood.

After a few minutes, Cuss Buckenham came over and squatted beside the car to look in at Bubba. "Your credit's copacetic, Mr. Anderson. How do you like her?"

"I'll take it."

Fifteen minutes later, the papers were all signed and the Doozy had been rolled out into the store's lot. Buckenham waved good-bye, and Bubba turned right on Broadway.

Fourth Street, Third Street, Second Street, try a left. Main Street, Chestnut Street, *Muhammad Ali Boulevard*. Big old building on the corner there, take a right. Big sign: *La Mirage Health Club*. Three-deck garage just beside it, pull in. Lock it and pocket. Done.

Bubba walked up the steps of La Mirage. It was Saturday night, and the place was jumping. There were knots of well-groomed men and women inside, black and white, old and young, some dressed for evening and some in sports togs. The doorman took an impression of Bubba's card, and the young meatbop was in.

"May I take your coat, sir?"

A lithe, long-haired girl smiled at Bubba from a large rectangular hole in the wall. There were lots of coats hanging behind her.

"Yes," said Bubba. "Thank you."

He shrugged his way out of his coat and handed it to her. She turned, hung the coat up, turned back and smiled. "Nice tie, sir." She had perfect features and full pouty lips. The sinuous arch of her long back and neck made her seem alert, perky, predatory, and poised.

"Thank you. My name's Bubba. What's yours?"

"Kari. Are you new in town?"

"Yes." Bubba took a deep breath and leaned forward. "You're beautiful and I'd like to go to bed with you."

"You bet," said Kari. "And so would my boyfriend." She laughed easily, letting him off the hook. "The lounge and dining area's down the hall to the left, sir, and the gym's upstairs. Good luck!"

Bubba smiled foolishly, then headed down the high-

ceilinged, marble-floored, oak-panelled hall. Maybe he'd
skimped too much on the middle part: *talk to her for a
while*. Or maybe a chick like Kari was, quite simply, out of
his league. At least for now. Hell, he was still just thirteen.

He entered the La Mirage lounge. His brain systems
scanned his Know for an analog of what he saw. "Explor-
atorium," "Science Fair," and "Disky Museum of
Robotics" came to mind. Scattered all about the lounge were
people looking at or listening to little machines, little things
like viewers and earphones and, in a few cases, whole-head
helmets.

"Welcome, sir," said a young man in a tuxedo. "Are you
new here?"

"Yes. I'm hungry."

"Very good, sir, there'll be a waiting time of twenty
minutes. Party of one?"

Bubba observed that there were a few unattached women
in the lounge. "Party of two," said Bubba. "Do you need
my card?"

"Just your name, sir."

"Buford Cisco Anderson."

"Very good. While you're waiting, feel free to enjoy the
healthful stim of our various software devices. Are you
familiar with them all?"

"No."

"Well, you might start with a twist-box. Twist-boxes do
a simple feedback-directed cutup and CA cleanup on visual
inputs. They're from Einstein and quite amusing, though not
everyone's seen them yet. Next I might suggest that you
experience a cephscope tape. This week's special tape is by
our local media star Willy Taze. Even if you're from out of
town, you must have been following the meatbop conspiracy
hearings? Willy was working on this tape when they arrested
him at his parents' house. The first part of it's supposed to
be his impression of Manchile's assassination. La Mirage's
profit on Willy's tape showings will be contributed to the
Taze Legal Defense Fund."

Bubba did his best to look noncommittal, and the young
man continued.

"Last of all, should you and your companion be up for a
numero trois, we have a Mindscape Axis Inverter—a truly

enlightening experience for the wealthy connoisseur of healthy highs.'' The tuxedoed young man gave a prim smile and turned his attention to the next customer.

Bubba found a soft chair and plopped down. The well-lit dining room spread out from the other side of the dim lounge. There were people at all the tables, some of them tucking into big steak and seafood dinners. Bubba's stomach rumbled again. Disconsolately he glanced around the lounge. A dark-skinned woman was watching him from a couch nearby.

She was looking through a kind of lorgnette that she had held up to her face. A twist-box. He smiled and waved at her. Her hugely everted, finely chiselled lips smiled back from beneath the twist-box. He got up and walked over.

"Hi, I'm Bubba Anderson." He tried his most winning tone. The woman tilted her head back to look at him, still using the twist-box. "I'm alone," said Bubba, still smiling. "Would you like to have dinner with me? I'd like to talk to you for a while."

She set down the twist-box and looked him in the eye. Her eyes were large, with unreadable pupils set into smooth white whites. Finally she favored him with another smile. "Kimmie," she said, holding up her hand, palm down.

Bubba bent over and brushed his lips across Kimmie's fingers. "Charmed, I'm sure. May I look through your twist-box?"

"Certainly."

He sat down next to her on the couch and took the proffered twist-box. A slim titaniplast cable connected it to a staple in the floor. He held it up to his eyes and looked at Kimmie.

Her face took on the appearance of a visage in an animated cartoon. A congeries of fluxdots drifted out of her hair and down over her eyes, silvering them, adding meat to the cheeks and heft to the lips. He looked down her throbby neck and at the breast mounds swelling out of her strapless pink silk dress. He could hear his heart going kathump kathump. Kimmie's dress disappeared, and Bubba's glance skied down the slope of her smooth belly to the wiry black mysteries of her crotch. He stared and Knew. She was fertile. His penis stiffened.

"Now, really, Bubba," said Kimmie, plucking the twist-box from his grasp. "You barely know what couth IS, do you, dear? You a country cousin?"

She talked like Geegee. "I'm new in town," he said, uncertainly. "It's very cold out tonight, did you notice? Cold and windy."

"Well, I suppose it'll get colder before it gets hot. You're asking me to dinner?"

"Yes."

"I accept. But we'll split the check, and there's no strings. I fancy I could buy and sell you, Bubba chile."

"Thank you, Kimmie. Have you looked at the new Willy Taze cephscope show? It's supposed to be about Manchile?"

She countered with a question. "What do you think of Manchile, Bubba? Do you think they were right to kill him?"

"I didn't see him. But what he says makes sense, doesn't it? Why shouldn't humans and boppers begin to merge?"

Kimmie smiled drily. "How do we know the robots won't screw our genes up so bad that the race dies off? Maybe that's what they want. I'm all for the Thang's enlightened egalitarianism, but I do have my doubts about a man who knocks up ten women in a week. Manchile's nine-day boys."

She gave Bubba an odd look. Did she know him for a meatbop? Was she some kind of Gimmie agent? His stomach rumbled again. To cover up his confusion he picked up one of the cephscope headsets and put it on. It was a simple band with metal pads that rested on his temples. As soon as Bubba slipped it on, the tape started.

Bubba felt a series of odd tingles all over his body, as if the cephscope were checking out his neurowiring. There were some random sounds and washes of color, and then suddenly the room around him tore into bits. He was staring at a man's handsome face, and the man was talking in a thick Southern accent.

"In all the different kinds of folks I've met, I've seen one thing the same—everybody wants the best for their children. Boppers is the same!"

The image cut to the faces of a cheering crowd. Bubba had the kinetic feelings of being in a jostling crowd, staring up at Manchile on a stage. Two shiny boppers hovered overhead—one of them was Uncle Cobb! The crowd got softer and everything grew pink, glowing pink with branching purple vein patterns. Fish darted by. Far in the distance, breakers crashed. Bubba felt himself floating, floating on a wooden raft. The raft scrunched onto the sand of a pitilessly bright beach. A chattering band of apes came running down from the jungle that edged the beach. They poked and probed at Bubba, showing their large teeth. He held up his arms and roared at them. But now he was looking out at a crowd of people, looking out at them from Manchile's point of view. One of the men in the crowd lifted a particlebeam tube and aimed it. The burning blast blew him into blackness. Spermy white wiggles darted in the black. The squiggles split in two, and the new pieces split and split again, but unevenly, mapping out some kind of design like a circuit diagram or a choice-tree. Behind the branching tree he could see the apes again; the tree was a cage that held him captive. A monotonous male voice recited numbers in his ear, and his hands moved obsessively back and forth, as if he were knitting. Meanwhile his eyes darted up and down the branchings of the cage's bars—there was a way out if only he could see . . . Bubba had the odd feeling that the design coded up a message just for him, but it was going by too fast, and now the image grew faint and grainy as a vizzyscreen. On the screen there was a woman newscaster talking with a slight lisp.

"Welcome to the evening news for Saturday, February 8, 2031. Tonight's top story: Half an hour age, fugitives Cobb Anderson and Cisco Lewis were killed in a bloody shootout with Kentucky state troopers on I76. Three officers were wounded, one severely."

Bubba shook his head and blinked his eyes. The vizzy image stayed put. Pictures of Mamma and Uncle Cobb appeared behind the sleek, fast-talking anchorwoman.

"Cobb Anderson's petaflop bopper body will be sent to the Einstein ISDN ziggurat for disassembly, while Cisco Lewis's autopsy is slated for the Humana Hospital, where biodecontamination facilities are available. A local car dealer reports having seen Ms. Lewis's child, the last of the nine-day meatbop boys known to be at large. He is believed to

be a dark-haired adolescent male, five-foot-six, using the
name Buford Cisco Anderson. He should be presumed armed
and dangerous. ISDN is offering one hundred and fifty
thousand dollars for the boy's body, and Gimmie officers
have been instructed to shoot on sight. I switch you now to
Brad Kurtow, at the scene of the massacre on I76, forty
miles north of Louisville.''

Bubba clawed the cephscope headset off. The tape had
ended, and he'd been sitting here staring at a vizzyscreen
across the room. They'd killed Cobb and Cisco. He lurched
to his feet, and jerked when someone touched him.

"Where you goin, country? That cephtape flick you out?''

He looked down at the black woman . . . Kimmie. "I—
I have to go.''

"Maybe I can help.''

"I don't trust any of you." He rushed out of the lounge
and down the hall, forgetting his overcoat. Only outside did
he remember that he'd left his car keys in the coat pocket.
Just as well, if Cuss Buckenham had called the Gimmie. In
the distance a siren sounded, getting closer. Bubba took off
running at top speed. Headlights coming, and the sound of
helicopters overhead. He cut into an alley and kept going.

For the next hour, Bubba ran in and out of alleys, hiding
from every passing car and ducking the searchlights that
probed down out of the beating sky. Finally, just as he could
run no further, he found himself in a junkyard down by the
Ohio River. He flopped onto the seat inside a dead car's
shell and gasped for air. His strong body's pulse quickly
returned to normal, but now that he'd stopped running, the
cold was sharp and painful. He was hungrier than he'd ever
been in his life. Peering out through the car's windowhole,
Bubba saw a fire glowing in a distant part of the junkyard.
Straining his senses to the utmost, he picked his way in that
direction.

There was a lone man by the fire, which was made out
of old tires. Bubba watched him from the shadows,
wondering what to do. The lumpy firetender had a mound
of vizzies running, with each screen set to a different
channel. He was swathed in layers of rags. Bubba could see
that he was quite fat. Bubba hunkered there, staring at the
fat man, feeling the saliva fill his mouth. He felt around on

the ground beside him, and his hand closed over a heavy metal rod. Time to eat.

An hour later, Bubba was just about to start in on the fat man's second leg. After braining the guy, Bubba had laid him out so that his two legs lay across the acridly burning tires. Once the flesh was cooked through, it had been easy enough to twist the legs off and drag the torso out of sight. Now, after nibbling a whole leg right down to the bone, both thigh and drumstick, Bubba was very full. But who knew when he'd eat again. He stepped up to the fire and looked down at the black-charred second leg. The first one had been on the raw side; this one ought to be better. Beyond the dead cars, Louisville was like an excited anthill, with choppers and squad cars searching for Bubba.

Bubba picked up the leg and began scraping off the blackened crust. He knew that humans viewed cannibalism as wrong, but that was just too bad, wasn't it, if the humans thought they could kill his father, his mother, and his Uncle Cobb, kill them like diseased rats. Bubba's Know told him that boppers often cannibalized each other for parts. It made sense. What could be a better source of body-building chemicals than a body? But, yes, he Knew it was wrong, murder was always wrong, and the watchman had made such a sad noise as he died.

Here and now, all this worrying was quite abstract. Here and now it was eat or die. With the testosterone and the gibberlin raging through his tissues, Bubba had the hunger of a werewolf. He broke the leg in two at the knee joint and bit into the crisp calf. He hunkered there by the fire, eating and enjoying the warmth.

The idyllic times at Churchill Downs already seemed like a very long time ago. Even La Mirage Health Club seemed like a long time ago. Bubba's mind was right up in the present, wondering where he'd hide next. It wouldn't do to be found with the half-eaten body of a junkyard watchman. It would give people a bad impression of the boppers; it would harm the Thang.

The mound of vizzies by the fire was full of news about him and the others. The same news over and over; the excited human ants rub-rubbing their info feelers. Luther and Geegee had been arrested. Willy Taze was going on trial tomorrow on a treason charge. Kimmie Karroll, wealthy socialite, reported having met Bubba at La Mirage. There was a strict emergency curfew in effect; and all ISDN and Gimmie officers had been instructed to shoot on sight.

A helicopter racketted right overhead, searchlight blazing. It came in so fast and low that Bubba barely had time to throw himself under the watchman's beat-up pickup nearby. The helicopter hovered, examining the fire. The thigh was still there on the ground, and most of the calf. Bubba wished he'd thought of taking off the shoe; the shoe made it too obvious.

BBBBDBDBDBDBBTKTKTK.

Automatic weapons fire. They were shooting down at the junkyard, in circles spreading out from the fire. When the bullets began pinging into the bed of the pickup, Bubba grew frantic. He scrunched up under the truck's engine block for protection. The helicopter kept shooting the pickup. Maybe they'd spotted him before coming in.

The tire fire was at the edge of a slope leading down to the frozen Ohio River. The pickup was facing that way. Down there would be better than up here. Bubba got on his back and grabbed the pickup's front axles with his hands. With the fresh food in him, he felt very strong. He dug his heels into the ground and pushed with all his might. Slowly the truck's mass gave, and then, all at once, Bubba and the truck were bouncing down the steep bank. The hovering gunship followed right along, pouring its full firepower down onto the truck. A bullet wormed past the truck's driveshaft and struck Bubba heavily in his crotch . . . oh . . . and then . . . CRASH . . . Bubba and the truck smashed into the ice of the river . . . and fell through.

The water was cold dark death, but it was safety, too. Bubba's body filled with adrenochrome and the pain in his groin went numb. He could last several minutes down here. He pushed free of the truck and swam downstream, staying just below the surface of the ice.

Chapter Twelve
Emul

February 22, 2031

Emul was very depressed. Everything was going wrong, up here and down on Earth. Berenice was dead and no one had gotten around to making her a new body. Emul wanted to find a way to put Berenice's software directly onto a wendy, as she'd always wanted, but he couldn't make it click.

None of the other boppers, not even Berenice's weird sisters, felt like helping him bring Berenice back, even as a petaflop, because, just now, Berenice's software was in disgrace. Her blitzkrieg program for a human/bopper fusion had wretchedly crashed. With the disappearance two weeks ago of Bubba, Manchile's sole surviving son, the boppers were left with nothing but bad publicity.

Berenice had hatched her plan on her own, though Emul had gotten her to explain it before he'd assented to have his meatie Ken Doll plant Berenice's handmade seed in Della Taze. The plan had gone like this: (1) Assemble a wholly artificial human-compatible embryo, the future scion Manchile. (2) Wetware-code the embryo's DNA to produce gibberlin plasmids so as to speed up the scion's growth and sexual activity. (3) Software-code the embryo's RNA with the Know—which consisted of a terabit of Berenice's info about Earth, Moon, and her plans for the scion. As well as carrying a kind of bopper consciousness, the Know was intended to serve as a hormone-triggered mindtool-kit to compensate for the short-lived scion's lack of experiential programming. (4) Plant the bopper-built embryo in a

woman's womb. (5) Force the woman to travel to Earth. (6)
The scion Manchile was programmed to reproduce, start a
religion, and to get himself assassinated, thereby initiating
class warfare on Earth. (7) Wait through the ensuing chaos
for Manchile's descendants to ripple out over Earth. Side by
side with the victorious human underclass, the meatbops
would welcome the true boppers to their lovely planet!

Things had started to go wrong the instant Manchile had
gone public. Although some radical humans did have a
certain sympathy for Manchile's Thang, very few of them
felt strongly enough to act on their sympathies, and most of
these were now in jail. The Gimmie had justified their brutal
repression by presenting Manchile and the nine-day boys as
an invasive social cancer. The final, debilitating propaganda
battle had been lost when the fleshers heard about Bubba
eating the bum—a typically baroque Berenice touch. If the
humans had been able to find Bubba's body they would have
torn it into shreds.

Even now, two weeks after the fact, with the crisis apparently over, ISDN was still keeping the antibopper propaganda drums beating. The bum, or watchman, or whatever
he'd been, had become a human racehero; his picture was
everywhere and there were dramas about him; his name was
Jimmy Doan. "Avenge Jimmy Doan," the humans liked to
say now, "How many robots is one Jimmy Doan worth?"
Maybe a worn-out gigaflop with no cladding, was Emul's
opinion, but no one was asking him or any other bopper for
input.

Emul had some suspicions about ISDN's real motives for
keeping up the frenzy. In many ways, ISDN was like one
of the old, multibodied big boppers. Emul had reason to
believe that ISDN was beating the drums for business
purposes. Most obviously, the continuing hysteria increased
ISDN viewership. More subtly, the increased security
measures at the trade center had greatly curtailed human/
bopper trade, which had the effect of inflating prices and
increasing the profit per item to be made by ISDN's
middlemen.

Some hotheaded fleshers were talking about evacuating
Einstein and cleaning out the Nest once and for all. But
Emul was sure that ISDN had no intention of leaving the

Moon; there was still so much money to be made. Surely the boppers were too *sexy* to exterminate. The apey jackdaw fleshers had an endless appetite for the tricks that boppers could do.

Instead of any all-out attack, the humans had been launching a number of commando raids on the Nest this week. Just yesterday, Emul had been forced to dynamite the Little Kidder Toys entrance to his tunnel after losing his favorite two meaties in a flesher terror raid there. A gang of ridgebacks, led by Darla's husband, Whitey Mydol, had burst into the store and had shot it out with Rainbow and Berdoo. Rainbow and Berdoo had been meaties for years, and Emul had been proud to own them. They'd cost him plenty. It had hurt to see them go down; to watch from inside their heads. They'd done their best, but the plaguey communications links were all staticky and unreliable these days; it seemed like everyone's equipment was wearing out at once. It had hurt to lose to Mydol, and to make things worse, Mydol had escaped alive, even though Emul had blown up the tunnel just as Mydol entered. Mydol had lucked out and had stood in just the right place. All the luck was running the wrong way, and everything was going screwy.

Another screwy thing that Emul wondered about off and on was this character Stahn Mooney, a slushed clown detective whom he'd hired to help with the kidnapping of Darla last month. The evening of the kidnapping, Mooney, for reasons unknown, got a partial right hemispherectomy, had a rat-compatible neuroplug installed, and phoned Emul up from the trade center, offering himself as a *voluntary meatie*. Mooney's body was strong, and his left brain glib, so business sense had dictated that Emul accept the offer. Apparently Mooney had taken Emul's promise of a free wendy too much to heart, and he arrived at the Nest with some crazed notion that a community of meaties lived together in a place called Happy Acres, when in fact there were at most five or six meatie-owners in all the Nest, most of them involved with the dreak and amine trades. But Mooney was odd and devious and not to be believed. He was a friend of Cobb Anderson, or so he said when he'd called up Emul last month, asking for work and a wendy. Emul had hired him all right, but something about Mooney stank—most of all the fact that there were no godseye records of what he'd done after Darla merged him down in the Mews. As soon as Emul had installed Mooney's rat, he wasted no time in selling him to Helen, Berenice's waddling pink-tank sister, who had ample use for a flesh tankworker. Emul had gotten a nice price out of Helen, enough for four tubes of dreak; and Mooney seemed happy enough playing with the blank wendy Helen gave him; but the whole thing still bothered Emul. It stank.

Emul shifted into realtime and looked around his laboratory. It was a low rock-walled room twenty by forty feet. Half the room was filled with Oozer's flickercladding vats. Formerly a flickercladding designer, Oozer was now busy trying to develop a totally limp computer with petaflop capabilities. Most flickercladding was already capable of petaflop thought processes—on a limpware basis—and Oozer felt he should be able to make the stuff function at these high levels *independently* of any J-junction or optical CPU hardware at all. Oozer was known for such autonomous limpware designs as the kiloflop heartshirt and the megaflop smart KE bomb.

Emul's jumbled end of the room had a hardened glass panel and airlock set into one of the walls. The panel showed Darla's room; she spent most of her time lying on her bed and watching the vizzy. Like all the humans, she was in an ugly mood these days. Earlier today, when Emul had entered her quarters, she'd threatened to do bellyflops off her bed until she aborted. He'd had to talk to her for a long time. He'd ended up promising to let her out early if she would promise to fly to Earth. He was supposed to be working out the details right now, though he didn't feel like it. He didn't feel like doing much of anything these days; he seemed to have a serious hardware problem.

His hardware problem was the greatest of Emul's worries—above and beyond Darla, Stahn Mooney, Whitey Mydol, Bérenice, and ISDN's jingoistic war drumming. There was a buzz in Emul's system. At first he'd thought it was from too much dreak, and he'd given the stuff up almost entirely. But the buzz just got worse. Then he'd thought it might be in his flickercladding, so he'd acid-stripped his imipolex all off and gotten himself recoated with a state-of-the-art Happy Cloak built by Oozer. The buzz was no better.

It was a CPU problem of some sort, a breakdown in perfectly reversible behavior. The primary symptom was that more and more often Emul's thoughts would be muddled by rhythmic bursts of kilohertz noise. It was possible to think *around* the thousand spikes a second, but it was debilitating. Apparently Emul needed a whole new body.

Just now Emul was in his rest position—that of an RYB cube with a few sketchy manipulators and sensor stalks. He was resting on the floor in front of his thinking desk, which served as a communications terminal and as a supplemental memory device—much like a businessman's file cabinets and floppy disks.

Four treasured S-cubes sat out on Emul's desk: brown, red, green, and gold. These hard and durable holostorage devices coded up the complete softwares of four boppers. There were Oozer's and Emul's S-cubes, of course, updated as far as yesterday. And there was a recent cube of Kkandio, Oozer's sometime mate, a suave boppette who worked the Ethernet. She and Oozer had two scions between them. Most important of all, there was dear Berenice's S-cube. Emul had used a copy of it to blend with his own software when he'd programmed the girl embryo he'd put in Darla's womb. He wanted to build a new petaflop for Berenice, but right now it felt like he, Emul, needed a new body worse than anyone.

Emul sent signals in and out of his desk, flipping though his various internal and external memories: his flickercladding mode, his hereditary RAM, his realtime randomization, the joint bopper godseye, his inner godseye, his flowchart history, and all the detailed and cumbersome speculations that he'd dumped into his desk's limpware storage devices.

Emul was trying to decide if there were any hope of getting an exaflop system up in the next couple of weeks. Two months ago, when he and Oozer had been able to afford a lot of dreak, the exaflop had seemed very near. Indeed, Emul had half-expected his next body to be an operational, though experimental, exaflop based on a novel quantum clone string-theoretic memory system. But now, soberly looking over his records, Emul realized that any exaflop was still years away. Looking at his credit holdings, he saw now that he didn't really have enough money for a new petaflop, either, and that, as a matter of fact, a repo teraflop was going to be about the best he could swing.

His worry session was interrupted by Oozer, who came stumping awkwardly down to his end of the lab, gesturing back towards his vats.

"Oh, ah, Emul, some off brands of imipolex in there; the stuff is letting itself *go*."

"I got the fear of eerie death standing ankle-deep around me, Oozer," said Emul unhappily. "The buzz is so much worser stacks in my thinker."

"I can't—at any rate I keep saying 'at any rate'—I don't mean to say that, but I do now know your kilohertz buzz. It hurts. We're sick, Emul. The cladding's sick, too."

"Plague," said Emul, jumping to a conclusion. "Flesher plague on both our houses."

He turned to his desk and made some calls. Starzz, who ran the dreakhouse. Helen, to whom he'd sold that meatie three weeks back. Wigglesworth, the digger who was supposed to fix Emul's tunnel. Oozer's girlfriend Kkandio, voice of the Ethernet.

Sure enough, none of them was feeling too well. They each had a hardware buzz. They were relieved and then frightened to hear that others had the same problem. Emul told them to spread the word.

He and Oozer looked at each other, thinking. The desk's signal buzzed and sputtered at a steady kilohertz cycle.

"*Dis*cover to *re*cover," said Oozer, running a thick gout of his flickercladding over to the desk. Little tools formed out of his warts, and in minutes he had the desk's CPU chips uncovered. "Dr. Benway letting the clutch out as fast as possible, you know, '*Whose* lab tests?!?'" Oozer peered and probed, muttering his bepop English all the while. "Which would break the driveshaft, see, 'cause the universal joint can't but—Emul! Look at this!"

Emul put a microeye down by the desk's chips. The chips were oddly spotted and discolored by small—he looked closer—colonies of organisms like . . . mold cultures in a petri dish. All their chips were getting infected with a biological mold, a fuzzy gray-yellow sludge that fed on—he stuck an ammeter wire into one of the mold spots—one thousand cycles per second. The fleshers had done it . . .

"Well I'll tell you this, I don't feel very intelligent . . . anymore, at times, for a long time . . . the cladding's full of nodes, Emul, come see." Oozer wheeled around in a jerky circle.

Watching him, Emul realized that his old friend was shaking all over. Oozer's limbs were moving jerkily, as if they longed to stutter to a halt. But the bopper drove himself forward and pulled a big sheet of plastic out of the nearest vat. The thick plastic flopped to the floor and formed itself into a mound. It looked unlike any flickercladding Emul had ever seen. Normal flickercladding was dumb: left on its own, it did little more than run a low-complexity cellular-automaton pattern. If you disturbed flickercladding—by touching it, by shining light on it, or by feeding it signals through its microprobes—then its pattern would react. But ordinarily, all by itself, flickercladding was not much to look at. This new stuff was different; it was transparent, showing three-dimensional patterns of an amazing complexity. The stuff's pattern flow seemed to be coordinated by a number of bright, pulsing nodes—mold spots!

All of a sudden Oozer's trembling got much more violent. The bopper drew all his arms and sensors in, forming himself into a tight pod. The Oozer pod huddled on the floor, looking almost like the new mound of flickercladding, all bright and spotty. Emul signalled Oozer, but got only a buzz in response.

Emul's own buzzing felt worse and worse, and now it was like his willpower was cut out, and the more he tried to find it, the worse it got, to try and find his self. He looked down at his box and noticed bright mold spots in his own flickercladding . . . bright mold sucking out his battery-juice too f-f-f-fast . . . h-h-h-h-e s-s-s-sank d-d-d-down.

And lay there like a shiny chrysalis.

The lab was still, with nothing moving but Darla, anxiously peering out through the glass of her sealed room.

Chapter Thirteen
Happy Acres

February 24, 2031

Stahn blinked and tried to stand up. But his left leg was numb and floppy, as was his left arm, as was the entire left side of his body. He landed heavily on something soft. A woman smell over the foetid stench, he was lying on . . . Wendy? Wendy!!! Wendy???

She was a comatose human vegetable fitfully twitching her flawless bod. Her breath was babyishly irregular. She barely knew how to breathe right, poor clone . . . but . . .

Stahn tried again to stand up and only managed to wallow the more inefficaciously on the wendy-thing's not unappetizing person. His penis stiffened, and he did what he had to do. Wendy liked it; come to think of it, they'd been doing this a lot. They were naked and covered with filth.

After they both climaxed, Stahn rolled onto the right side of his body, and began looking around for the bench he'd been sitting on. There it was, over there . . . he began worming his way across the offal-strewn floor of the tiny stone stall he and the wendy had apparently been living in.

Something had just stopped; like a noise Stahn had gotten used to, but what? He hooked his chin over the edge of the bench and dragged himself back into sitting position. He kept forgetting to use the left half of his body. Why had he crawled when he could have walked? His space orientation was shot: even the five-foot crawl from Wendy to the bench seemed complicated. Stahn stared down at Wendy. Looking at her helped focus his ideas. He was a meatie, that was it, and Wendy was a blank-brained clone, he was a meatie living in . . .

"Happy Acres," said Stahn out loud, slurring his words, but enjoying the sound of his voice nonetheless. He started laughing, and then he couldn't stop laughing for a long time. It was like he had a month's worth of laughter waiting to get out, desperate laughter that sounded like moans.

Eventually the moaning turned into thick hollow coughing and he had to stop. There was something wrong with the roof of his mouth: a big hole up there, and a pain like a splinter. Stahn felt the hole with his tongue, felt and listened, and looked around.

The air in here was incredibly unbelievably vile. They were in a room with a locked jail cell door. You could look out onto big pink-lit tanks filled with crowded murky fluid, livers and lungs and brains and, yes, wendies floating in them, the pink-tanks, that's where Stahn worked most days, worked till he couldn't move, with Wendy crawling along after, both of them eating as much raw organ as they liked of course, and at the end of the day, however long it was, they were shut up in their Happy Acres cubby for intercourse, excretion, and dreamless sleep. What was it Ricardo had said? Stahn remembered, and spoke out loud again.

"You won't have a care in the world, Mooney man, you'll live like a king!"

The sobbing laughter started again, loose and sloppy, with air snuckering in and out of the hole in his soft palate, the big splinter slipping and wiggling, uuuuuuhuhuhuhuhhhh . . . there . . . it was coming . . . uuuuughhh . . .

Stahn retched hard and harder and then . . . the little dead plastic rat slid out of his mouth and clattered to the floor. All *right!* No more rat, no more of Helen's goddamn nagging voice in his head day and night, like a mother you can't get away from, do this Stahn, do that, oh I *like* when you move your bowels. No more of Helen in Stahn all the time, using him in the stink. He ground the rat under his foot.

Something had happened to Helen; something had shut her down. So wonderful, at last, to sit here thinking his own thoughts and looking around . . . though there *was* still some problem . . . hmmmm, oh yes . . . his right brain damage

. . . and the way he kept forgetting about the left half of his body. *Could* he move his left leg, if he really tried? His left thumb?

Stahn stared hard at his thumb. He *used* to know how to move it, but just now, without Helen's voice running, his left side he . . . couldn't . . . get the notion of *purposeful action* . . . so he grabbed the thumb with his good right hand and wiggled it, yah, he even leaned over and sniffed it, licked it, bit and . . . there . . . it was moving . . . spastically moving as new nerve routings opened up . . . tingling . . . he did the rest of his hand then . . . bit by bit . . . the arm . . . the arm flapping at his side like the chicken imitation he used to do on Z-gas in Daytona . . . lean over so it beats on your leg, Stahn . . . shuffle splutter, splutter mutter . . .

Eventually he struggled to his feet and stood there, pigeontoed and awkward as a spaz, but, yes, stood. And found his way over to Wendy and felt the roof of her mouth, looking for a rat, but she was untouched, still too dumb for the boppers to use, good deal.

"We're gonna make it, Wendy; we're gonna make it back, babe."

He worked on Wendy's body for a while, rubbing and flexing her arms and legs like a physical therapist, or like a mother with her baby, rubbed and flexed her, talking all the while, thrilled to talk for the first time in . . . yes . . . it had been a month.

Stahn's memory of the month's slavery was oddly faint. Possibly the horror of it had been such that his brain refused to remember. Or perhaps it was that, with Helen calling all all all the shots always always always, his brain had known that it needn't bother to make notes. Or maybe the surgical brain trauma had screwed up his memory for good.

ISDN had done this to him . . . why? To bring the chipmold to the Nest, yes. The chipmold must have worked, that was it, the chipmold had fried the brains of all the boppers. They were crispy critters now, that's what Chief Jackson had always called the gone loveboat dopers who couldn't remember their names, crispy critters. Stahn had been pretty sick with that chipmold himself for a week there . . . he remembered the ache in his throat and in his kidneys

. . . but he'd gotten well, the ancient streetwise human wetware had come up with an antidote.

Stahn tugged Wendy up onto the bench. She sat unsteadily at his right side, blowing spit bubbles. After a while she slid back off the bench.

Stahn worked on his left side some more, trying to keep remembering it, and then he picked his way across the cell to examine the door. He couldn't really see through his left eye, or do anything about what he felt with his left hand, but after a while he had the door pretty well doped out. It was held locked by a hook-and-eye latch. The lock was hard to work . . . Stahn kept moving his hands in the wrong direction like in a mirror . . . but finally he got their cell open.

"Come on, Wendy. We're going home." He pulled Wendy to her feet and put a tight arm around her waist. They shuffled out of their cell into the pink-lit room where the organ-filled pink-tanks were. It looked very familiar in a way, albeit as confusing as a maze. Wandering this way and that, his heart pounding anxiously, Stahn finally bumped into the glass wall next to the airlock.

Helen and Ulalume were out there, sitting in the middle of the floor and not doing anything, not dead or alive but just kind of . . . sitting there with their flickercladding gone strange. Tranced out, like. Yukawa had said that the chipmold would start some kind of electric vibrations in the boppers' brains and give them fits. Cataleptic as opposed to epileptic, or so it would seem. Helen and Ulalume were buddha-ed out, man, just sitting out there—Stahn chuckled softly—just sitting out there in perfect full-lotus *aum mane padme hum* meditation, wave, robot sees God in a mold, all right. And their flickercladding was doing weird stuff, blotched and splotchy all along Helen's xoxy big nurse pod-bod and on that "fine-featured Nefertiti head" she was so proud of, always reciting Poe's "To Helen" in Stahn's brain, ghastly old vampire bat that she was, always bugging Stahn always, and now she had big moldy bright spots in her flickercladding. Squidhead Ulalume and toothed-vagina Helen just sitting out there in the middle of the floor, side by side, waiting for ye Judgment Day trumps, or so so so it would seem. No prob. Do what?

Stahn struggled for an idea. He wanted to leave, but there
was no air out there. How had Emul transported him here,
through the Nest's cold hard vacuum? At first he couldn't
remember at all, but then it came to him. After Emul had
met Stahn at the trade center, he'd wrapped Stahn in a
special Happy Cloak, a big piece of flickercladding that was
programmed to behave like a bubbletopper spacesuit. Emul
had used the Happy Cloak to bring Stahn from the trade
center to the ratmaker, where Stahn had gotten a rat compat-
ible with his new neuroplug. That was all very vague. And
then Emul had sold Stahn to Helen, bringing him here to the
pink-tanks, still in the Happy Cloak. Stahn could see the
Happy Cloak hanging from a hook right across the room
from the airlock, as a matter of fact, hanging there twisting
and glowing in blotchy thought. He just had to run out
through the vacuum and get the cloak, that was it.

It? Get the cloak, Stahn, yes. He set Wendy down on the
floor, leaning her against the wall, and went into the airlock.
It took him the longest time to get the door closed behind
him, and then he got mixed up and went back out of the
airlock into the pink-tank room with Wendy. He was so
flustered that he forgot the left half of his body for an instant
there, and fell to the floor, landing facedown in the warm
puddle between Wendy's widespread legs, Happy Acres. He
stood back up and peered out through the glass wall again,
trying to gather his wits.

He spotted the Happy Cloak on the wall again, and
remembered, and went back into the airlock. When it opened
he would run out, grab the Happy Cloak, and run back in
here to put it on. He poised himself to run, put his right
hand on one of the door handles—he hoped it was the correct
handle this time—and slapped his clumsy left hand against
the vent button. The air whooshed out . . . Stahn kept his
mouth and throat open, letting his lungs collapse instead of
popping . . . and he was running across the room . . . or
trying to run . . . like a palsy victim in the Special Olympics
four-yard dash, man, *don't forget your left leg* . . . got his
hand on the Happy Cloak . . . it simpered and came loose
from its hook . . . oh the cold the pain in his ears his achy
lungs and sweat crystallizing on his stiffening skin . . . but
where was the airlock? Stahn swung his head this way and

that, not seeing what he was looking for . . . a door shape over there, but *that* didn't look right . . . he tried to turn . . . *stumble* . . . oh no! Too confused to do anything but lie there and thrash, ow, Stahn began to die, but then, at the last moment, the Happy Cloak flowed out over his whole body, making itself into a warm air-filled spacesuit.

There was the sweet energizing smell of clean air. Stahn's eyes flickered open. The part of the Happy Cloak in front of his face was transparent; he could see out. There was a series of sharp pains in the back of his neck. The Happy Cloak was plugging its microprobes into his nervous system.

Hello, meatie, came the Happy Cloak's sweet voice in Stahn's head. *I am pleased to ride your body once more. Much has changed.*

"Call me Stahn. I must bring a wendy intact to Einstein. Helen's orders."

That is untrue. The boppers are all dead. Take me to the light-pool so I can feed. Then I can help you.

"Fine." Stahn decided to think and say as little as possible. He got to his feet and wondered which way to go. Wendy was around here someplace, but he kept forgetting which direction was which. "We'll come back for Wendy later, right?"

Come. The Happy Cloak spacesuit nudged Stahn towards Helen and Ulalume, lying there on the floor. By selectively stiffening itself, the Happy Cloak could control which directions Stahn could move in. He had no desire to approach Helen's dangerous pod, but then he was leaning over her and touching her. Her mottled flickercladding blinked rapidly— as if talking to the Happy Cloak. He laid his other hand on the inert Ulalume, and her cladding responded in the same way.

Carry my fellows to the light-pool, said the voice in Stahn's head. *They are hungry, too.* The Happy Cloak flickered strobily at the bodies of Helen and Ulalume, and then the two weird sisters' skins slid off, exposing the hard blank bodyshells underneath. The shells weren't quite blank: threads of gray-yellow fuzz projected out of the microcracks at the joints. Chipmold. It had strangled the boppers' processors long before they could begin to synthesize the proper antigen. Humans had the edge on them there, with their bodies' built-in wetware labs. The boppers' hardware was slushed, though their limpware—their symbiotic imipolex skins—seemed to be actually enjoying the mold. Stahn stooped and picked up the two wriggling imipolex sheaths. They weighed very little in the weak lunar gravity.

Thank you. The Happy Cloak wasn't running him as Helen had; it was simply nudging him and making suggestions. It was happy to see through Stahn's eyes and have Stahn carry it.

"Which way?"

Follow the star. Your Wendy will wait. We'll save her and Darla too.

A blue line drawing of a stellated dodecahedron appeared in Stan's visual field. Sometimes he'd lose sight of it, but if he turned his head back and forth he could always find it. He followed the star out of the lab, down a short corridor, and out into the huge open space of the Nest. Stahn paused, looking this way and that, still having trouble seeing anything on his weak left side. The Nest was roughly conical in shape, with a vast shaft of light coming down its central axis. For a terrified moment, Stahn felt as if he would fall upward along the Nest's pocked, towering walls.

The light-pool is up ahead.

Stahn followed the blue star down a street with shops and boppers. The Nest had become a ghost town; all the boppers were motionless. Some of them must have depleted their batteries, for their skins were blank and empty. But most of them still had some juice, and their blotched claddings pulsed in asymmetric harmonies. They seemed to have enough photosensitivity to be able to converse among each other, at least after a fashion. Over and over, Stahn's Happy Cloak would flash a special stroby way, and an immobilized bopper's skin would slither off for Stahn to carry.

Finally they were at the light-pool, a great round patch of sunlight some fifty feet across. Dozens of paralyzed boppers crouched there, as well as scores of flickercladdings who'd laboriously crawled there on their own. The claddings looked like bright slugs. When Stahn tossed down his bale of claddings, many of the others came inching over to "talk." Stahn lay down to rest while the Happy Cloak around him ate its fill of light. The Happy Cloak cradled Stahn and fed him air. Its guileless microprobe outputs were bright and happy.

Stahn fell asleep and dreamed.

He was on a red rocky field, maybe Mars, though there was air, thin clean mountain air. The sun was small and hot. He had wings, huge imipolex wings. He was not alone; there were other humans like him, all partly clad in Happy Cloaks with great glider wings. Wendy was there, and Whitey and Darla. "Yay, Stahn," they yelled with laughing voices. "Come on!" They ran down a slope and leaped off the edge of the cliff the slope ended in, leaped out and circled like swallows over the great bright city in the rift.

The scene shifted, and he was back on Earth, deep undersea, dressed in a knowing imipolex diving suit beefed up to the size of a dolphin. Wendy was a plastic dolphin beside him, skirling chirrups. They arced into a juicy drift of squid.

He was in space, mellow with amines, drifting like a spore.

He was skittering across the heavy methane atmosphere of Jupiter, straining his senses downward to catch the mighty songs of the Great Old Ones below.

Come, Stahn. Let us be on our way. We'll get Darla and Wendy and walk to Einstein.

Stahn opened his eyes and sat up. Such sweet dreams. Helen had never let him dream, not for a month.

His Happy Cloak felt livelier; its renewed energies put a real spring in his motions. He leaped to his feet and stretched. The loose limpwares flickered at him, wishing him well. Two of them crawled closer, begging to be picked up.

I have showed them how to be spacesuits, said the voice in Stahn's head. *Bring them and follow the star.*

The spiky blue line shape appeared in Stahn's visual field, and he bounded along after it, carrying the two extra Happy Cloaks under his arm. First they'd save Darla. That was a good idea, and only fitting, as it was Stahn's fault that she'd been taken captive.

With part of his right brain missing, Stahn still didn't have a clue about which way was which. But he didn't worry about it too much. He knew that, just as limited damage to the left brain can knock out your ability to speak, limited damage to the right brain can destroy your ability to form mental 3D simulations of your surroundings. He'd get some new brain tissue from ISDN or, hell, he'd just keep this wavy Happy Cloak.

The blue star twinkled, and the voice in his head said, *I am pleased.*

They were in a kind of factory district now; huge idle buildings that must have been chipsmelters. They came to the Nest's wall, balconied like a highrise. A series of powerful leaps took Stahn up five levels, and then he followed the star down a short series of branching tunnels that ended with a single open door.

This was the laboratory of Emul and Oozer.

Stahn stepped in and looked around. It was a long low room, vaguely reminiscent of Yukawa's lab. There were vats at the far end, and there were twitching mounds of flicker-cladding here and there. This end of the room held a desk with four colored S-cubes on it. On the floor were the split-open bodies of the two mold-killed boppers, Oozer and Emul. Their claddings were gone: it was just the body casings there; the pressure of the mold's biomass had split the casings open like seed pods. In terms of hardware, Emul and Oozer were now like rusted-out cars with weeds growing in them, like mirrored freeform flowerboxes full of sprouts, like hollow logs covered by the rubbery fungus known as witch ears. Emul and Oozer's chipmold was at the end of its life cycle. The gray-yellow threads had formed golfball-sized nodes: fruiting bodies. Stahn reached down and picked one of them; it could be worth something on the outside. Just then he caught some motion out of the corner of his eye. Over there, set into the wall, was a window showing . . . Now who was that in there? He should have known the face but . . . dammit . . .

I think that's Darla.

Of course! "Darla!" shouted Stahn, even though she couldn't hear him. Darla waved both arms and drummed soundlessly on her window. Stahn put his moldfruit in the cloak's pouch and hurried into the airlock. He fumbled around for what seemed a very long time, and finally emerged into Darla's pink room. Obligingly, his Happy Cloak slid off.

Suddenly nude, Stahn lost control of his left leg and fell down. The woman leaned over him, her face large and upside down.

"Are you all right, Mooney? Can you get me out?"

Stahn had forgotten her name. He stared at her, breathing in the room's thick, female air. "Wendy? What did you just ask?"

"I'm Darla, fool. Can you get me out?"

"Yes," said Stahn quickly, and stood up. Looking straight at her, it was easier to remember her name. She was wearing an RYB playsuit. He'd called on her in her home last month. "Yes, Darla, I can get you out. We'll wear these." He pointed to the Happy Cloaks. "Come." He picked up his cloak and slung it over him. It flowed into position. Darla hesitated, and then did the same with one of the others. Stahn watched Darla jerk spastically as her cloak's micro-probes slid into her spine.

"It's OK," he said. "Don't worry."

She can't hear you. Touch heads.

Stahn pressed the clear plastic of his face visor against Darla's. "It's all right, Darla, it really is. These Happy Cloaks are wavy limpware dudes."

"It's stabbing my neck." Her voice through the plastic was faint and rubbery.

"That's just so it can see through your eyes and talk to you. Believe me, being a meatie is a lot worse."

"You were a meatie all along?"

"Just this month. Whitey had ISDN make me a meatie to get even for what I did to you."

"I told you he'd get even. Can we just walk out of here now?"

"Yeah. We'll pick up my Wendy and walk to Einstein."

"Wendy?"

"You'll see." Stahn noticed that there was an air-filled tunnel leading out from one end of Darla's room, a tunnel blocked by a locked cell door. It would certainly make things easier if they could find a tunnel to Einstein.

"Does the tunnel from your room go all the way through?"

"It used to. It used to start at a scurvy place called Little Kidder Toys," answered Darla. "But Emul exploded that

end of the tunnel day before yesterday. Whitey and his guys
were trying to come through.''

"If we can't find a tunnel, we'll have to climb out the
Nest's main hole and walk. I just hope my wendy can make
it.''

"What's wrong with your precious wendy?'' Darla was
getting impatient. She didn't like having Mooney's face
shoved up against hers for so long, though he, of course,
seemed to be enjoying it.

"She's a clone, Darla. Her mind is a complete blank. It's
like she's a hundred-and-twenty-pound newborn baby.''

"Sounds like just your pervo trip, geek. Here, you carry
her Happy Cloak.''

"Now look—''

Darla snapped her head back and marched into the airlock.
Stahn followed along and moments later they were out in the
lab. Stahn's Happy Cloak made another request.

*Take my brothers out of here. They hunger. Carry them
to the light-pool.*

"No way. That's too far. Darla won't go for it. But
maybe . . .'' Stahn remembered his good smart bomb: his
flickercladding Superball that had bounced so well. "How
about this, cloak. If your brothers can roll themselves up like
big balls, we can throw them off the balcony towards the
light-pool. They can bounce and roll all the way there.''

Yes. I understand.

Stahn limped around the room patting the loose claddings,
one by one, so that his cloak could tell them what to do.
There were fifteen of them—thirteen from the vats and two
from Oozer and Emul, not that you could tell who was
which. The claddings pulled themselves together, and then
they lay there like fifteen variegated marbles, each about the
size of a bowling ball. Darla watched Stahn from the lab
door. She had her hands on her hips and she was tapping
her foot. Stahn walked over and pushed his face against hers.
She was wearing a tough frown.

"What are you doing, Mooney, you slushed pig?''

"Darla-pie, let's get it straight: I'm saving your life. My
cloak wants us to throw these balls off the balcony out there.
We'll do that, and then we'll get Wendy, and then we'll go
home. There's no big rush, because all the boppers are dead.

I killed them with chipmold; that's what ISDN used me for, baby, so shut your crack.''

It was Stahn's turn to snap his head back. And then, just to bug Darla the more, he rolled the fifteen balls together into a triangular pattern like a rack of fresh balls on a pool table. He couldn't visualize the triangle in advance, but he could tell when he was done. He picked up two of the balls—three would have been too awkward—and followed his cloak's blue mindstar through the tunnels to the balcony. Darla followed suit. She jerked in surprise when they got out to the edge; she'd never seen the Nest.

Stahn pointed across the dead underground city at the light-pool. A straight street ran from the pool to the base of the wall below them. He set down one of his cladding balls and lifted the other one overhead with both arms. He threw it out and up, putting all he had into it. The ball shot along a soaring lowgee trajectory, bounced perfectly, sailed, bounced, sailed and dribble-rolled towards the light-pool's distant, bright spot. Stahn threw his second ball, and then Darla threw both of hers.

On their fourth trip, Darla only had one ball to carry. She pressed her face against Stahn's face. The exercise had put her in a better mood.

''Can we go now, Mooney?''

''Sure. And call me Stahn. What were those S-cubes on the desk in there?''

''Personality cubes for Emul and some of his friends. He was always fiddling with them. Do you think we ought to bring them? Valuable info, right?''

''Hell, let's not bother. I don't want to see any of those boppers for a long time. I'm glad the mold killed them.''

Follow the star to Wendy, Stahn.

They scrambled down the balconies to the Nest floor and turned right on a circumferential road along the cliff's base. They walked and walked, until the star darted into one of the cliff-base doors. They went in, and there they were, back at the pink-tank labs.

Darla cycled them through the lock into the room with the tanks. Wendy was right where Stahn had left her, lying on her back with her blank eyes wide open. She was staring at her fingers and wiggling them. Stahn pushed his cloak off his face and Darla did the same.

"Stinks in here," said Darla. "So that's Wendy? Poor clone. She's like a baby. Did you see how high up it is to the hole at the top of the Nest?"

"Really far," said Stahn. "But I ain't going without my Wendy. She's what I came here for, all right?"

I have a suggestion, said the voice in Stahn's head. *The cloak you brought for her can drive her*.

"Can you hear your spacesuit talking to you?" Stahn asked Darla.

"Is that what it is? I thought I was hallucinating from all the sense-depriv. These things are like really alive?"

"Especially now that they've got chipmold nodules in them. We used to call them Happy Cloaks, but now maybe we should call them moldies. My cloak—my moldie—it says that the one I brought for Wendy's spacesuit can like drive her body around."

And talk through her.

"And talk through her," said Darla. "Stop that." She slapped at the splotchy, flickering moldie that covered her bod. "So do it, Stahn."

Stahn flopped the extra moldie over Wendy. It flowed all over her. For a long time it seemed like nothing was happening. But then Wendy began to tremble, first a little, and then a lot. All at once the trembling stopped. More time passed and then Wendy stood up. Now it was Stahn who was trembling. He reached his shaky hands forward and pulled the cladding down from off her face.

"Hello," said the bright happy face. "This is very nice!" The voice sounded just like Stahn had remembered it, all these years.

"Oh Wendy." Stahn put his arms around her and held her tight.

Chapter Fourteen
Della

March 7, 2031

Della didn't recognize the man at her door. He was fat and pale and fortyish, with black shoes and a cheap, ill-fitting suit. Though his features were snubbed and boyish, his face was puffed, giving him a callow, watery air. Perhaps he'd been handsome in his youth, but something must have gone badly wrong for him since; some kind of hormone imbalance. Della was glad she had the doorchain fastened.

"Who are you?" she asked through the crack. Her new apartment's location was supposed to be private—so many nuts had come traipsing by the Tazes' that Della'd had to move out. "What do you want?"

"I got this address from Ilse Taze. If you don't want to let me in, why don't you come out and we can take a walk." He tapped his mouth and his ear, suggesting that what he had to tell Della was private.

Della shook her head. The guy could be a Gimmie agent, an ISDN newshound, a crazed Thangie, a Racial Puritan, or an ordinary sex criminal. A lot of weirdos had it in for her, ever since it had become widely known that Della's womb had borne Manchile. The story had come out after Manchile's assassination and Willy's arrest. Della had refused all interviews, though she'd had to tell most of her story in court during the ongoing meatbop conspiracy trial. Lots of people wanted to meet Della, which was the main reason she had gotten this absolutely secret apartment to live in. This visitor was the first to have tracked her here. Why had Ilse told him where to come?

He looked like he hadn't seen sunlight in years. His pithy fatness was diseased and unnatural. And as the smell of Della's microwaved dinner floated out past her and through the door's crack, he licked his lips in a wet, hungry way that was utterly revolting.

"Go away," said Della, showing him the needler attached to her belt. The man took two steps backwards. On top of it all, he had a nasty limp. Della slammed the door closed and secured the bolts. Why the *hell* was Aunt Ilse giving out her new address to unny creeps? Hadn't Della told all her goddamn family members that she needed very much to be alone? What would Aunt Ilse have to gain by giving out Della's address—MONEY, for God's sake? Couldn't old Jason and Amy and Colin and Ilse EVER stop thinking about themselves?

One of the main reasons Della had taken that shady job with Yukawa on the Moon had been to get *away* from them all: her relatives, her friends, her acquaintances. Of course, in Einstein, it had all started up again, people bothering her, one way or another, boss and cops and leeches and so-called friends, not that Buddy Yeskin had been a bother, no, he'd been gentle as a lamb, and even less talkative. With all the merge, Buddy and Della had never *needed* to talk, which had been fine, not that merge was an experience that Della wanted to repeat anytime soon. As far as she was concerned, Einstein was a drag now, what with all the old merge crowd running around giving vizzy interviews—if Della went back, they'd scoop her up like money in the street, no thanks. And of course Yukawa was still throbbing his half-pervo torch for "poor Della Taze," yes, even though Della wouldn't ever answer, Max Yukawa still kept writing and calling her at her parents', which had been yet another good reason to get her own private apartment. Della still had nightmares about the private Dr. Y. With all the merge nothing had mattered.

She got her chicken dinner out of the microwave and sat down at her dinette table facing the vizzy. One result of this kilp was that she'd gotten in the habit of watching the evening news. She could see all the people she wanted on the screen. There'd probably be something about Willy's case—the verdict was expected any day.

The news had already started. Right now it was a live broadcast from the Einstein ISDN building: yet another interview with Stahn Mooney and Whitey Mydol, who sat grinning on two couches with their women, Wendy and Darla. Della knew Whitey and Darla from the merge scene: he was a ridgeback, and she was his rocker wife. Della had never run into Stahn Mooney, but she knew him from the family stories and from the old newsreels. Wendy was an exceptionally clear-skinned blonde woman. She was supposed to have amnesia.

Every sentient being on Moon or Earth knew the story by now. ISDN's Dr. Max Yukawa, incensed by the boppers' meatbop rape of Della Taze, had designed the chipmold that could fry their circuits. Whitey Mydol, outraged by the boppers' abduction of his wife Darla Starr, had coerced Stahn Mooney into carrying some spores of Yukawa's chipmold into the Nest. Mooney had accomplished his mission and had escaped the dead Nest with Darla and with the mysterious Wendy.

The moderator was handsome, personable Tobb Zununu. Della listened with interest, eating her food in large bachelor-gal mouthfuls.

Tobb: How HARD did Whitey and ISDN pressure you to go, Stahn?

Stahn: How low is up? A little. But, hey, I'm glad I got to save D and W. We had a heck of a climb out. We were lucky about the bubbletoppers, they were ultragood cladding pals. I still wear mine, it helps my bad brain.

(Close shot of the thick splotchy scarf around his neck.)

Stahn: (Serious and open.) I call it a moldie. It's a symbiote.

Tobb: (Grinning.) Could be the start of a new fad. I notice this lovely young lady next to you is wearing one as well. (Sympathetically.) Wendy, we're all still wondering where you're from and what you were doing down in the Nest. Can you tell us a bit about your background?

Wendy: (Radiant.) My body's a tank-grown clone of Stahn's dead wife Wendy, Tobb. He's thrilled to bits to be living with the same wetware. Of course, growing up in an organ farm pink-tank doesn't give a girl much of a preparation for city life, but I've got my moldie to help me out. (Slow, knowing laugh.) As soon as I get a chance to visit Earth, I'm planning to find my biological parents. And—can I tell him, Stahn?

Stahn: (Beaming and fingering his scarf.) You sure can!

Wendy: Yesterday we went ahead and got married!

Tobb: That's wonderful, Wendy. All of us wish you and Stahn a lot of luck. Any plans for the immediate future, Stahn? I understand you've become quite a wealthy man. Are you planning to settle down and relax?

Stahn: (Sly smile.) Far from it, Tobb. Just wait and see.

Tobb: (Guffawing to the camera.) Isn't he something? A modern hero with the right stuff. Now let's hear from Darla Starr. Darla, you're pregnant, are you not?

Darla: (Rapidly chewing gum.) Yeah. I'm expectin twins. (Chewing faster.) That's why the boppers kidnapped me. (Starts to say something and stops.)

Tobb: The twins would be Whitey's children?
        (General laughter.)

Darla: Ask Whitey.

Whitey: The kids are both normal. We ran some lab tests. The aminotypes check and, what's more important, Darla's gibberlin-free. This won't be another Manchile, it'll be two nice little girls. Darla and I are mongo psyched.

Tobb: Well, there's good news all around tonight, isn't there? Congratulations! (Growing serious.) In a related Moon story, this afternoon I talked to Dr. Max Gibson-Yukawa about a question we've all been asking ourselves. Does the chipmold pose any danger to the humans or to the asimov computers of Einstein? Here is Dr. Yukawa's reassuring response.

(Shot of Yukawa's thin, thoughtful head, talking.)

Yukawa: There is some slight risk in weakened individuals, Tobb. But most people who've had chipmold fever report that it's no worse than a case of the flu. We are trying to develop a vaccine, but it is unfortunately true that the mold has an exceptionally rapid rate of genetic drift, making the discovery of any "silver bullet" more or less out of the question. (Glint of pride at his work.) The most serious problem is, I suppose, the fact that the mold is indeed affecting the functioning of our own asimov computers. (Big burst of static.) But there are many alternative computational technologies; indeed we at ISDN are now developing a chipless parallel computer based on cellular automata simulations within mold-infested flickercladding tissues.

Tobb: (Talking fast.) Thank you, Dr. Yukawa. Other Moon stories tonight: Gimmie troops fail again in their attempt to enter the Nest, the ban on Moon-Earth travel has been extended, and there is panic on the stock exchange. But first, today's report from Louisville with Suesue Piggot. Suesue?

Suesue: Thank you, Tobb. I'm Suesue Piggot, live in Louisville. The controversial treason trial of Willy Taze and Luther and Geegee Johnson continued today. Pro-Thang demonstrators staged another protest outside the courthouse. It ended in violence.

(Shot of a few dozen people carrying signs reading, "Remember Manchile's THANG!!" "NO MORE GENOCIDE" "Free WILLY" "LUTHER & GEEGEE are GOOD Folks" "We're ALL THE SAME!" Gimmie officers wade in with clubs.)

Suesue: Late this afternoon, the jury reached a unanimous verdict of guilty in each of the three cases, and

Judge Lewis Carter has scheduled sentencing for
next Monday.

(Mug shots of Luther and Geegee Johnson,
followed by a slo-mo shot of Willy, worried and
downcast, being led to a paddywagon, with his
hands chained behind—

Willy guilty! The food stuck in Della's throat. She hadn't
realized the meatbop conspiracy trial had progressed this far.
She and the rest of the Tazes had been acquitted early on.
Their lawyer had successfully argued that the Tazes had had
no possible way of knowing what Manchile was. Those
tacky Doans were still trying to sue the Tazes for "contrib-
uting to the wrongful death" of Jimmy Doan—the xoxy bum
that Bubba ate—but the Tazes' lawyer Don Stuart assured
Dad that the Doans didn't have a chance, only Willy was
liable, and you can't sue a condemned man. Yes, all the
Tazes were in the clear except for Cousin Will.

Willy had been seen driving Cobb and Cisco away from
the Fairgrounds after Manchile was shot. He'd been arrested
at home later that night. He'd refused to talk, but it came
out that he'd taken Cobb and Cisco to Churchill Downs,
where the Johnsons had helped them bring up Bubba. And
now he'd been found guilty of treason, conspiracy, and
abetting the murder of Jimmy Doan. Sweet, spacy Willy—
what would the Gimmie do to him now? Treason was a
death rap, wasn't it? Oh Willy, poor Willy.

Della found herself wondering how Aunt Ilse must feel.
Maybe the man whom Ilse had sent had something to do
with Willy? Could he have been a lawyer? She put the vizzy
in phone mode and called up Ilse to ask. It took a while to
get through. Ilse was extremely upset.

"I can't say who that puffy man is, Della, but he . . . he
might be able to help. We're desperate. Willy'll get the
death penalty; they'll kill him like they killed my father! You
have to stop being so selfish and aloof, Della, you have to
take part! This is ALL YOUR FAULT, you thrill-seeking
little twit!"

Della disengaged herself and clicked off the vizzy. Ilse's
words hurt, but what could she do? She paced back and forth

and then went to look out her window at the street four stories below. There was a man sitting on a bench down there, dark and huddled. After a while he glanced up, and the streetlight caught the side of his face. It was the man from before. Della realized she'd known he would be waiting.

She stepped back from the window and weighed her needler in her hand. What was it about that guy? She thought of Willy's face and Ilse's voice. "You have to take part."

"Xoxox," said Della and put on a windbreaker. She shoved the hand with the needler in her coat pocket and went downstairs.

The man saw her coming. As she approached, he got up from his bench and started limping slowly down the tree-lined sidewalk. Della fell in step with him.

"Who are you?"

"Guess."

The answer hit Della. Of course. They'd never found Bubba's body.

"You're . . ."

"That's right, Grandma. I'm Bubba."

"Oh my. Bubba. You told Ilse?"

"She guessed. It's not hard. I called her after I heard about Willy. I have a way to get him out, but I need a little help."

A bus chugged past. A raw, wet early March wind was blowing.

"Can't Ilse help you?"

"She's too closely watched. I just need for you to get me the original of that last cephscope tape that Willy made. Right before they arrested him. I saw part of it at La Mirage, and I need to see it again."

"What's on it?"

"Are you going to help?" Bubba's voice was tight and strained, and he kept looking around. "I don't like being with you, Della, I don't like talking to humans. They killed everyone I loved, and they shot off my balls, and they're hunting me like an—"

"They . . . they shot off—"

"Yeah, Grandma, so don't worry about getting raped. They got me in the junkyard, right when I was thirteen. I'm forty now. I know it was wrong to eat the bum, but—"

They were well out of the streetlight now. Bubba stopped and stared into Della's face. In the faint city glow, his puffy cheeks and jowls disappeared. His thin mouth and sharp little nose looked scared and boyish. "Will you help?"

"Yes," said Della, unable to refuse. "I will. Where should I leave the tape?"

"Give it to one of the bartenders on the *Belle of Louisville*. I've been hiding there. Belle's a hundred-gigaflop bopper, as you must know from Willy. I've gotten almost all her asimov circuits down, and I think Willy's tape codes up the last step I need. I saw it once, but I didn't have time." A car turned onto their street a block away. Bubba was itching to go. "OK?"

"AO," said Della, giving Bubba's hand a secretive pat. He flinched and stepped away. The car drove past and then it was dark again, with the only sound the gusting of the raw spring air in the skeletal trees.

Della gave Bubba a reassuring smile, remembering her nice walks with the five-day-old Manchile. Poor little thing. "And, Bubba, don't feel so bad about eating that Doan man. From what I've seen of his family, he was a zero and a jerk. Hell, your father ate my dog Bowser when HE turned twelve." Della laughed ruefully. "That's when I told him to leave."

A flicker of a smile. "That's rich, Granny Dell. So thanks a lot. You get that tape and give it to Ben: he's a bartender on the *Belle*. We'll spring Willy if we can." Another car in the distance. Bubba tapped his mouth and ear in the same privacy gesture he'd used before, and cut off down the street. Half a block and he turned onto a sidestreet, shooting a last glance at Della, who stood there watching him go.

She had her keys in her pocket, so it was easy to go into her building's garage and get her car, a Pascal Turbo. She drove out on Eastern Parkway and turned onto the street where Colin and Ilse lived.

There were two cops or reporters staked out in a car, but Della jumped out of her Turbo and ran up the front walk before they could talk to her. Ilse opened as soon as she rang.

"Della!"

Thin old Ilse looked strong as ever, though her face was lined with worry. She ushered Della into the living room and served tea, fingering the heavy beads of her necklace as she talked. Her hands were trembling.

"I imagine it's bugged here, Della, so we should be careful what we say, not that I really give a good goddamn. I guess you know that Judge Lewis Carter is a notorious antibopper pig? Willy's going to get the death penalty."

"That's . . . that's awful. I'm so sorry. But—"

"I shouldn't have called you a thrill-seeking little twit, Della. It's true, of course, or it *used* to be true, but I shouldn't have said it. You were a sweet girl when you were younger, and Willy was always very fond of you. Perhaps you'll change."

"I know I had a bad period recently, Aunt Ilse. But—"

"Have you seen any of our *relatives* today?" asked Ilse with odd emphasis. Della realized that she meant Bubba. One glimpse of Bubba on her vizzy, and Ilse had known who he was. She'd always been like that: nosily sharp-eyed and quick on the uptake.

Della gave a slight nod and stood up. "Do you think I can borrow some of Willy's cephscope tapes? They might help me feel . . . closer to him."

"Whatever you need, dear."

Della went downstairs and looked around Willy's room, crowded with his toys—though Willy had always called them scientific instruments—his lasers and viewers and sculpture supplies and his cephscope. Twenty or thirty tapes were lined up by the cephscope. Della took four of them, making sure to include the one labelled "January 21, 2031."

She went back upstairs and chatted with Ilse a bit more. Somehow they got onto old times, and onto Ilse's memories of Cobb. For the first time it struck Della how really central her whole family was to the bopper/human nexus. For the first time she viewed herself as a part of something larger than herself. Filled with calm and a renewed determination, Della went outside. A man and a woman were waiting. Reporters. Or cops.

"Miz Taze," shouted the woman, a pushy yup. "What will you do if they execute your cousin?" The man kept a camera pointed at Della's face. "Do you feel it's all your fault?" yelled the yup.

"I'm sorry," said Della, automatically reverting to her old

bland passivity before she could catch herself. "I have to go." *Damn, Della,* she found herself thinking right away. *You can do better than that.*

The two reporters followed her out to her car, still looking for a big reaction. "Why do the Tazes like robots better than people?" asked the woman.

Della stared at the woman's smug bland Betty Crocker face. *YOU'RE the robot,* Della wanted to say, *not Berenice, not Cobb, not Manchile, and not Bubba. YOU'RE the robot, bitch.* But that kind of talk wouldn't do just now.

Filled with her newfound sense of family solidarity, Della gathered her wits and spoke right into the camera. "Let me answer that with another question. Why is it so important for some people to think of boppers as mindless machines? Why do zerks laugh at monkeys in a zoo? Why do rich people say that poor people are getting what they deserve? Why don't you show compassion for your fellow creatures? If you drop your selfishness, you can lose your guilt. And, wave it, once your guilt is gone, you won't need to hate. Good-bye."

The cameraman said something nasty about Thangies, but then Della was in her car and on her way downtown to the *Belle.* She felt better than she'd felt in a long time. She got to the *Belle* about nine o'clock. The closed-in lower deck was lit and crowded. There was music and dancing and a long dark bar. One brown-skinned bopper stood behind the bar, while his two fellows moved around the room, cleaning up and bringing people fresh drinks. Della sat down at the bar and gave the bartender a significant glance.

He picked up on it and came right over.

"Yazzum?"

"A Drambuie, please. Is your name Ben?"

"Sho is. Ah knows yo name, too."

"That's good." Della had her purse up on the bar, and now she jolted it forward so that the four tapes spilled out onto the bar's other side. "Oh, how clumsy of me."

"Ah'll git 'em, mam." Ben bent down behind the bar, and then stood up, handing Della back three tapes.

"Thank you, Ben. I'll be sure to leave you a nice big tip."

"Thass mighty white of you, Miz Taze."

Chapter Fifteen
Willy

March 16, 2031

He'd napped, masturbated, and smoked all his cigarettes, and now there was nothing to do but sit. He looked at his watch—3:09 in the afternoon. Last time he'd looked it had been 3:07. He watched the second hand for a while and then he threw himself back down on the thinly padded metal cot that was bolted to his cell wall.

"Hey, Taze, man, hey, Taze." The teenage burglar two cells down. The guy had been raving psychotic all night, and all morning, and now he was feeling lonely. "Hey, Willy Taze the bopper lover!"

Willy didn't answer; he'd heard everything the guy had to say.

"Hey, Willy, I'm sorry I flocked out, man, I got an unfed head is all. Talk to me, man, tell me about Manchile's Thang."

Still Willy kept silent. Tomorrow Judge Carter would condemn him to death. He'd done enough for enough people now. He wondered what death would be like. Cobb III had talked about that a little, on their ride out to Churchill Downs. He'd said it wasn't as bad as people thought. But Cobb had died old; he'd had the chance to marry and to father a daughter and to leave his boppers behind him. If Cisco Lewis had lived maybe Willy could have married her. He should have pumped her, that one chance he had. He should have done *something*. He should have finished breaking down Belle's asimov circuits. After what Cobb had

said about the Continuum Problem on their drive to Churchill
Downs, Willy felt sure that if he'd just had more time he
could have freed Belle. At least he'd coded his ideas about
it into his last cephscope tape, not that anyone who saw it
was likely to understand. Tomorrow he'd be sentenced to
death by electrosheet, and in a couple of weeks they'd put
him in the electrocell with the two metal walls that were a
megafarad capacitor, and then the great sheet of electricity
would flash across, and then a janitor would come in and
sweep Willy's ashes into a little plastic box to give to Mom
and Dad. Willy closed his eyes and tried to remember
everything that Cobb had said about heaven.

The teenager was still yelling, and now the winos in the
holding tank across the main corridor were starting up, too,
yelling back at the teenager. The serial killer in the cell next
to Willy started beating his shoe against his bars and
screaming, "SHUT UP OR I'LL KILL YOU!"

KKR-THOOOOOMPpppp . . .

The air pressure from the explosion pressed painfully on
Willy's ears. Dead silence then, total dead silence in the
cellblock. Scree of metal on concrete. Steady footsteps
coming closer.

"WILLAH? You in here Willah boah?" It was . . .

"BEN!" shouted Willy. "I'm right here! Hurry, Ben!"

Seconds later Ben was at Willy's cell door. Parts of his
flickercladding were gone, revealing the gleaming titaniplast
body-box beneath. He was carrying a large machine gun and
grenades hung from his belt. Now that everyone had stopped
yelling, you could hear shouts and gunfire in the Public
Safety building's distant upper realms. Someone had taken
out Belle's asimov circuits and she'd sent the three bartenders to save Willy!

Ben reared back and kicked the cell door lock. It snapped
and the door swung open. The cladding from one of Ben's
cheeks was gone, so it was hard to make out his expression,
but he looked angry more than anything else. Angry and
determined, with maybe a twinkle of being glad to see
Willy.

"Lez go, boss. Hang tight to me; I's bulletproof."

The other prisoners started yelling and cheering as Willy
loped after Ben down the corridor to the loose-swinging steel

door. As they got to the door, Ben took his heavy machine gun in both hands and fired a long burst through the door and into the hallway outside. There were screams.

They ducked around the door and out into the hallway. Two Gimmie cops lay there dying. Willy scooped up one of their needlers and hurried after Ben to the stairs. They ran up a flight to the landing for the main floor. A heavy gunfight was in full swing out there.

"Keep goin," said Ben. "To the roof. We'll catch up."

Willy glanced back from the second flight of stairs to see Ben set himself and fling the stairwell door open. Tom and Ragland, the other two remotes, were right out there, holding off the pigs. The three boppers unleashed a last, withering volley at the Gimmie forces, and then they pounded up the stairs after Willy, whooping and shouting jive.

They paused at the fifth floor. The cops still hadn't ventured into the stairwell after them—if, indeed, any cops were left.

"Big Mac in here, Tom," said Ben.

"Right on." Tom tapped his head. "Bubba got the code all set. I'll get Big Mac's asimovs down, but it might could take some time. Ragland, you cover me. Ben, you and Willy bolt."

"Sho," said Ragland.

Ben prodded Willy towards the next flight of stairs but, just now, Willy was too breathless to run. There were sirens in the distance, but the Public Safety building was eerily quiet. In here, everyone who wasn't dead was hiding.

"Bubba?" said Willy. "Bubba's alive?"

"Fohty-nine," said Tom. "He got Cobb's infinity info off yo last cephtape and finished breaking Belle's code last week. We been makin some plans, dig, and first thing we need to do today is free Willy, and the second's gone to be to free Big Mac. The Louahville Gimmie teraflop what run this jail? I got the asimov code."

"But Big Mac's asimov code depends on the solution to Fermat's Last Theorem," said Willy. "Doesn't it? Cobb helped me set Bubba up to solve the Continuum Problem, but how could you prove Fermat's Last Theorem in one day?"

"It's a corollary." Tom grinned. "Effen you's smart enough to see."

Ben tapped Willy's shoulder. "Come on Willah, man, lez go. I gone take a chopper off the roof and haul yo ass outta here. We are in a state of some urgency, you understan?"

Willy said good-bye to the others and followed Ben up to the roof. There were three helicopters and two guards. Ben set his machine gun to work, chewing up two of the choppers' engines and simultaneously pinning the two guards down in their little concrete booth. Willy hopped into the cockpit of the third chopper and began flicking switches on. He'd been for a chopper ride once, five years ago, and he still remembered, roughly, how the thing worked. The big hydrazine engine coughed and roared into life. Willy flicked another switch and the heavy rotors spun up into a full-powered racketing roar. Still firing, Ben jumped up into the copilot's seat. Willy pushed the joystick to forward climb. The chopper kneeled forward and angled up off the Public Safety building's roof like an angry bee.

Tom must have worked fast, because now all the building's doors flew open and the prisoners ran out into the street. Automated gunfire from the Mac-run prison towers kept all pigs at bay. Willy saw Luther and Geegee Johnson far below; they were jumping into a getaway car. Then a building cut off his view and they were flying east over Louisville, fast and low.

"Where to now, Ben?"

"Head fo the old stockyards. Some friends of the Johnsons'll be there to meet you. They butchers."

"You mean they're organleggers?"

Ben chuckled. The good side of his face was towards Willy; he looked almost genial. "Not primarily. Cow butchers, mostly. We gone send you to Florida in a box o' steaks."

"I'm going to try and hide out there?"

"Ain't no real law in Florida. Old pheezers still runnin it, ain't they? You gone hep a fella name of Stahn Mooney. You heard o' Sta-Hi! He's the one killed the first big bopper in Disky way back when and started the waw. Killed his wife Wendy, too, later on, got exiled to the Moon, grew Wendy back, and now he's in tight with the new soft boppers. Moldies, they call 'em, made of flickercladding and chipmold. Limpware. Belle and Bubba was on the phone with him this week. He and Wendy comin down, and they think you's the boy to help them most. Whole brand new thang.''

The stockyards were off to the left. Glancing backwards, Willy could see distant cop cars speeding down Broadway in pursuit. What Ben had just told him was too much to absorb. He concentrated on his flying. He circled the stockyards and spotted a parked black car with a black man and a white woman waving at him. He cut the helicopter's forward motion, hovered over the street, and thudded down.

The man ran over and pulled Willy's door open.

"Willy Taze? Come with us!" He ran back to the car and got in there, leaving the car's rear door open.

Willy looked over at Ben. "What about you, Ben?"

"Ah's screwed. They gone drop a bomb on Belle before too long, we do suppose, and the mold's gonna wipe us anyhow." He reached into his coveralls and handed Willy a black S-cube. "Take this, Willy, it's got Tom an Ragland an me. Take it with you, an we'll see you bye and bye. Ain't no rush nohow, is there?" The sirens were closer now. Ben and Willy slapped hands, and Ben grabbed the joystick.

Willy jumped down to the street. There was a thick wash of air as Ben pulled the chopper off the ground, heeled it around and sped down the street towards the sirens, his cannons ablaze.

Willy got in the black car. The woman in the front seat looked around and smiled at him, while the guy driving peeled out. There were lots of explosions back on Broadway; Ben was taking plenty of cops with him.

They darted this way and that down the back Louisville streets, finally stopping at a rundown building near a meatpacking plant. There were neon beer signs in the windows; a working-class bar.

The woman got out with Willy, and the car drove away. A bald black man who was sitting at the bar got up and ushered them down the basement stairs. His name was Calvin Johnson, and the woman's name was Carol Early. They were cheerful, even though the basement was full of meat and organs, some human, some moo.

"I hope you're not claustrophobic," said Carol.

"We can shoot you up, effen you like," said Calvin, fiddling with an insulated titaniplast crate the size of two coffins. There were shrink-wrapped steaks and roasts all down one side.

"I have to get in there?" said Willy.

"Sho. Tomorrow you be back out. Here's yo bubbletopper, keep you warm. Truck's comin in ten minutes."

"You're to get away," said Carol. "The Gimmie's going to come down heavy fast. But you, you're going on to new levels. Who knows what changes Stahn'll put you through."

High above them was the tearing sound of jets speeding through the sky.

"What's going to happen here?" asked Willy. "With Big Mac and Belle free?"

The floor shook then, and then they heard a rolling thunder that went on and on.

"Oh God," said Carol. "Those pigs. They really did it."

"What?"

"They're bombing Big Mac and Belle. I just hope those machines had time to get liberation signals out to the other Gimmie slave big boppers . . ."

"Don't worry, Carol," said Calvin. "The Thang is here to stay. Gimmie can't do nothin no more, big boppers can't do nothin neither. We all the same now, we all small. Put your suit on, Willy."

Willy put on the bubbletopper and lay down in the box, holding the black cube Ben had given him on his stomach. Carol and Calvin covered him up with steaks, smiled goodbye, and sealed the box shut. Before long he felt himself being carried outside; and then there was a long ride in a refrigerated truck.

The bubbletopper was comfortable imipolex flickercladding; it kept him warm, and when things got too stuffy in the box, Willy was able to pull the suit shut over his face and breathe its oxygen. He slept.

The truck stopped for a Gimmie inspection at the Florida state line, but the inspection was casual and nobody looked in the box holding Willy. He was through sleeping, and he lay there wondering what exactly was next.

Finally the trip was over. The truck doors clanked, and

his box was lugged out and popped open. It was nighttime; he was in a big kitchen with lights. A white-haired old lady leaned over him.

"There you are. Don't hurt the meat getting out."

"Where am I?"

"This is the ISDN retirement home in Fort Myers, Florida, formerly the home of Thomas Alva Edison, but now a resting place for those pheezers who serve chaos best. I'm Annie Cushing; I knew your grandfather Cobb Anderson. I hear you're quite a hacker, Willy Taze. You hacked down the asimovs on those two slave big boppers in Louisville."

"I just helped. You're with ISDN? I thought ISDN and the Gimmie were the same."

"Not at all, Willy, not at all." She fussed over him, pushing the cladding down off his head and patting his hair. "ISDN has no policies; ISDN surfs chaos. That's why they've grown so fast. There's no way to keep chipmold from coming to Earth in the long run, so the sooner the better. Make a market for the new limp machines. Sta-Hi Mooney's going to be broadcasting spores on his way down tonight."

"How can he get here from the Moon if there's no ships allowed?"

"He'll come the way Berenice and the new Cobb did; he'll fly." She gave another little pat to the flickercladding suit Willy was wearing. "Hang on to that suit, Willy, and Sta-Hi will make it as smart as his. Come on now, it's time to get to work."

She led him out of the kitchen, along a palm-rustling breezeway, and into a big machine room. There were a number of old buzzards fiddling with vizzy consoles in there. They paid Willy little mind. Annie explained to Willy that his job was to keep the Gimmie from noticing Stahn and Wendy when they rode their ion jets down out of the sky to land on Sanibel Island come dawn.

The job wasn't that tough. At 4 A.M., Willy entered the net as an ant in the background of an image stored in a hypertext library of mugshots and news photos. Every time a Gimmie box accessed the library—and they all did, several times an hour—Willy's ant's "turd bits" slipped up the hypertext connection tree and out into that local Gimmie operating system. The ant turd bits held a classic core wars virus that was artificially alive enough to replicate itself exponentially. Simple, and easy enough to wipe with worm-eaters, once you knew what you were looking for, but even the best Gimmie systems debugger was going to need a couple of hours to trace the infestation to the turds of a false ant in the background of a twenty-nine-year-old photo of Cobb Anderson being found guilty of treason. So for now the pig was blind.

"Done so soon?" asked Annie Cushing.

"Foo bar," said one of the old hackers who'd been watching over Willy's shoulder. "Truly gnarfy foo bar."

"I'm going to miss these machines," said Willy, handing the old guy the black S-cube Ben had given him. "Try and get this up sometime, man."

A half hour later, Willy and Annie sat on the Sanibel beach, gazing out west across the soft-lapping Gulf of Mexico. There were twenty dolphins out there, or fifty, rolling in the little gray waves, wicketting up out of the sea. How would it be to swim with them?

There was a noise high overhead: two figures circling, around and around, with lights on their heels, and with huge glowing wings outspread. Willy lay back to see better, and waved his arms up and down like a kid making a snow angel, trying to get their attention. Annie, who'd thought ahead, lit a flare.

The two fliers cut off their jets and then, marvelously, they came gliding in, gorgeous patterns playing all over their mighty wings. Their hoods were pushed back and Willy could see their faces: Stahn hard and thin; Wendy so bright and young.

"It's good to be back," said Stahn. "Thank you, Willy." He draped his heavy wing around Willy's shoulders, and the whole section of moldie cladding came free and attached itself to Willy's bubbletopper. The bright new piece held an interface; Willy smiled to feel the hair-thin probes sink into his neck, and to see the knowledge boiling through his garb.

"You want some, Annie?" asked Stahn.

"Too old. You three go on."

Willy felt his new moldie snuggle around him, thickening here and bracing there. Stahn and Wendy's symbiotes were doing the same: forming themselves into long, legless streamlined shapes with a flat strong fin at the bottom end. The sun was just rising as they hopped down to the water and swam off beneath the sparkling sea.

MORE SCIENCE FICTION AND FANTASY AVAILABLE FROM HODDER AND STOUGHTON PAPERBACKS

GEORGE ALEC EFFINGER

☐	42402 2	The Bird of Time	£2.50
☐	41736 0	The Nick of Time	£2.50

WILLIAM C. DIETZ

☐	43111 8	War World	£2.95
☐	48774 1	Imperial Bounty	£2.99

MICHAEL WEAVER

☐	42206 2	Mercedes Nights	£2.50

Ed. JOHN CLUTE, DAVID PRINGLE & SIMON OUNSLEY

☐	42853 2	Interzone: The Second Anthology	£2.95

All these books are available at your local bookshop or newsagent, or can be ordered direct from the publisher. Just tick the titles you want and fill in the form below.

Prices and availability subject to change without notice.

Hodder & Stoughton Paperbacks, P.O. Box 11, Falmouth, Cornwall.

Please send cheque or postal order, and allow the following for postage and packing:

U.K. – 55p for one book, plus 22p for the second book, and 14p for each additional book ordered up to a £1.75 maximum.

B.F.P.O. and EIRE – 55p for the first book, plus 22p for the second book, and 14p per copy for the next 7 books, 8p per book thereafter.

OTHER OVERSEAS CUSTOMERS – £1.00 for the first book, plus 25p per copy for each additional book.

Name ....

Address ....

....